FREEFALL

Also by Joshua David Bellin

Survival Colony 9
Scavenger of Souls

FREEFALL

Joshua David Bellin

Margaret K. McElderry Books

NEW YORK   LONDON   TORONTO   SYDNEY   NEW DELHI

MARGARET K. McELDERRY BOOKS
An imprint of Simon & Schuster Children's Publishing Division
1230 Avenue of the Americas, New York, New York 10020
This book is a work of fiction. Any references to historical events, real people, or real places
are used fictitiously. Other names, characters, places, and events are products of the author's
imagination, and any resemblance to actual events or places or persons,
living or dead, is entirely coincidental.
Text copyright © 2017 by Joshua David Bellin
Jacket photographs © 2017 by Thinkstock
All rights reserved, including the right of reproduction in whole or in part in any form.
MARGARET K. McELDERRY BOOKS is a trademark of Simon & Schuster, Inc.
For information about special discounts for bulk purchases, please contact Simon & Schuster
Special Sales at 1-866-506-1949 or business@simonandschuster.com.
The Simon & Schuster Speakers Bureau can bring authors to your live event. For more
information or to book an event, contact the Simon & Schuster Speakers Bureau at
1-866-248-3049 or visit our website at www.simonspeakers.com.
Book design by Greg Stadnyk
The text for this book was set in Electra.
Manufactured in the United States of America
First Edition
2 4 6 8 10 9 7 5 3 1
CIP data for this book is available from the Library of Congress.
ISBN 978-1-4814-9165-5
ISBN 978-1-4814-9167-9 (eBook)

For Christine

Earth, 2151

Upperworld

I told Sofie I loved her the day we boarded the ships.

I sidled close to her in the loading bay. She was easy to spot, even with the massive crowd, thanks to the worldlink lenses that surrounded her. The Peace Corp. stood on alert, but they let me be. "There's something I have to tell you."

She stiffened. Her black braid curled down her back. The jewel on her forehead flashed red. We hadn't seen each other since that night, months ago, when she'd lied to me and led me to believe she might one day be mine.

"I love you," I said. "I know that doesn't matter anymore. I just needed to tell you."

She wouldn't look at me. Her pod stood ready to receive her. Across the bay, separated by a distance infinitely smaller than the one that would soon divide us, I knew mine waited for me, too.

"Cameron," she said. "You did not need to tell me that."

"Actually," I said, "I really kind of think I did."

She looked at me then, and smiled. I tried to hold on to that smile, knowing I'd never see her again.

Not in a thousand years.

PART ONE

Sun Orbits Moon

Not for the love of a husband is a husband dear, but for the love of the soul a husband is dear.

Not for the love of a wife is a wife dear, but for the love of the soul a wife is dear.

—Maitreyi-Yajnavalkya dialogue,
from the *Brihadaranyaka Upanishad*

Otherworld

Earth Year 3151

Night

I wake with her name on my lips.

And the feeling that something's gone terribly wrong.

But I don't know what. My mind's cloudy, my thoughts scattered and unreal. My throat burns. My eyes blink open, but total darkness wraps me. Darkness and dizziness. Closing my eyes doesn't help with the sensation that everything's spinning. My heart races, and the first thought that makes sense is that I must have been having a nightmare. But I can't remember it, not one detail. I can't even remember going to sleep.

I try to think. The effort doubles my nausea, and I dry heave into the dark. Why can't I see anything? What's happened to me? Where am I?

When am I?

The fog rolls back slowly, and it starts to make sense.

I'm in my pod. The place where I was put into deepsleep and then into storage aboard the Upperworld starship, the

Executor. Me, and close to a million others. Each of us in our own pod, sleeping through the endless vacancies of space until our ship was pulled by its target star's gravitational field to its destination, the Earth-analog planet Tau Ceti e. If I'm awake, that must mean we're here.

But there's still something wrong. My pounding heart is a sure sign the pod's given me an adrenaline injection. No gradual slide from slumber to wakefulness, the way it worked back on Earth when they put us into a week of deepsleep to test our response to total physiological hibernation. I've been wrenched awake, and that can mean only one thing.

The mission's failed. The pods have ejected. And I could be a million light-years from where I'm supposed to be.

Golden lights dance around me as the pod's systems spring to life. The front panel displays my personal information, reminding me, in case of a rocky awakening, who I am:

PASSENGER: NEWELL, C.

DOB: 05022134

CLASSIFICATION AT DEPARTURE: 17 EY

HT: 1.75 m

WT: 68.49 kg

HAIR: brown

EYES: brown

CORPONATION OF ORIGIN: Can-Do Amortization

GENETIC SCREEN: within designated parameters

PSYCHOLOGICAL PROFILE: within designated parameters

It gets dizzying reading all the data, but I turn my attention to the display that shows my vitals: heart, breathing, muscle tone, bone density. According to the numbers, I've lost very little in however long I've been in deepsleep, which means the pod's nanotechnology has done its job, continuously monitoring calcium, muscle fiber, organ systems. My vision's blurry, like looking through goggles, but I can see enough to scan the instrument panel, passing over the silver-and-black JIPOC logo, seeking the time log.

When I find it, I'm both relieved and shocked.

EY 3151.

The exact year we were meant to arrive. Precisely a thousand Earth-years after we left. The math of relativity was always slippery to me, so I won't try to figure out how long that was for my sleeping body. But so far as Earth is concerned, I've survived a voyage that lasted more than twelve human life spans. And that means that if the readout's accurate, the pods ejected at the end of the mission, when we'd reached our target.

I'm here. I'm where I'm meant to be. But if I'm where I'm meant to be, I can't understand why I'm alone and locked in the life pod.

I try to sit. There's not much room to maneuver, and despite the pod's best efforts to revive me, I'm clumsy and uncoordinated from all the time in deepsleep. But after a few minutes of me struggling like a bug on its back, my muscles respond the way they're supposed to, enabling me to lift my head and get into a hunched squat. That brings me face-to-face with the readout for my location, and when I see it, I blink and shake my head, thinking my eyes must be betraying me.

The screen's blank.

Or not exactly blank. There's a weak blue light emanating from it. But empty. No coordinates. No map. Nothing to tell me whether I've reached Tau Ceti e or not.

That could mean a number of things: I'm not where I'm supposed to be. I'm where I'm supposed to be, but the system's malfunctioning. I'm where I'm supposed to be, but the sensors think I'm not.

Which could mean a number of other things. Deep-space travel's brand-new—or was when the *Executor* left. There were no guarantees our destination would end up being what we'd been led to believe. All the data told us Tau Ceti e was sustainable—but then so was Earth, and we saw how well that turned out. So maybe I *am* here, but the computer's telling me *here* doesn't match what it expected to find.

The dizziness returns as I check the environmental readouts: atmospheric composition and pressure, water, life-forms. They, too, are blank.

I'm faced with a decision. I'm upright, breathing, blinking, moving. All systems go. The emergency release lies within reach. But if I pop the top and I'm not where I'm supposed to be, I'm screwed. Excessive or inadequate pressure. Radiation. Microorganisms. Lots of ways for me to die. And some of them slow and messy.

But the alternative isn't any prettier. The pod could have

kept me alive indefinitely in a suspended state. But now that I'm awake, my body's clamoring for attention. My stomach cramps from eons of emptiness. My lungs strain to pull oxygen from the enclosed space. Embarrassingly, my bladder feels ready to explode. (Or maybe not so embarrassingly. You try holding it for a thousand years.) If I stay here, within a matter of days or hours I'll be dead.

My mind is coming clear. It hurts to concentrate, but that's an unavoidable side effect of not thinking for a millennium. I know what the pods are designed to do. In an emergency scenario, they abandon ship to seek planetary conditions meeting certain minimum requirements for human life. If they don't find it, they don't touch down. They wander forever, or at least until they run out of fuel. No one told us how long that was.

So, assuming the pod's working, it's set me down somewhere it thinks I can survive. Maybe where it was meant to. The *Executor* might have experienced trouble in orbit, and the pods responded on cue: eject, search for the right environment, wake the sleeper. Everything might be all right.

Or everything might have failed, theory and/or execution, and the moment I open the door, my head might get sucked off my body.

I take a deep breath. Or try to. The oxygen's wearing thin. It's like breathing through a paper mask, the kind people in the Lowerworld used to wear. The kind that got thicker and thicker as the air got less and less breathable.

That settles it. I've seen people hacking up lungs. If it's

a choice between that kind of death and the instantaneous, head-sucking kind, I'll take the latter.

But I'm not a complete idiot. I listened to the JIPOC trainers. The pod carries a self-contained oxygen unit, good for up to twenty-four hours (depending on exertion and anxiety). Another safety feature in case one of the pods gets thrown clear of the ship during touchdown. If I'm where I'm supposed to be, and if the gravitation and air pressure are nearly Earth-normal, and if the *Executor*'s not far off, the mask should keep me breathing long enough to find it.

Lots of ifs. But at the moment, they're all I've got.

I scan my thumbprint against an icon on the control panel, and the oxygen unit pops out. It slips easily around the back of my head, the mask covering my nose and mouth, the valve fitting between my teeth. I breathe in, and the unit delivers a jolt of O_2. It's as good as the adrenaline, maybe better. My vision is clear and my mind as sharp as it's going to get.

It's now or never.

I grip the release, pull the handle up. It moves easily. There's a tiny pop of air as the pod's shell opens, the panels folding back like the petals of an elaborate mechanical flower. I raise myself above the level of the pod and take a look around.

The good news is my head stays in place.

The bad news is I can't see a damn thing.

The weak lights of the pod show me nothing except my own hands and arms and legs. My one-piece gray jumpsuit. The curve of the pod's innards, the etched letters *JIPOC* on the front panel of the open shell. Beyond that, total darkness.

And silence. I don't know what I expect to hear. But whatever it is, I don't hear it.

I take another deep breath. My lungs expand, not quite as fully as they did in a CanAm Freshen Air apartment back on Earth, but it'll have to do. For the next twenty-four hours, give or take, I'm not going to suffocate in this place.

After that, if I haven't found the ship, I'm going to be faced with another choice. But I'll cross that galaxy when I come to it.

I swing my legs over the lip of the pod and feel for whatever surface it's resting on. My nerves don't register anything particularly worrisome, excessive heat or moisture, so I complete the step, planting a foot on solid ground. It's the tiniest bit spongy, but it holds my weight, even with my out-of-practice muscles feeling stiff and rubbery at the same time. I bring the rest of me out of the pod and stand.

Darkness envelops me. The air feels cold and clammy. I might be standing on the only patch of solid ground in a hundred kilometers for all I can see. There's a speaker in the oxygen mask, so assuming a sufficient atmosphere to carry the sound, I should be able to communicate. If, that is, there's anyone within earshot to hear me.

"Hello?" I call out, not too loud. My voice sounds weak and tentative. But I can hear it, slightly distorted by the speaker, which encourages me to try a little louder. "Anyone?"

No answer. I didn't really expect one. But it feels like an

eternity of loneliness has settled on my chest when the only thing that returns to my ears is silence.

I lean into the pod's pale amber glow. It's not entirely unequipped for this. A flashlight, a few days' rations, a syringe. Not much else. The ship was loaded down with everything we needed to terraform Tau Ceti e. But an ejection scenario in deep space is totally different from an emergency situation on Earth. There, if your privacar breaks down outside a safe area, all you need to do is survive a couple of hours until the rescue squad arrives. Out here, if things go wrong, you don't expect anyone to come to your rescue.

Which means there's not much point in keeping yourself alive.

The syringe, for example. The trainers said it was for injecting intravenous antibiotics. But Griff insisted it was for what you did when you realized you weren't going to make it.

Still, I take the supply pouch out of the pod and empty it of its contents. A drinking tube built into the mask enables me to take a swig of water, and that refreshes my throat, though I can't help recalling as it goes down that my jumpsuit has no waste-processing capabilities. The flashlight shows me a bare patch of rock at my feet, or at least what looks like rock, though it's got that strange spongy feel. No vegetation that I can see. Mist or fog gathers in the air, its source indeterminate, too thick for the beam to penetrate more than a few meters in any direction. Whichever way I decide to go, I'll be a moving island of light in a sea of darkness.

Unless, of course, I decide not to move at all.

I sit on the spongy ground. It's not wet that I can tell, just porous and yielding. I could be imagining this, but it seems to pulse underneath me, like tremors from deep down.

My second decision tonight looks no better than my first.

In fact, it looks a lot worse.

I'm alone. Everyone I know is either dead or scattered across the planet, or more likely the galaxy. Could be I'm the sole human being not only on this world, but on any world. The billions we left behind, they're long gone. According to the chief catastrologist for the entire Upperworld, Earth had maybe fifty good years left in it. "Good" being a relative term.

I take out the syringe, the vial of clear liquid that goes with it. If Griff's right, death will be quick and painless. If he's wrong, I'll be pumped up on enough antibiotics to fight off an infection I don't stand a chance of living long enough to contract. In which case death from anoxia will be mine to enjoy, unless the atmosphere is toxic enough to kill me with a single unprotected breath.

I laugh out loud. The sound emerges as a short, ugly squawk.

I'm seventeen Earth-years old. I've survived a journey more than fifty times that long. And all I get to do at the end is choose how I'm going to die.

I stare at the syringe in the flashlight's glow. The liquid has a rainbow in it from the light, which means the visible spectrum on this place is comparable to Earth's. For all the good that does me. I remember the stories people back home told about rainbows. With all the doomsday predictions on the worldlink, I guess they were looking for hope.

Hope, Sofie used to say, *means nothing without struggle.*

Her image flashes into my mind. I can see her face, hear her voice. My heart yanks at my chest as I realize this is the first time I've thought of her since waking up. I feel unbelievably guilty, as if remembering her now means I'd forgotten her before. I wonder if, wherever she is, she's thought of me.

When I lost her, I think, *I lost everything.*

I indulge myself in that thought for about two seconds, then let it go. I'm not willing to give up. I knew when I stepped aboard the *Executor* that I'd never see her again. I also knew I might never wake, or that if I did, it might have been better if I hadn't. But I got into the pod anyway. If I learned anything from her, it's that even when life looks bleakest, there's a reason to go on.

I swing the flashlight, willing it to penetrate the dark and fog. I shout into the night as loudly as the microphone will let me. "Adrian! Griffin! Anyone!" My voice sounds like I'm pleading.

But I get no reply.

Or that's not entirely true.

I do get a sound, coming out of the dark and fog. A soft sound, a low sound, a rattling sound. A sound that doesn't come from a human throat.

The darkness gathers itself to spring.

I guess I was wrong.

I'm not alone here after all.

Upperworld

first saw the girl on the worldlink. That was the only place I could have seen her, considering. But I wasn't supposed to see her at all.

I had my two best friends to thank for that.

Adrian Conroy, best friend number one. Friends since before either of us could remember. Friends in our very first Classification, where the grown-ups took embarrassing shots of us hugging each other, the way little kids hug, with our arms wrapped around each other's necks and enormous goofy smiles on our faces. "Regular lovebirds," Griff said, and maybe he was a little jealous because (being best friend number two) he came into the picture a few years later. Knowing Griff, though, he was just calling it like he saw it. And anyway, after Griff's mom died and his dad got his transfer, the three of us were inseparable. Birthday parties, sleepovers, ball games, the whole deal. When we got older, there were more sports, hanging out, talking about girls, dating and dumping girls, copying off each other on tests, cruising around the walled outskirts of CanAm Capital in our dads' privacars, daring each other to drive up to the guard station at the wall (but never doing it). When it came time to prep for the Otherworld Colonization Protocol, the three of us signed up on the same day. Not that there was any doubt we'd be on the command ship, what with Adrian's dad being chairman of the board of JIPOC and my parents and Griff's dad being high up in the ranks of CanAm, but Adrian said his dad told him everyone had to take the OCP for security reasons. So the three of us crammed for two months, with the same corponation trainer and access to the testing protocol via our dads' private codes on the worldlink, and then we took it.

And aced it. Together. Of course.

"That was, like, a year of my life I'll never get back," Adrian said to me and Griff the day our scores came in. The three of us went out that night in Adrian's dad's privacar and got trashed at one of the clubs only corponation officials could get into. And their sons, with fake ID codes. I don't remember how we got back home. All I know is we must have dinged up the car, because the next day Adrian showed up driving a brand-new one.

Here was the thing, though: If passing the test was cake, training for the colonization was torture. You couldn't get around it the way we'd done with the OCP. You had to prep your body for the things you might have to deal with in deep space, your mind for the shock you might have to handle when you woke up a thousand Earth-years after the ship departed. Even more than that, you had to *prove* you belonged. Adrian said his dad didn't want any deadweight on his ship. He wanted people who'd demonstrated their loyalty to the Upperworld—which meant people willing to bust their asses for the mission. As it was, less than 1 percent of our population was going to fit on the *Executor*, which a lot of people bitched about. But that's life: Everyone's competing for the same limited resources, and only the strong survive. With our dads' connections, the three of us could cut some corners—scoring nanoroids through their corponation accounts to build muscle mass, for example—but we still had to *work*. The year before the ship was scheduled to take off in midsummer 2151, our parents pulled us from our Classification like all the other upper-echelon kids, and we went into training overdrive.

Colonization Preparation—or ColPrep for short—was brutal. Endless workouts in the weight room. Running treads and stairs. Climbing, rappelling, zip-lining. The nanoroids were nice and all, but we discovered that they didn't activate unless you gave them lots of torn muscle fiber to repair. And then there was all the testing of emergency scenarios, from fire in the command ship to depressurization on the planet surface. Not to mention getting our heads scrambled by some over-aggressive PMP's experimental deep-space drugs, then getting our balls busted by some hard-ass trainer's twisted idea of playtime. At the end of each day, we came home and collapsed, our legs like jelly and the trainers' spit dribbling from our foreheads.

"Kill me, Cam," Griff would groan. "Put me out of my misery." He was barely kidding. We felt like zombies. Zombies who'd totally pissed off someone and were getting the beating of their undead lives.

The day I first saw her, the three of us had crawled back to Adrian's apartment after a grueling session in the zero-gravity gym. If you think zero-G is all about floating around and doing effortless backflips like they show in the promos, think again. It's mostly about having trainers fire projectiles at you while you spin out of control and try to keep everything in your stomach from spewing out of your ribcage. Griff was particularly inept at batting away missiles, which didn't surprise anyone who'd seen him play ball. He'd taken a nasty blow to the gut, and he kept jumping up to run to the bathroom.

"Check this out, dude," Adrian said to me during one of Griff's unscheduled breaks. He was stretched out on his bed, with the worldlink up and streaming live video.

I stared at the screen that filled an entire wall of his bedroom. "How'd you get into that, man?"

"With extreme caution, my friend."

"Seriously," I said.

"I believe the polite term is 'hacking.'"

"You hacked a CanAm server?"

"I hacked *the* CanAm server," he said. "Which is easy enough to do, if you've got a genius friend who owes you big time."

For a second I couldn't think who he meant, but then it

came to me. Or the sound of him puking in the room next door did. "Griff? What've you got on him this time?"

Adrian laughed. "Let's just say I caught our little friend red-handed."

I decided not to pursue that one, because I didn't want to know. "Since when is Griff a worldlink genius?"

"Since his dad's one of our top tech guys," Adrian said. "Mr. Griffin Senior must have passed along some very choice genes."

"Or some degenerate ones," I said. But I had to admit, I was impressed. I'd never come close to breaching the Ultimate Security Wall on the worldlink, not even when I was studying—aka cheating—for the OCP. No one in the Upperworld had access to Lowerworld feeds except the top corponation officials. The CEO and sub-CEO of the four Upperworld corponations, the VP of operations (i.e., my dad), the top top guys. The chief catastrologist and his catastruarial team, probably. I knew Griff's dad was head honcho when it came to JIPOC starship technology, very hush-hush stuff, so I guess I should have figured he'd have the clearances to keep an eye on the Lowerworld. But my dad had never let me watch a restricted channel, and I doubted Griff's dad would be happy if he knew his sixteen-year-old son had stolen his codes and was using them to snoop on Lower-worlders through the link. "That's crazy, man," I said.

"You want to see crazy," Adrian said, "just get a load of what these Lower-lifes are up to."

I watched. Most of the screen was dedicated to an approved channel, with promos for Otherworld Colonization fluttering across the feed like brightly colored streamers: *Out of This World!* and *Get Away from It All!* But way down in the corner, squeezed into a little box, Adrian had managed to hack into something I'd never seen before: a live, for-top-guys-only feed on the Lowerworld. The place-stamp said it was from SubCon, but it could have been anywhere outside the Upperworld for all I knew. Adrian performed some more hacking gymnastics and maximized the lens, crowding out the approved channel and using the 3-D function to make the Lowerworld feed pop off the screen. The image was grainy, the sound bad, a crackle like constant throat clearing. I made out a crowd of Lowerworlders—they had to be Lowerworlders, with their brown skin and robes and veils—standing in some soggy, polluted street, trash piled to the windowsills of their chicken-coop houses. Or maybe their houses were made of trash. That's what everyone said, and I had nothing to prove them wrong. The crowd was big, hundreds of them at least, and more kept coming as I watched, streaming in from the corners of the screen. I didn't get how they'd been allowed to gather, so many of them in one place, without the Peace Corp. coming to clean them out.

I watched, fascinated. I'd heard countless stories about the Lowerworld in Two Worlds History and watched stock footage on the approved sites, but those were all the same. The Lowerworlders had wrecked the planet, they were trying to get their hands on nukes to blow the whole place up, they lived across the ocean, safely walled off from the Upperworld, in the ruins of the once-beautiful cities they'd bombed to pieces after the

Upperworld corporations pulled out. I'd memorized those stories well enough to pass the Separate Destinies module of the OCP, but I'd always wondered what it would be like to see the place for real. Bad as the feed was, the image on Adrian's screen seemed like the answer I'd been waiting for. It was as if I'd stepped out of my own world and been let in on some huge secret they'd kept from me my entire life.

Then one man with a pile of rags wrapped around his head climbed on top of what looked like a collapsed house and started talking, waving his arms as he spoke. He had a high-pitched, squeaky voice, and I couldn't understand a word of it.

"What's he so worked up about?"

"Probably has to take a piss," Adrian said with a laugh.

"TranSpeak, please?"

"Come on, man, this is classic."

"I want to know what he's saying, dude."

"Oh, all right," he said, and clicked the link.

"Otherworld colonization," the guy on top of the rubble said, shouting in a voice so loud you could hear the strain even over the TranSpeaker, "is a right, not a privilege."

The crowd cheered. Some held signs with marks that looked like red crayon squiggles scrawled on dirty white cardboard. When Adrian hovered the cursor over the signs, I saw that the marks formed words, reading *Justice Now* and *Our World Too, Not Two Worlds* and something I didn't recognize, the word "Sumati."

"The Upperworld has taken this planet's riches from us,

retreating to their walled citadels to lap up their ill-gotten wealth, and now they intend to leave us behind to face the ruin they have created," the speaker continued, his voice rising impossibly high. "They are like locusts, traveling from world to world, using up each in turn and moving on to another."

"It gets better," Adrian said.

"Is this on a loop?"

"It's the same thing every day. They've been at it for months."

"The Upperworld corponations believe that only the wealthiest few should have access to Otherworld colonization!" the guy screamed. "But the prophet Sumati speaks differently."

The crowd cheered so loud at this final statement it was deafening, even on Adrian's screen.

"Sumati?"

"The top Lower-life," Adrian said. "The one they're so excited about."

"What, is he some kind of Terrarist big shot?"

"She," he said. "But yeah, they're all Terrarists."

We watched some more. The guy on the trash pile got even more excited. His voice rose to a pitch where you couldn't make out the words even with the TranSpeak function. Maybe he'd run out of things to say and was just screaming. The crowd went crazy. They waved their handmade signs and jumped up and down in their bedsheet clothing, and some of them did this strange dance, dipping forward at the waist and bobbing up and down. It was mesmerizing and exciting and a little bit scary all at the same time. Adrian said that when they got really worked up, they threw themselves in the dirt and rolled around in their own garbage.

The toilet flushed, and Griff came out, looking queasy. "Damn, Adrian. Haven't you watched enough of this shit?"

"You missed most of the show," Adrian said. "But the best part's coming."

Griff grabbed a chair and sat, the material shaping itself to his body. It must have detected how messed up his biorhythms were, because it started to massage him until he shut it off.

"You realize we are totally screwed if my dad finds out," he said.

"*You're* screwed," Adrian said. "I'm just an innocent victim of your criminal propensities."

"Thanks a lot, man," Griff said, flipping Adrian the bird.

But he watched while the scene unfolded. Many of the people on-screen were down on their knees in the dirt like Adrian said, except they weren't rolling around, more like bowing to the ground with their hands spread in front of them. The speaker waved his arms so wildly he lost his balance and slipped, which made Adrian crack up. Flames appeared in the corners of the screen, torches held high by some of the people in the crowd. Then, all at once, the sounds from the crowd ended and it got really quiet, so quiet I thought the audio had gone dead. But I could hear a sort of hissing, which might have been static or might have been the light rain that had begun to fall over the bodies and the muddy streets and the piles of trash.

"What's going on?" I said.

"Just wait," Adrian said, his voice and eyes eager.

I watched. The feeling that I was about to be let in on something hidden made my heart pound.

A small knot of men was moving toward the place where the speaker stood. They looked like the rest, brown skin and sharp dark beards, but the way they walked and the identical white jackets and pants they wore gave them the appearance of private mercenaries in uniform, marching to the front of the crowd. In their center stood a dark figure, much smaller than them, and in purple instead of white. I couldn't see the person's face, but I could see enough to tell she was a woman.

When the men in white got to the front of the crowd, they spread out in a line behind the woman, giving me my first clear look at her. She was short, dumpy, maybe sixty years old. A purple sheet fringed in gold wrapped her, muddy where it dragged on the ground. Her graying hair hung over one shoulder in a single long braid. She had a spot of red centered on her forehead. I thought it was blood at first, but looking closely, I saw it was too perfect for that. A single spot, like a laser scope about to put a bullet in her brain.

"Sumati?"

"How'd you guess?"

She raised her hands, palms out. The crowd had fallen to the ground, but they weren't moving. In fact they held themselves perfectly still, with their heads pressed to the muddy street. They looked like they were riveted by the woman's presence, waiting for her to say something. The man who'd done all the screaming had come down from his perch and joined the others, and like them, he was too busy bowing to say anything more.

I held my breath. For a second I felt like I was there, waiting with the silent crowd for the woman to speak.

But she didn't. She just stood there in front of them, with her hands in the air, and they stayed on the ground like she was holding them motionless. All the Two Worlds sites said that Terrarist leaders exercised absolute control over their recruits, making them do anything they wanted, like strap explosives to their chests and blow themselves up in the middle of a hotel or a shopping center. They'd get their underlings strung out on crystal death or worked up on some ancient religious bullshit—who could tell the difference?—and have them run around dressed in costumes or covered with tattoos of extinct animals before their leaders blew them up from the safety of their headquarters. And then the leaders would claim they'd done it because they loved the planet Terra, and that the animal trappings were a way of showing their great love for the beauty that was gone, which made a whole lot of sense when they were the ones blowing things up. It was why the Upperworld corporations had pulled back behind walled cities, and why the Lowerworld cities were piles of rubble like this one.

But if Sumati was giving the people in the street some kind of order, it wasn't evident to me. And the people weren't running around wild. They were bowing. Listening. Waiting.

Like me.

"Is something supposed to happen?" I said.

"Any second," Adrian said tensely, almost a whisper.

A shot rang out. I flinched, thinking it came from the room and not the screen. The crowd leaped to their feet and scattered, muddy robes flying behind them, shrieks filling the air. Some of them scaled the walls of garbage and took off across the rusted tin roofs, while others threw themselves into doorways or alleys or any crack that appeared in their maze of a city. In seconds the crowd had disappeared. I expected to see Sumati and her heavies break for cover next.

But they didn't.

I could see the Peace Corp. approaching, a whole squadron in glistening white uniforms marching in tight formation, rifles at the ready, the yellow-and-green SubCon logo emblazoned on their chests and on the energy shields some of them carried. It was bizarre, this show of force against one old woman who stood there silent and frozen, arms raised. I knew that corporations like SubCon and Frackia had a much tougher job than CanAm, since it was their responsibility to keep peace in the sprawling, unruly geography of the Lowerworld. But it still didn't make sense. The crowd was gone. The woman stood unmoving, unresisting. What had she done, and what were they about to do to her?

The Peace Corp. snapped their black visors down to shield their faces. They leveled their rifles, taking aim. I leaned forward, a sick feeling in my stomach, unable to stop myself from watching.

But then something tore my attention away from the old woman and the guns trained on her.

Coming up behind Sumati, in an identical purple robe fringed with gold and a long braid of jet-black hair, was another woman, much smaller and slimmer. With a shock, I realized she wasn't a woman but a teenage girl, no older than me. Her skin was the same pale brown as Sumati's, and she had the same single red dot on her forehead. Even in the grainy worldlink video, I could tell that she was beautiful: high cheekbones, full red lips, curves beneath her robe. The way she moved made it look like she was floating, like she was the ghost of the old woman from years before. She hadn't covered half the distance to where Sumati stood when she held up her hands as well, and with my gaze fixed on her, I saw that her eyes met the Peace Corp. calmly and without fear.

Her eyes.

Their intensity shot through me like an electric current. They were a color I'd never seen in a human being, a summer sunset gold. My heart beat faster, and though I knew this was impossible, I couldn't get over the feeling that those incredible eyes were looking not at the Peace Corp. but at me.

Then her voice rang out, loud and clear but in a language I couldn't understand, as if the TranSpeaker had jammed or something. I heard her say the word "Sumati," and I thought— but this made no sense—she said "CanAm," too, but the rest was beyond me.

"TranSpeak—" I said.

There was a buzz and the image slanted and broke up, and the next thing I knew we were staring at a blank screen.

"What the hell?" I said.

Adrian shrugged. "It's always like that. They're about to take Sumati down, then we lose the feed. Then the next day, she pops up in some other Lowerworld hellhole, and the same thing happens all over again."

"But what happened to the girl?"

"Girl?" Adrian toyed with the link, trying to bring the feed back up. "Dude, did you get a look at that hag?"

"I saw her," I said. "But there was a girl. Dressed the same way. She said something. In their language."

"Damn it," Griff said, and jumped up to hustle to the bathroom again. Adrian laughed as the door slammed.

"There's six billion breeders over there," he said. "The Lowerworld population's, like, totally out of control. You expect me to keep track of one in particular?"

"No, but . . ."

He had the feed back on and was surfing sports channels. I figured I could get in one more question before the subject was done. "How does Sumati get away?"

"How the hell do I know?" he said, eyes fixed on the on-screen menu. "Maybe they've got some escape route. Or maybe there's a whole bunch of them dressed up the same. All I know is she shows up in a different Lowerworld corponation every day, from ConGlo to MicroNasia. The local Lower-lifes are dancing around in their skivvies, listening to some hopped-up street preacher, and then she comes along and stands there until the cops show. It's like she's their god or something. And they can't wait to hear what she has to say."

"The girl was the one who talked," I said, but he wasn't listening anymore. I settled back in my chair, which hummed comfortingly. If Adrian noticed, he didn't say anything. We watched sports, bitched about our trainers, then his parents showed up and I went home. Griff didn't leave the bathroom the rest of the time I was there. I called out to him as I left, but he only groaned in response.

Back at my apartment, I programmed something to eat and tried to forget about the video. Laugh it off, like Adrian would. Focus on my own life, not some street scene taking place thousands of kilometers away.

But it stayed with me. The crowd, the preacher, his speech, then the bodyguards, Sumati, the Peace Corp. . . . And last of all the girl with the golden eyes, the girl who'd called out in a voice so clear it was as if she was standing in the room with me—yet somehow it hadn't made an impression on Adrian or, so far as I could tell, Griff. They hadn't seen her, much less heard her. It was as if she was speaking only to me, looking out from the screen across all that distance with something to tell me.

Like she was there *for* me.

I knew it sounded crazy. But a voice inside kept whispering that there was something there, something I'd missed. Something I'd known before but forgotten, like a password you make up with your friends when you're little and then drop out of your memory banks when you don't have any more use for it. It danced on the edge of my mind, maddening when I couldn't pin it down. I knew I'd have to come back and see the video again, see *her* again, if only to see if anything was there.

Adrian thought I enjoyed the show, so he hacked in and let me watch a bunch of other times. I laughed along with him while he joked about Terrarists and Lower-life messiahs. I kept my mouth shut when he cheered the Peace Corp., when he shouted at them to take Sumati down. I didn't say another word about the girl.

But I saw her every time. I heard her speak. I waited to receive her message, but the TranSpeaker always died just before the words left her mouth.

And the whole time she was talking in a language I felt I should know, her eyes never left mine.

Otherworld

Earth Year 3151

Night

The thing made of mist and shadows leaps at me, and it's not made of mist and shadows anymore.

A body, hard and fast as a bullet, slams me to the ground. My flashlight flies free. Something makes a scraping noise, like knives being sharpened. Then pain worse than anything I've ever felt impales my left shoulder, and I can't help the scream that tears from my throat.

Hot liquid coats my face. It burns. My shoulder blazes as if the muscle is being opened by a scalpel.

The thing chatters in my face as it leans over to feed.

Then the night explodes in a brief, bright flare, showing me a confused image of the creature that hangs above me, gunmetal-gray flesh and a face that's all teeth. It emits a startled scream before flinging itself away and vanishing into the mist. I hear swift, soft footpads for a second, then all is still again.

My shoulder's on fire. I reach for it with my right hand,

touch the stickiness of blood. I press hard against the wound, gasping at the pain. My eyes burn so much from whatever dripped in them, I can barely keep them open. I can't see well enough to know how bad the shoulder is, but I know it's bad. I wish my heart would stop pumping so fast, since I know it's pumping my life away.

Every movement I make feels like it's going to rip my arm from my body. But I sit up, try to dig through my supply pouch for a bandage. The pain nearly makes me pass out, and with only the weak beam of the flashlight on the ground nearby to aid my burning eyes, I can't find what I need. Sitting has made the blood pour down my arm onto my hands, and it's getting too slippery for me to hold on to anything. I lie back down, feeling dizzy, the mist swooping unnaturally over my head. My brain's moving in slow motion, my eyes squeezing shut. I press my hand against the wound, unable to feel the pain or pressure anymore. All I feel is cold.

I'm going to die here. I knew it all along. Bleeding to death wasn't on my original list, but that's exactly what's going to happen. And then the thing will come back and scavenge what's left.

The thought makes me struggle to stand. But my legs are rubber, and they collapse under me.

I'll never see Sofie again.

I knew I'd never see her again the day we boarded the ships. Maybe I'll see her on one of the worlds she used to speak of.

There's the sound of something scuffing rock. The thing's

back. I force my eyes open, try to raise my head to face it, but I'm too weak to do even that.

A beam cuts the darkness, fog swirling overhead in the fan of yellow light. Then a voice. A human voice. Two.

"Did you get it?"

"Ran off, I think."

"Wounded?"

"How the hell do I know?"

"What are they?"

"My friend, we're in the middle of freaking nowhere. I'm afraid I didn't ask the tour guide for a rundown on the local wildlife."

I try to call out. My throat is as weak as the rest of me, and all that emerges is a soft groan. The voices pause then resume.

"Did you hear that?"

"What am I, deaf?"

"Is it the thing?"

"If it is, our worries are over. Sounds half-dead."

I summon all my remaining strength and call out again. I know those voices, their banter, their back-and-forth. I can't believe my luck. A thousand years and a hundred trillion kilometers from home, and it's the two people I've known the longest on Earth.

"Adrian!" I call out. "Griffin!"

The footsteps stop, but the flashlight beam swings a wide arc through the mist. When it shines in my face, erasing what little I can see of the world, I hear their cries.

"It's one of ours!"

"Gee, you think so?"

The footsteps become louder. The light dances in front of my eyes, so painful I have to shut them again. Something falls to the ground beside me, a body. Hands prod me. I'm too numb and cold to feel them.

"Holy—!" the one on his knees swears. "It's Cam!"

I squint, force a smile. I can't see his face beneath the helmet and oxygen mask he wears. "Hey, Griff."

"You're hurt."

"Been better."

"Can you stand?"

"I'm not . . ." He gets his arm under mine, lifts. My legs aren't there. I stumble and fall. Blood smears his boots. He doesn't back away.

"Adrian, get over here. Cam's hurt."

The flashlight moves closer. I can't see the face of the one holding it, but I can see his hand.

"Hey, Adrian."

"Hey." There's a long silence, broken only by the sound of Griff's heavy breathing.

"Well, for God's sake, don't just stand there," he says. "Help me out."

"We shouldn't move him," Adrian says.

"Well, we can't just leave him."

"I'll stay," Adrian says. "Go back and find my dad. Tell him you need a medkit. And a stretcher."

Griff says nothing, but I can hear his hesitation.

"Get moving, Griffin," Adrian says. "Take the light," he adds, and the beam sails into the air, swinging wildly before settling. Griff must have fumbled it.

"You sure you two—"

"Move!" Adrian says, and this time Griff's feet take off, fast, the sound getting softer before dying out completely.

Adrian drops beside me. I can't see a thing, but I feel his hands on my wounded shoulder. He's putting steady pressure there, and it should hurt, but that entire side of my body is as numb as a stone.

"How bad is it?" I ask.

"Let's just say you won't be our starting second baseman this season."

"It's my left arm."

"Then there's still hope."

He's silent, leaning his weight on me, using his hands to stop the flow. I can't tell if it's working. The world seems a little less distant, but my ears are ringing and I feel sick to my stomach. I wish I could see Adrian's face, say something to him like I used to back on Earth. Some joke, something.

Finally, I say the first thing on my mind, the last thing before I lose consciousness. "Where are we?"

"We're in hell," he says, his voice ringing like everything else. "But you already knew that."

I'm not expecting to wake up. Not on this planet, anyway. Not on any planet, really.

But I do. I come to in brightness. There's no mist, no nothing. This place is as empty with light as the other was with dark.

A shadow falls on me. A body. I flinch, thinking it's the thing from the fog. But it's human. It speaks with a human voice, a concerned voice.

"How are you feeling?"

I can't feel anything, and I think I've gone mostly blind. Could it have been some kind of acid that spilled in my eyes? "I feel . . . better," I say.

"Good," the voice says. "The wound looked ugly. We weren't sure about toxins. Can you sit?"

Hands grip my back. I feel them but don't feel them, like they're separated from my skin by a wall of water. They guide me upright. I'm afraid I'm going to get sick, but then my head and stomach settle.

"You'll be fine," the voice says. "Assuming we're right about the toxins. Did you get a good look at it?"

"It was dark. I saw . . ." Why can't I see? "It was too dark."

"The nights are very dark," the voice says. "The atmosphere, you know. By the same token, the days are very clear."

"Is that why it's so"—I feel and sound stupid—"so bright?"

There's a short laugh. "I nearly forgot." Fingers fumble around my face, and I realize there's some sort of material stretched across my eyes, too lightweight to feel. Tape, maybe. A tearing sound gives way to varied light and shadow. "There."

I blink at the face in front of me. I don't know him, but I recognize the silver-and-black JIPOC crest on his lab coat. One of the primary medical personnel who put us into deepsleep on Earth. One of many brought along to minister to Upperworld passengers numbering in the hundreds of thousands.

"We found traces of an organic compound on your face," the PMP says. "We've taken it to the lab for analysis. We were concerned about its effect on your eyes."

"My eyes are fine." I blink again and realize it's true.

"And the arm?"

I'm about to tell him my arm's not there when I realize it is. It hugs my side, wrapped tightly in gauze and tape, and though it tingles a little, I can't feel any pain. Drugs, probably. "Arm, eyes, both fine."

"But you didn't see what attacked you."

"I told you, it was too dark."

He nods, sighs. "We know so little about this place. Officially, we're not even supposed to be here." Then he looks abashed, like he realizes he just said a no-no.

I can't help laughing. "Officially, was I attacked last night?"

"Of course." He purses his lips, his expression turning from embarrassed to offended. "I filed an incident report."

That makes me laugh even harder, which wakes up the arm enough to cause me the first actual pain I've felt since I came to. "What's it say? Unknown assailant kicks teen's ass at undisclosed location?"

He bustles around me, which is probably his way of avoiding eye contact. "I'm sorry I can't be more helpful. Until there's a statement from Chairman Conroy, all I can say is that we have, *officially*, touched down on an unidentified interstellar location. Which," he adds, glancing up for a second, "plain to see, may not have been our scheduled final destination."

Plain to see. Unless every reading we took on Earth set new records for wrongness, our scheduled final destination wouldn't have rocks that are more like sponges, nights without moon or stars, swift things that shape themselves into hard-edged predators out of swirling mist. I'm about to say something else when he signals, and the auxiliary medical personnel I hadn't noticed standing behind the head of the bed moves to put his hands on my left side.

"Can you stand?" the PMP asks, supporting me on the right. With the help of him and his AMP assistant, I slide from the bed, which is cold and metallic like an examining table. It's then that my muddy mind puts his words together, and I realize where I am: in the *Executor's* sick bay. I've never been here before, but I've seen the video. Antiseptic white and endless rows of cubicles, enough for anything short of a major epidemic. We're in one of the cubicles now.

So the *Executor* did land. But—I'd laugh again if it wasn't for the arm—not *officially* on the planet it was shooting for. And apparently with no better reading on where we are than my pod could supply. "How many of us made it?"

The PMP looks surprised. "Your pod ejected at some point before the *Executor* touched down. But otherwise, the entire company arrived safely several days ago. We've been recovering passengers from deepsleep ever since. We were fortunate to have found you before . . . well."

Before the thing made out of mist finished with my arm and started in on my face. "Why would my pod eject if the others didn't?"

"Some sort of malfunction," he says. "We've brought it on board for diagnostics. But so far as our records show, yours is the only pod that ejected prematurely."

"So far as your records show?"

He won't meet my eye. "We're still tabulating the data. There's been some trouble with the computers. . . ."

I shake my head, trying not to laugh at the whole sorry mess. But really, what did I expect? As the trainers we left behind on Earth told us until we were sick of listening, anything was possible. "What about the other ship?"

"The other ship?"

"The Lowerworld ship," I say. *Sofie's ship.* "Has there been any communication with them?"

He gives me a long, hard look before exchanging glances with the AMP. Then he says, "Maybe it's better if you rest a while longer," before leading me back to the exam table/bed. I consider resisting, but the truth is I'm too exhausted from three minutes of standing to fight him. Once he's got me settled in and the AMP has done all the fluttery things with my arm that auxiliary medical personnel do best, he pulls a screen around a metal rod that circles the cubicle.

"We'll check on you again soon," he says. "And I'm sure your friend Adrian will be able to answer all of your questions."

I'm about to ask whether Adrian's coming to visit when he

flicks the curtain closed and the two of them are gone.

I lie back against the stiff regulation pillow, my good arm behind my head, the bad one taped rigidly at my side. There's no way Adrian will answer my questions, no way Adrian will show up for me to ask them. He saved me out there in the mist, sure, but that was only because Griff was with him, only because he was caught off guard. There's no way his dad will report on the Lowerworld ship, even when he's ready to confirm what went wrong with the mission, where in the universe we are. There's no way I'll learn what happened to them, to her.

Too many things can change in a thousand years. You can lose your best friend. You can lose your way across the galaxy. You can lose the girl you love.

But I know, deep down, it doesn't take anywhere near that long for those things to happen. Most of it can happen in a day. A minute. A heartbeat.

By the time I left Earth, most of it already had.

Upperworld

When I wasn't hanging out with Adrian and Griff, training my ass off, or sleeping/doping off the effects of the training, I spent every spare moment trying to track down video of the golden-eyed girl I'd viewed for those few precious seconds of cross-world screen time.

Which, it turned out, was practically impossible.

Unless they were expert hackers like Griff apparently was, Upperworld teens didn't exactly have unlimited access to the worldlink. The only channels I could view were the regulated ones, and all they offered were the standard catastrology chatshows and Otherworld colonization banners and promos for CanAm and the rest of the Upperworld corponations (except UniVers, because there was some kind of hostile-takeover thing going on between us and them). The content on the Two Worlds sites told me nothing I hadn't heard a million times before: how in the closing decades of the twenty-first century, the civilized world finally progressed beyond the sixteenth-century concept of the nation-state and put corporate know-how to the business of running society. There'd been such success with everything else—the incorporation of health care, education, defense, entertainment, transportation, construction, spaceflight, you name it—it made sense to go all the way. Corporations knew how to run things, always had. They knew how to make money work for the one percent who worked to make money. When the CEO of Can-Do Amortization wanted to tear down a bunch of firetraps and gentrify the neighborhood, he didn't have to sit around waiting for the latest public opinion poll or cut some kind of lame deal with the CEO of Continental/Global Communications. He just did it. And it got done.

Problem was, by the time the Upperworld corponations of CanAm, Exceptional Content, Uniform Versatility, and Medical/Territorial Risk Management finished cleaning up their own house, the corponations they'd commissioned to run the rest of the world—ConGlo, MexSanto, SubCon, Frackia, and MicroNasia—had spiraled completely out of control. Probably it wasn't the Lowerworld corponations' fault. The areas they were trying to administer were just too damn big. With a peak population of eleven billion by the start of the twenty-second century, the ninety-nine percent of the world's people who lived in the continents of the Lowerworld had spent the past five hundred years burning up the planet, tearing down forests, driving most life-forms to extinction, dirtying their own water and everyone else's, swamping the sky with toxic gases. The Upperworld did everything financially feasible to arrest the damage—built more prisons, deported illegals in the millions, put together articulation agreements to support the policing efforts of the Lowerworld corponations—but no go: Planet Earth was trashed, and it was only a matter of time before it became uninhabitable for us as well as them. A hundred years tops, the chief catastrologist calculated. So CanAm fortified the wall that had been built in the previous century between us and MexSanto, erected similar barriers around the few of our cities that remained, and with the doomsday clock ticking down, convened the Joint Intercorponational Panel on Otherworld Colonization (JIPOC) in a last-ditch effort to save the human race.

The panel's objective was clear and straightforward. Hunt the galaxy. Find a new planet. And go there, leaving Earth and its unwelcome billions behind.

Mars seemed the likeliest candidate at first, but it turned out to be a bust, arid and hot and deadly to anything that preferred oxygen over arsenic. The panel cast a wider net, found a bunch of Earth-analog planets outside our own solar system, each one heralding jubilation until the final reports came in: gas-based instead of rock-based, too close to a star, tidal-locked instead of rotating. The killer was the one that lay twenty-plus light-years away, well outside the range of our ships' gravitational drives: Gliese 667Cc, which was by far the most promising site we'd identified to that point. *Close to Home, Too Far from Home*, the worldlink banners read when the bad news broke. But Tau Ceti e, less than twelve light-years away, was the next best thing, with breathable atmosphere, abundant supplies of potable water, nutrient-rich soil, microscopic life, metals, and minerals. Not as fully developed as Earth, much earlier in the evolutionary process—but that was actually a bonus, considering how much the Lowerworld had fouled up our home planet. Tower City, some people called it, and they weren't hearing the name wrong. They were thinking of it as another city on a hill, another place to rebuild human civilization. A chance to start again.

I knew that history the way I knew the two guys I'd grown up with, knew it like everyone else in the Upperworld did, which meant I knew it well enough to breeze through the Two Worlds/ New Worlds module of the Otherworld Colonization Protocol. I liked to think I didn't buy into it wholesale like Adrian, who recited corporational slogans—the Way of Wealth, the Survival of the Richest—as if they were some kind of personal creed. But I wasn't like Griff, either, who'd gotten into conspiracy theories in the past year and started talking about how everything we'd learned in Two Worlds History was a load of crap. I'd always pretty much ignored the Lowerworld, never had a beef against the Lower-lifes as long as they didn't bomb my parents' apartment or hurt my chances of making it off-planet. I wasn't about to flush my entire past—and, more importantly, my future— down the toilet because of some brown-skinned girl's haunting eyes.

That's what I told myself, anyway.

But no matter how hard I tried, I couldn't get over the impulse to stream video of her. To see her again, hear her speak, even if the damn technology wouldn't let me understand more than two words of what she was saying. Every time I went over to Adrian's apartment, I vowed that one final glimpse of her would satisfy me, that I'd be able to brush her off as another anonymous Lowerworlder who'd disappear from my life the moment the screen went dark—but every time the screen went dark, the need to see her again grew stronger. Maybe it was because she was inaccessible that I was so frantic to access her. But it felt like more than that. It felt like I was on the verge of something huge—what, I didn't know—and she was at the center of it.

I wrestled with myself time and again, but every time, I got pinned. So like some pathetic Lower-life Terrarist strung out on crystal death, I kept going back to Adrian, begging for my next fix.

But finally, he cut me off. He'd been watching the videos for months, and—being Adrian—he'd decided right when someone else got interested that there was nothing to see. "They're just pissed because we're leaving and they're screwed," he said. "The sooner we forget them, the sooner we'll be able to fly out of this hellhole." I could have tried joking him into it, reminding him of the times we'd stumbled across banned content on the worldlink, like the rogue side channel we discovered at age fourteen that documented how all the ballplayers we worshiped were pumped up on nanoroids. Finding that report had been a real blow to me, but Adrian had laughed and said, "Look, dude, if everyone's doing it, then no one's doing it," and I'd let him convince me. After that conversation, though I knew the games were fake, I still felt a thrill watching the pure white ball sail out of CanAm Clippers Stadium into a simulated perfect blue twilight.

But this time a sixth sense I didn't know I had told me I needed to be careful around my best friend. It wasn't anything specific he said or did, but after a lifetime of feeling free to share pretty much whatever I wanted to with Adrian, this time it felt different: dangerous, taboo. I'd noticed he seemed to think it was up to him to correct any misconceptions about JIPOC he heard from kids in our Classification. Anything controversial, any doubts or misgivings they expressed, he'd be up in their face, telling them if they didn't like the way things were being run, maybe they should go roll around in the garbage with the rest of the Lower-lifes. He'd never needed to say anything like that to me, of course, because I'd never said anything that sounded like I was questioning him or his dad or the entire colonization effort. Even Griff had enough sense to keep the conspiracy talk between the two of us. But now an uncomfortable feeling told me I couldn't press Adrian too far, couldn't risk him finding out what my real interest in the Lowerworld videos was. If I was going to find the girl, I was going to have to do it some other way.

I couldn't ask my parents. Even if I could talk to them about something like this, I never talked to them these days. Never saw them. When I was little, we used to be pretty close—they'd take me to Clippers games, cheer for me in Little League. My mom had this thing about eating dinner together and talking about our lives the way all the programmable-food promos showed families doing, which wasn't as dorky and painful as it sounds. But in the past year, my dad had been too busy stocking the Otherworld ships to spend any time at home, while my mom had been holed up around the clock in her Data Recruitment lab, fine-tuning the deepsleep technology she'd helped design. I'd kept my dad's worldlink access code, which had let me in on some good tricks for beating the OCP. I didn't bother with my mom's code, which was too science-y for me to make heads or tails of the sites it gave me access to. But I thought if I dug a little deeper, my dad's code might show me a way to find the girl.

I was wrong.

Even though his code was a hundred steps up from mine, it turned out to be a nonstarter too. Probably he had a higher-level code he wasn't letting me in on. Whatever, the only things I could access were decades-old footage of Lowerworld riots and the weekly report of mass executions, Terrarists the Intercorponational Colonization Protection Agency (INTERCOLPA) had caught plotting to set off a nuclear bomb in an Upperworld city or conspiring to steal the plans for our ships' gravitational drive. I couldn't even find any references to Sumati, which either meant she wasn't classified as a Terrarist—which I couldn't believe—or, more likely, that her profile was so highly classified I couldn't get at it. With Griff's help, Adrian had hacked into the heart of the CanAm security network, so it wasn't surprising that every time I ran a search for "current Terrarist attacks" or "active ConGlo cells" or any of a million other keyword combinations, the best I got was an *Access Restricted* message. Most of the time I didn't get that much. The link simply snapped, and I was left staring at a blank screen.

After weeks of trying every search strategy I could think of and getting nowhere, I realized there was only one way I was going to find the sites I was looking for. If I couldn't work through Adrian, I was going to have to get Griff to show me the way in.

Me and Griff—or Richard Griffin III, but I'd always known him as Griff—went back almost as far as me and Adrian. Twelve years to be exact, ever since his dad took the JIPOC job after years of hopping between corponational positions in the Lowerworld. Griff's mom had died a few months before they moved, so I guess his dad decided to settle in one place so Griff wouldn't have to keep joining new Classifications. If Adrian's first appearance in my life was just off the edge of the memory map, Griff arrived right when I was starting to make firm connections, which meant that when I thought about my childhood, it was Adrian's outline but Griff's face that popped up. Like he was a mirror to my past, and I was seeing my own life in his face.

And what a face. Griff never quite settled into the looks he was given, not when he was a pudgy, buck-toothed kid, not after he transformed into a scrawny, snout-nosed teen. There were no pictures of his mom around his apartment, but I always hoped for her sake she didn't look anything like her son. Red hair and freckles everywhere, like his freckles had hair or his hair had freckles. I never figured out which. He told me once, laughing at himself, that his dad had invested in nanocosmetics for his thirteenth birthday, but those had only made matters worse. "The bots took one look at me and ran screaming," he said. Griff laughed all the time, but not like Adrian, the way Adrian's laugh had that commanding tone to it, like: *I'm laughing—you'd better laugh too.* Griff laughed because he found the world ridiculous, because he was convinced it was all a cosmic gag some shadowy forces were playing on everyone else. At least, that's what he said, him and his conspiracy-nut theories. With Griff, you could never tell if he was bullshitting. I don't think I'd ever had a serious conversation with him, and that was fine with me. I certainly didn't intend to have one now.

"Dude," I said to him one day after ColPrep. We were hanging out in his room, Adrian off doing something with his dad for a change, which made me feel relatively safe. Still, I tried to approach the subject like it was no big deal. "I was thinking about that video we watched with Adrian."

"You had to remind me?" Griff said. "As I recall, I was puking my guts out at the time."

"They've got to toughen us up somehow, man."

"Yeah, but what's the rush?" he said. "They can't bioengineer the hell out of us while we're drifting through space? By the time we step off the ships, we could be freaking supermen."

"Maybe there's something they're not telling us," I said in

a spooky voice. "Isn't that what Cons Piracy is always saying?"

"There's a million things they're not telling us," Griff said with a laugh that came mostly out of his nose. "You know, about Survival of the Fattest and all."

"Survival of the Fattest?"

"Yeah, how the fattest cat squashes all the scrawny little kittens," he said. "Isn't that the way it works?"

I cracked up. This was vintage Griff. "Anything else?"

"I could write a book," he said. "Corponational corruption, insider deals. The whole thing's more a leveraged buyout of space than an attempt to save humanity. But none of you pretty boys seem to care about that as long as you get your free ride off of this dump."

I laughed along with him for a minute more. Then, trying to make my voice sound nonchalant while my heart thumped wildly, I said, "But seriously, how'd you get into that shit? It was wild."

For a second Griff looked startled, then he laughed again. "The video? I don't know, I was fooling around one day, and that's what popped up. There's a lot of crazy stuff out there. As all good conspiracy theorists know."

"But how'd Adrian find out about it?" I asked, feeling both nervous and giddy, the way you feel when you do your first drop in zero-G.

Griff stopped laughing—instantly, like my question had cut the power to his face—and the smile slid away. "What did Adrian tell you?"

"Nothing, man."

"He must have told you something."

I shrugged, tried to steer us into safer waters. "He said you were, like, the hacking king."

Griff didn't say anything for a minute. Then he exploded. "Goddamn it. I should have known he'd . . . What *exactly* did he tell you?"

"He didn't tell me anything, man," I said. "Not one goddamn thing. He said you showed him how to get into the Lowerworld videos. So you two could piss your pants laughing at the Lower-lifes behind my back." All of a sudden I felt myself getting angry. "Were you ever planning to let me in on it? Or was it supposed to stay your little secret?"

"God, Cam," Griff said. "It wasn't like that."

"Oh, so what was it?"

"It wasn't anything. At first. But I'm in deep shit if my dad finds out that Adrian knows. It's not a game anymore, dude."

"It's a bunch of Lower-lifes shouting crap from a pile of garbage," I said. "Isn't that what Adrian says?"

Griff shook his head. "You don't get it, man. Adrian doesn't either. It's different this time. Bigger. With Sumati and her disciple—"

My heart jumped. "I want to see it again."

"No way." He shook his head, over and over, like that might physically stop me. "This is why I didn't want to show Adrian. You see this stuff, it gets inside you. You're not the same afterward. You—"

"I said I want to see it again."

Griff tried a smile and a change of direction. "I can also hack into the smut sites. The really hardcore ones. With inter-activity."

"*Now*, Griff," I said, handing him the link controller. "The same site. The crowd, the guards, Sumati, and—the other one."

"God," Griff said, taking the controller. His hand shook. Realizing I'd accidentally intimidated him into doing what I'd tried to do with finesse made me feel ridiculously good, the way—it hit me—Adrian felt most of the time. Strong. Powerful. In control.

Forget finesse. I just wanted in.

And I got in. Griff muttered to himself as he fooled with the link for a minute or two, and one by one all of the lenses showing the permitted sites blinked out, like city lights disappearing before the dawn comes. What was left was a massive glowing silvery field, a nebula on his bedroom wall, and with the controller in his hand, Griff reassembled the pulsing bits of stardust until they formed an image, much clearer and sharper than on Adrian's screen, so highly defined I was half convinced the people from that faraway world could step through the wall and stand right in front of me. "Surround," Griff said, and the figures did step off the screen—or, instead, we sat in the middle of them, with projected bodies all around his room, so close I could have touched them if they'd actually been there. I stood and walked among them, through them, their flesh offering no more resistance than ghosts. Nothing had changed—the muddy streets, the tin-roofed houses, the veils and turbans, the street preacher, the torches, the bowing and silent crowd. The feeling of déjà vu was so strong it felt like it came from somewhere much deeper than the weeks I'd been watching this scene on Adrian's bedroom wall.

But it wasn't a replay. It was somewhere else. It was live. And it was real. It was, I felt, more real than anything I'd seen on the worldlink. Maybe more real than anything I'd seen off the link as well.

And she was there.

The girl, coming up behind Sumati. The black hair and purple robe. The red jewel flashing above her golden eyes. I stood right in front of her, so close I would have felt her breath if there'd been anything to feel. This time, when she stretched her hands out in a copy of the old woman's gesture and spoke the words I couldn't understand—"Sumati" and "CanAm" and a bunch of sounds that meant nothing to me, though I knew instinctively they were the same as before—I imagined the air stirred by her voice.

"Something's wrong with the TranSpeaker," Griff groused, monkeying with the controller. "It always cuts out on her."

When the girl's eyes rose to confront the Peace Corp., I expected those eyes to stare straight through me, at the soldiers who were their real target. I was on the other side of the world, after all, and though I could see her, she couldn't possibly see me.

But her eyes shifted, focused, fell on mine. Up close, their golden irises were rimmed in a shade of green or blue. They locked on me, and my heart caught in my throat.

She *saw*.

The thing I'd buried at the core of my being. The thing I couldn't see by myself, though I knew now that it was there.

She saw *me*.

"Satisfied?" Griff mumbled, looking down at the controller in his hand.

I sat, legs trembling, as the video disintegrated and the girl was swept away like a handful of stars. Now that my high was fading, I thought about apologizing to Griff, saying something to soften the blow, but I knew anything I said would make it worse. We hung out for another hour, not talking much, not watching much, and when I left, he threw me a half wave that looked like a plea.

That night, alone in my room, while I tried to rinse the foul taste of what I'd done out of my mouth with CanAm AquaNova water that had been distilled and purified and desalinated and I hardly knew what else, I struggled to understand what was happening to me. It seemed like, up to this point, I'd been watching it happen, careening along behind it as if it wasn't really me. But it *was* me. It *was* happening.

The only question was, what was it?

For the past few weeks, I'd been watching a beautiful girl on the worldlink. That was nothing new. I'd watched beautiful girls on the link all my life: in colonization promos, in flicks and techgames. If I'd taken Griff up on his offer to show me the smut sites, I'd have seen more beautiful girls, and I could have made them say and do pretty much whatever I wanted. But there was nothing real about that, nothing worth risking anything for. Even the girls I'd dated had been like the videos: surgically reconstructed princesses on an interplanetary ego trip. A week after I cleaned their data out of my selfone, I couldn't remember their faces.

So, why was this girl different? Why did it feel like, with *this* girl, I had to see her again, no matter what the risk? How could a girl who was nothing but an image on a screen mean more to me than girls I'd seen in real life?

All of a sudden, I remembered Griff's words. They joined with the cryptic words of the girl in the video, and together they slammed into me, an asteroid striking in the middle of interstellar space.

It gets inside you, Griff had said. *You're not the same afterward.*

I knew he was right. And I knew what I had to do.

I was going to *find* that girl. Stand in front of her and look into her eyes, the way she'd looked into mine. If I could, speak to her.

I was going to meet that girl.

Which, I knew, was even more impossible than seeing her on the screen. Because that girl wasn't only on the other side of the world.

That girl was on the other side of everything.

Otherworld

Earth Year 3151

Day

Griff visits me every day in sick bay. The shoulder's healing slowly, and the PMP insists I need rest. I'm eager to get out of bed, look around the ship, find out what's going on, but I'm on orders. Also on drugs, which make me drowsy and disinclined to fight the orders. So I stay, and Griff tries to make the time pass as quickly as possible.

Like I said, a lot can change in a thousand years. But that doesn't apply to Griff. He never once got angry at me for that day in his room when I forced him to play the worldlink video. I know he hasn't forgotten, but at least he's forgiven. In fact, he's forgiven not only that but a whole lot more.

That's another way he's different from Adrian.

Today he's cracking up as he tells me the story of how the two of them found me that first night.

"We're on patrol, right?" he says. "Us and about fifty other teams. The last thing we're looking for is castaways. I mean, no offense, but when your pod turned up missing, we figured that was the end of that. We were just going to have to figure out some way to survive on this dump without your brains and bubbly personality."

"You're breaking my heart, man."

Griff pantomimes playing the violin. "So anyway, we're out in the middle of nowhere trying to track those things, the ones that come swooping past the ship all night, moving too fast to get a lock on them. Like I'm looking forward to this, right? But the little monsters don't have the decency to show up in the daylight, so the patrols have to go out after dark. And I'm on patrol because, guess what, Adrian's dad is in charge, and he says everyone has to take turns being out there, no exceptions."

"Except him?"

"And you'd think the top dog would be only too happy to risk his life for the rest of us peons," Griff says with a snort. "So, Adrian and me, we're stumbling around in the dark, maybe seeing those things swirling all around us, maybe not. Having absolutely no idea if they're things at all or if they're just in our minds, and if they aren't, whether they're harmless or plan to eat us for a bedtime snack."

"Thanks to me," I say, "I think we know the answer to that one."

"Give the man the Corporate Cross," Griff says, applauding. "Listen, dude, there's easier ways to impress Adrian's dad than getting your ass chomped."

I laugh for Griff's sake, but the thought of the thing that wounded me, or of sacrificing myself for the approval of Adrian's dad, makes me feel sick. The second probably more so than the first.

"Anyway," Griff goes on after he's had his laugh. "I was the one that heard the thing opening you up. They don't make any noise when they run past the ship, none we've heard anyway. But we're out there, and there's this click like a blade coming out, just a single click, and I'm like, 'Was that you?' And Adrian goes, 'What the hell do you think?' And I'm like, 'I think we're screwed.' And I'm about to crap my pants when Adrian starts shooting into the night, and then I'm like, 'My hero.'"

"You said that to him?"

"I think my actual words were 'Holy shit!'" Griff says, laughing. "But then Adrian insists on going to check it out, to see if he really got it. And I'm like, 'Enough macho bullshit for one night, I'm going home.'"

This time, my laugh's for real. Griff's acting the whole thing out with his face, going from scared shitless to mock heroic in a heartbeat, and though I know it's nothing like what actually happened, though he's turning my near evisceration into a comedy routine, I feel better than I've felt since my pod opened and I stumbled out onto extra-terra incognito. Griff reads my mood and keeps going, adding more ridiculous details to the story, like how Adrian blew on his piece like some gunslinger from the Wild West and how he, Griff, nearly forgot himself and grabbed Adrian's arm for support. It helps that Griff makes

Adrian the star and himself the sidekick. It also helps that, like all the patrols, he has to wear a regulation JIPOC helmet all the time in case Chairman Conroy needs to contact him, and on Griff the thing is so big he looks like a cross between a scarecrow and a bobblehead. With freckles.

Even Griff can't keep the yucks going forever, though. Or he could, but he sees I'm tired, and he knows there are things I want to talk about before I nod off. Griff would much rather keep it light. But cooped up like I am, he's my only source of information. And after spending thirteen years running interference between Adrian and me, I guess he's become an expert at reading my mind.

"Still no word on our location," he says. "Which either means they don't know where we are, or they know all too well."

"Too bad we don't have Cons Piracy around anymore."

"I'm thinking of starting a local chapter."

"Yeah? Sign me up."

"You know what people are saying, right?" he asks. "About the ship."

I sit up. Griff doesn't know any more about what happened to the mission than anyone, but he's been nosing around, and he's picked up plenty of rumors. "What are they saying?"

"Well, for starters, all our major systems are shot," he says. "Navigation and propulsion most obviously, but that's just the tip of the iceberg. The computers are all glitchy, and the hardware's not in any better shape. No operating vehicles, no loaders, no cranes, no nothing to get around outside, much less start fixing up this rock. Everything's just sitting around, and none of it will come online."

"Unreal." We came loaded with endless amounts of equipment to terraform the planet, grow our own food, extract water from air and rock, all that. How could everything be nonoperational? "You're sure about this?"

"No one's sure about anything," Griff says. "Except that we're royally screwed."

"What about your dad? Isn't he working on bringing stuff back online?"

"Yeah," he says. "One system at a time. Want to guess what Conroy has him working on first?"

"Weapons?"

"Bingo." Griff smiles witheringly. "But brilliant as my dad is, he's only one dude. He built in redundancies in case anything failed, but it seems the redundancies failed too. Which means that Rich Griffin, aka the Pride of CanAm, is as clueless as everyone."

He pauses to let his words sink in, but the conclusion is obvious. If the ship's drive isn't working, there's no way to leave this place. And though we knew we might encounter problems on our maiden voyage across light-years of vacuum, we did all our planning under the assumption that the *Executor* would be in shape to tackle those problems, not that it would *be* the problem. JIPOC figured we might need to stay on board while the terraforming got up and running, which is why they stocked the dispensary with enough food and water to last us for maybe five years. Or maybe one.

Or maybe less.

"Oh, and get this," Griff says. "Conroy's minions finally did a head count. Seems your pod wasn't the only one to go AWOL. Word on the street is we lost a hundred or more."

I'm shocked to hear that, though I don't know why I should be—this is just more icing on the cake. "And where'd they go?"

"That's the mystery, my friend." He smiles again, not like he's happy exactly. More like he's pleased to be proved right at last. "Ship's trashed, planet's a cesspool, and there's a hundred pods floating around somewhere in space. Lost. Gone. Like they never existed."

"Like what happened to the Lowerworld ship."

His face turns serious for the first time since coming in. "We're never going to find out what happened to them. They shot that ship as far away from us as they could, dude. Which isn't hard to do when you have the whole flipping universe to play with."

I'm reminded of the council that took place. The final council between Upperworld and Lowerworld. It wasn't pretty. No one expected it to be. Except, maybe, Sofie. Sofie and, possibly, me.

"It was totally messed up, Griff," I say. "Twelve billion human beings, and they screwed them all. And the only reason they got away with it is because they could."

Griff leans back, taking his helmet off so he can run a hand through the red mop he calls his hair. I think he's about to crack another joke when he plops the helmet back on and hunches forward, speaking in an angry undertone that's unlike anything I've heard come from his mouth.

"What goes around comes around," he says. "One percent of one percent of the world's population got to take this pleasure trip. That left a shitload of people with a major grievance against the Chosen Few. Lowerworlders. Or Upperworlders who lost out in the lottery. You don't think someone out there would see this as payback?"

I'm shocked by his tone, though of course the same thought has occurred to me. There's no way any of this was an accident. It had to be sabotage—an incredibly well-planned, incredibly thorough act of sabotage. But before I get a chance to say that, Griff breaks out in another laugh.

"Screw and thou shalt be screwed, as the Good Book says. That's from Saint Fat Cat's First Epistle to the Piss-poorlings, by the way. You can look it up."

And I bust out laughing, louder and longer than I have in centuries.

I'm out of sick bay in four days. More evidence of the sorry state the ship's in: If our medical nanotechnologies were working, treating a shoulder wound should have taken more like four minutes. The PMP insists on running some psychometrics before I go, and I put up with them patiently. I'm not sure what exactly he thinks happened out there—whether he has some nutty idea that I sliced open my own shoulder to get attention, or just for kicks—but he tells me it's routine to test people's mental state after all that time in deepsleep, and I don't make a fuss. He's been suspiciously quiet about the "organic compound" they removed from my eyes, so to paraphrase Griff, he either doesn't know what the stuff is, or he knows all too well. But making a big scene about any of these irregularities will earn me more time in sick bay, where he'll probe deeper, and that's the last thing I want. Plus, plain and simple, I'm dying to get up and get out.

Once I'm cleared to go, I have pretty much all the free time I want. I'm supposed to check back in with the PMP for weekly psychometrics, but that has the sound of something no one's going to hold me to. I'm assigned a cubicle in the ship's living quarters, a personal space not much bigger than the one in sick bay, but I'm not complaining about that, either. At least no one's prying. My living area is stocked with nothing but a neatly pressed jumpsuit and a selfone that won't work on this planet. Not my phone from Earth, either, but that's a long story. My parents could stop by for a visit, I suppose, but with the way it ended back home, I doubt they will. And I'm right: They don't. They do, however, send me a very nice note—handwritten, since all the personal comm devices are on the fritz too—in which they spell out what they told me on Earth: They want nothing to do with a disgrace to the Newell family name like me. Considering the good times we shared when I was younger, their abandonment makes me sad, I guess. Until I remember that I'm the one who abandoned them first, and with very good reason.

At this point, the only thing I have to worry about is Adrian's dad, who'll get word of my release eventually and add me to the roster for patrols. But it might take a while before that happens. He's a busy man, busier than ever now that his nice neat colonization has gone up in flames. Until he tracks me down, I'm essentially a ghost aboard the ship, not officially here. I can't leave the *Executor's* confines—no one can except the patrols, which go out every night to try to figure out where the hell we are or, failing that, at least to determine the identity of the things outside—and obviously there are places on board I'm not welcome. But other than that, I'm on my own clock and my own recognizance.

Griff's busy helping his dad on the day I get out, so I stroll over to the pod bay by myself. That's another bug in the system: The monorails that were supposed to shuttle us around the *Executor* are nonfunctional, which means people have to walk everywhere. The ship's strangely empty, with few fellow pedestrians out in the halls, most of them teens like me, the only difference being that all of them are wearing their identical gray JIPOC helmets. Turns out my friendly neighborhood PMP was exaggerating more than a little when he told me everyone arrived safely: Many of the pods didn't wake their occupants automatically the way they were supposed to, so the PMPs and AMPs, the ones who woke up, are busy rousing people from deepsleep. And lots of passengers, adults especially, are having a rough time with reentry and are stuck in sick bay, most of them coping with the mental stress of being alive long past the point

JOSHUA DAVID BELLIN

they should be dead. Some of them, Griff tells me, actually are dead. Plus, if his sources are right, there's the hundred or so pods that went missing. To no one's surprise, Conroy won't comment on them.

I expect to find the Peace Corp. guarding the bay, but they're nowhere to be seen. I guess after we boarded, they were one more group on a very long list of expendable personnel. Without the Lowerworld to worry about, the *Executor* didn't need them anymore.

I take my time exploring the bay. It's an enormous, canyon-like cavity, practically a city of its own, though a city where no one does anything but sleep. Docked pods climb the walls in rows of thousands, arching so high they get lost in the darkness that gathers beneath the silicone shell. Every so often, a pod drifts from its spot, then goes sailing down the hall to sick bay, where the medical staff are waiting. The pods' homing technology, at least, seems to be working. I search the rows for a cluster of empty slots, something to show me where my own pod and the hundred others ejected, wormed their way outside the hull, and drifted off into space. The bay's far too big for me to find a gap.

It chills me to think what might have happened to me, what did happen to the missing hundred. If my pod hadn't responded to something on this planet—the presence of the other pods, the traces of water that our science guys swear lie deep underground—I'd have become a wandering spirit like the rest, lost in interstellar space for all eternity. Or worse, I could have been stranded on some other planet where I was totally alone. Truth be told, with so many people relying on a technology we couldn't road test beforehand, it's a miracle any of us survived. A miracle that of all the hundreds of thousands of pods, only a handful malfunctioned as badly as mine. A miracle that Adrian and Griff found me right before I became a deep-space predator's bite-size man snack.

I wish I was in the mood to be thankful for miracles.

From the pod hangar, I make my way to the main concourse, which connects the *Executor*'s populated areas to the ship's guts, the mechanical rooms no one enters. Though narrower than the pod bay, the concourse is broad enough to park a battleship. Now that I think of it, I'm surprised Adrian's dad didn't think to bring a couple of those along. There's almost total silence in the concourse, with no moving vehicles, no squeaks or beeps from the robotic service stations, no sound of power tools being operated. Most of the overhead lights are on, but all of the doors are frozen in the open position, and the screens that are supposed to flash warnings and instructions are nothing but flat black squares. I peek into dining halls and common rooms, hear the whir of exercise equipment in use— basic stuff, stationary bikes and ellipticals—along with the buzz of handheld weapons being fired at the shooting range. I don't talk to anyone, and no one talks to me.

It's evening by the time I reach the observation deck midway between prow and stern. Through the glass-lined panels, shielded to protect the ship from radiation, I get my first good view of the planet where the *Executor* has deposited us.

It's not a pretty sight.

Spongiform rock rises in piles like tortured slag heaps. Bubbling vats of sulfurous mud shroud the valleys in fog, while volcanic cones spew yellow sludge as if they're puking the planet's guts. Here at the ship's midpoint, I can feel the floor quivering from all the geologic activity. Pale stars sprinkle the sky, and another heavenly body, much brighter than the stars against the gathering dusk, rides above the waves of mist. A distant moon or neighboring planet, from the looks of it. Even this late in the day, the rays of whatever star this planet circles glance sharply through the haze, warning me of a skimpy atmosphere unprepared to guard human bodies from UV. I was luckier than I knew that my two oldest friends went to check on Adrian's shooting skills before the sun rose, because I'd have been a piece of crispy bacon if they hadn't. Anyone who goes out before dark has to suit up in full radiation gear. Atmospheric pressure is roughly Earth-normal, but the science guys tell us there's not much in the way of oxygen, nitrogen, CO_2, and the other gases we need to survive. That would explain why there's no visible water, no sign of vegetation. Teams have gone out at daytime without collecting so much as a single microbe. Unless you count the night creatures, which no one can see clearly enough at dark to identify and which have eluded the search teams during the day, this planet's as devoid of life as the catastrologists told us Earth would be by now.

Actually, now that I look at the place, it's hard to believe large-scale predators could exist here at all. Hard to believe such a thing could have evolved in so harsh an environment, with nothing to feed on and nowhere to hide from the onslaught of the sun. Unless evolution has been supercharged by the UV barrage, you'd think anything that tried to live would have melted back into the soup before it had a chance to grow up. Tau Ceti e was supposed to be a young planet, an unfinished planet—a planet that could go either way, depending on fate and corpornational ingenuity. But as I study this place in the light of a star that for the moment can't kill me, it looks less like a planet in embryo than one on the verge of extinction. Not clay ready for the sculptor's hands, but ash awaiting the gust of wind that'll blow it back into the universal dust.

I can't be the first person aboard the *Executor* to notice this. If it's occurred to me, a guy who squeaked past the Worlds of Wonder module of the OCP only thanks to some very dedicated cheating, it must have occurred to Conroy and his geek squad. It must have occurred to half the other passengers as well—including Griff. They must be asking the same questions I'm asking right now.

Where do the night creatures come from? What are they doing on this barren world? How have they managed to survive?

And with our ship so completely incapacitated, how long can we last against them?

My breath escapes in a rush as something launches itself out of the mist right at me, as if it's the answer to my question. It moves so fast, and I'm so busy jerking away, I don't get a good look at it, seeing nothing but spidery limbs and a maw erupting with teeth like nails. It glances off the window, but it can't break through an alloy designed to withstand the impact of asteroids. It returns for another assault before spinning and vanishing into the fog. Dimly, I see other shapes moving below, shapes that seem little more than mist. And I hear the sound of them hammering the ship, percussion after percussion making the hull groan.

They've never attacked the ship before. And they've always waited for full dark to appear. But both of those things have changed.

They're out there right now.

And they're obviously trying to find a way to get in.

Upperworld

When the first pictures of Tau Ceti e appeared on the worldlink, everyone said it looked just like Earth.

That's what the banners said, too: *Earth in the Making! Our Home Away from Home!* Personally, I didn't think it looked like much of anything, only a tiny, faint bluish dot in the middle of empty space. But I could understand why people would say that. People always see what they want to see.

And so I wondered what people said when they saw me. Did they say, *He looks just like Cam?*

Maybe I did. Maybe, to the rest of the Upperworld, I looked the same.

But I wasn't the same.

The girl's face was burned into my consciousness. Her golden eyes stared at me in my dreams. The red dot on her forehead glowed like a heart. And the daytime was no better. Her face showed up in the faces of everyone I saw, as if she'd stepped off the screen and become a video overlay of my entire waking life. I didn't know her name—I always thought of her as Sumati's little sister, or daughter, or secretary—but whenever I thought of her, I knew I had to find her.

I also knew that the whole idea was crazy. I didn't need my two best friends to tell me that—and, after that day with Griff in his room, I vowed never to talk to either of them about her again. I knew there was no chance for me to meet a girl from halfway around the world, one single girl who lived in the midst of one Lowerworld city or another, who probably didn't speak my language and certainly didn't share my history or my future. The colonization was only seven months away, and travel between Upperworld and Lowerworld, which had never been easy except for corponational officials, had become practically unthinkable as CanAm and the other Upperworld corponations tightened security measures. The next trip I was taking was off-planet—and when I took that trip, I wouldn't be coming back. I knew it was crazy to dream about meeting a girl who was supported by Terrarist networks, even if I didn't believe, couldn't believe, that she was a Terrarist herself. But whether she was or wasn't, I'd never find her, and the only chance I'd have of seeing her again was if she showed up on the weekly tally of Lowerworld radicals who'd been earmarked by INTERCOLPA for execution.

That thought made me crazier than almost anything else. The thought that I would never meet her, never get a chance to learn what she was trying to tell me—and then she'd be gone, dangling from a rope in some SubCon square, her sightless eyes bulging and her black braid lopped off to be flung spitefully to the crowd. And I'd be expected to nod approvingly and get on with my life now that she was gone and her people—I always thought of them as *her* people, even though Sumati's name was the one she herself used—couldn't interfere with the Otherworld colonization anymore. We were enemies, and once she was gone, I would never discover whether we might have been anything else.

That thought made me even crazier.

I scoured the worldlink, hoping to find out where she was, though I knew that wherever she was, it was too far away. Maybe I wasn't trying to find *her* so much as I was trying to find proof that a guy like me and a girl like her could live in the same world. But every place I looked, all I found was the same Two Worlds propaganda, hammering home endlessly that the Lowerworld was the source of all the planet's problems and we'd be living in a paradise as soon as we left them behind for good. Without teachers—the Upperworld had gotten rid of them right from the start, along with classrooms and libraries and textbooks, all of which were unnecessary drains on prosperity—there was no one I could ask for an alternate version of events, nowhere I could turn with my questions and doubts. Classification had been about soaking up Two Worlds History and securing a lower-echelon corponational station by age twenty-one. ColPrep was about following orders—or getting an extra-heavy boot in your face when you didn't. My parents I saw three seconds a week if I was lucky, when I happened to pass them in the hallway going in and out of our apartment. But it wouldn't have been any different if we'd sat around the dinner table every night like we used to. My dad's access code had gotten me nothing but more JIPOC banners and slogans. If he didn't believe everything they said, then nobody did.

And from what I could tell, everybody did.

I'd take the moving walkway through the Two Worlds Center on my way to ColPrep, see everyone glued to their controllers and headsets, involved in their worldlink sessions or chats, and I'd get the strangest sense of distance, like I wasn't seeing actual people but simulations, holographic images on the link. Nobody was real to me. My oldest friend had become a risk to avoid, part of the chatter that played constantly over the lines and screens of the Upperworld, telling me to ignore, deny, revel in my own good fortune and forget about everything else. My second-oldest friend had never said anything like that to me, but he was just as much a danger as Adrian—in fact, he was even more, since it was entirely possible he knew what I was really looking for that day in his room. I felt rootless, like I didn't belong anywhere. I wasn't part of the Lowerworld—I couldn't imagine that, or at least, when I tried to, all I saw was her—but I wasn't part of the Upperworld, either. The only person who I felt would understand what was happening to me was the girl. *She*, I was sure, would see who I really was.

She already had. And I desperately needed her to tell me what she'd seen.

So I kept searching. I watched the link night and day. I blew off training sessions, and I suffered the trainers' wrath and my own body's rebellion the few times I did bother to show up. I slept—when I slept—with her image before my eyes, always there to remind me she existed, always there to remind me she was lost to me. In my dreams, I stood face-to-face with her, listening to the words she spoke—and though I couldn't understand what she said, I'd wake up believing she'd told me something too important to forget. I'd start the new day exactly where I'd finished the old, desperate to crack the riddle, praying the truth would be revealed the next time I brought up the feed.

But I found nothing.

And then, one day, she found me.

I woke up with my face plastered to the controller, an urgent call jangling in my ear. I realized I'd fallen asleep at the link. My mouth tasted stale and gummy from the night, and my head pounded. I reached blindly for my selfone and discovered it was Griff. We hadn't talked in weeks.

"Earth to Cam." His voice came through the ether. "You watching this, Cam?"

"Mm," I mumbled.

"Dude, you're a wreck," he said with a laugh. "Check this out." He sent me the link he was so eager for me to see. I blinked, clearing sleep from my eyes, and then I gasped.

"Historic, huh?" Griff said.

It was her.

I stared, speechless, as the screen on my bedroom wall filled with her face. She sat at a long wooden table, hands folded neatly on the top. They had a mike on her, and beside her sat Sumati, with her own mike. Both of them wore their purple robes, braided with gold. Her eyes flashed, and her teeth were sheer white when she spoke.

"It is a great honor," she said in perfect English but with an appealing lilt. "We wish to thank the Upperworld corporations who have offered us this chance to participate in the discourse of Otherworld colonization."

She talked like that, formal, as if she was reading from a script. But though she was speaking my language at last, her words didn't make sense in my half-conscious state. *Discourse of Otherworld colonization? Great honor? Chance to participate? In what?*

"Is this a secure channel?" I asked Griff.

"We wouldn't be watching if it wasn't," he shot back. "I learned my lesson the last time, bro."

I mumbled something, half apology, half nonsense. "Then how did Sumati . . . ?"

"They've opened up all the channels to the Lowerworlders. To announce the symposium."

Now it was Griff's words that didn't make sense.

"We have been disappointed by the response to our petitions thus far," the girl was saying on the screen. She spoke with a smile in her voice that barely touched her lips. "But we had faith that, with patience and persistence, the whole world would come to appreciate the justice of our cause."

"What do you want from this symposium?" a voice shouted from off screen.

"A seat at the table," she responded immediately. Sumati, I noticed, sat mutely behind her own microphone, heavy hands resting on the tabletop like two wooden weights. "An opportunity to discuss the grievances of the Lowerworld, and the prospects for an equitable, collaborative colonization. One that benefits all of humankind, not the select few."

I stared, the words beginning to make sense. But I could hardly believe I was hearing them. Mostly I watched her, and my heart soared.

"There was a demonstration," Griff said. "A major one. With, like, millions of protestors. There've been smaller demonstrations across the Lowerworld for weeks. All about colonization. Some of the speakers have been from the Upperworld, worldlink stars and stuff. Criticizing how exclusive the colonization protocol has been. Lots of arrests. But it's kind of tough to arrest twenty million people."

I said nothing, just watched her face. I couldn't believe I'd been searching the link for weeks and I'd missed all of this. Probably none of it had made the licensed channels. But it didn't matter, I told myself. All that mattered was that she was here now.

"Cons Piracy has been supporting the Lowerworld protests," Griff went on. "They hacked some key systems, threatened to go public with what they found, and that made the Upperworld corporations antsy. So CanAm and the others finally decided it was time to sit down with representatives from the Lowerworld. It was getting, I don't know, politically difficult for them? If there's still anything like politics. It was an embarrassment, at least. Bad for business. This whole symposium is probably some big PR move."

"Where's it going to be?"

"That's the thing," Griff's voice came. "Right here. In New York CITI. At the old UN building. They're bringing representatives from all the Lowerworld corponations, plus Sumati and her people. It's gonna be huge."

Heart pounding, I asked, "Is it open to the public?"

"Is anything?"

"I'm going," I said.

"Yeah, sure, me too. Want to book the next bullet?"

"I'm serious, Griff. I'm going."

Griff was quiet for a long time. The feed had frozen, and I studied the eyes of the girl on the link. She stared straight back at me, the way she always did, the way she had of reaching out through the screen to enter my world. Now that I was finally watching her on a crystal clear Upperworld channel, I saw that her eyes were even more striking than I'd imagined: eyes of pure gold, reflecting every color I could think of.

She was coming to the Upperworld. Against all odds, she was coming to *me*. New York CITI was the closest she'd be to my home by thousands of kilometers. I could do this. I had to.

As if reading my mind, Griff came back on. "Sounds like a blast. When do we leave?"

Otherworld

Earth Year 3151

Night

It's weeks before I'm sent out on my first patrol. I'm not sure if that's a precaution — to protect me, to protect the mission — or your typical bureaucratic red tape. Whatever, one evening I'm hanging out in the weight room, rebuilding muscle in my injured arm, when one of the nameless gray-suited minions of Chairman Conroy comes up to me and tags me for the night's patrol. No training, no instructions. Just grab a breathing mask, a helmet, and a flashlight from the commissary, meet my partner by Airlock Alpha 11 at shift change, and go. No weapon. I ask the girl at the window for a gun, but all I get is a frown. I guess they're playing it safe about that.

For a solid week after their first assault on the *Executor*, the creatures pounded away at the hull the moment the sun fell, moving too quickly to blast with the ion pistols we tried to use in place of our (nonfunctional) plasma cannons. Eventually, though, they must have realized they weren't getting in that way, and since then there's been no sign of them. No one thinks that means they've gone away for good, though. But Adrian's dad is using the breathing room to put a new plan into effect, one that involves planting what amounts to an electric fence around the ship. With a vessel the size of the *Executor*, that's going to take forever, even with the crews going out around the clock. Still, the chairman has a plan, and when the chairman has a plan, your best bet is to stick your head up your ass and not ask questions.

My partner for tonight's patrol, I discover when I arrive at the airlock, is Adrian. I don't ask questions about that, either.

I haven't seen him since the first night. Seen him to talk to, I mean. I've seen him around, but I'm not about to interrupt him in the middle of some drill or routine or whatever he does. I'm not sure what he does. Like everyone who's out of their pods and assigned to Conroy's patrols, he seems to move around a lot. With most people, that just looks like nervous energy. But maybe the commander's son has more of a purpose than the rest of us.

He throws me a look. I nod back. I'm excited to get out of the tin can—that's what everyone around the ship calls it—even if it means spending time with two of my least favorite organisms in the universe. You have no idea how stir-crazy you get when you're trapped with tens of thousands of other people who are suffering from the same toxic blend of boredom and anxiety as you are. My arm feels good, better than ever in fact thanks to my self-designed rehab. For a long time, longer than you'd think from an injury that didn't damage nerve or bone, the arm felt weak, uncoordinated. The PMP who was assigned to my case—or spying on me, depending—wondered at our first follow-up session if that had anything to do with the creature's venom, but obviously he didn't care that much, because he never ordered labs or anything. Not that I showed up for any of my other appointments after he wasted my time on the first one. But after a month or so, the numbness in my arm went away on its own, and after that the PMP vanished from my life the way you can aboard a ship that's as cold and anonymous as the rest of the Upperworld always was.

Adrian's been out on patrol multiple times since he and Griff found me. Griff tells me Chairman Conroy wants his son to set a good example, to prove no one's above doing the grunt work. All part of the chairman's attempt to spin the colossal blunder of landing a nonfunctional starship on this prime piece of space estate. But Adrian's as much a rookie as me when it comes to planting the perimeter fence. He's got about fifty of the fence posts, meter-long aluminum poles topped by silver-and-black flags, stacked on a little nonmotorized cart, and the look in his baby blues belies the sleepy arrogance on his face.

He's scared. And I don't blame him. But I can't begin to think of a way to say that to him.

Adrian clears the airlock. "Let's move." I hear his voice inside my headset, distorted by the microphone in his breathing mask. He rolls the cart down the ramp, with me following right behind.

We step out onto the planet surface. Shadows swirl around us. I can't tell if something's moving in the dark, or if our flashlights are rearranging the mist. Now that I've seen the planet by day, I'm not sure if it's completely solid or partly gaseous. If the latter, it won't make much difference what we do about the night creatures. It'll only be a matter of time before the ship is pulled all the way under.

"I never thanked you," I say.

It sounds formal. Adrian grunts.

"No, really," I say. "That night . . ."

"Forget it," he says.

We walk through the dark and fog. The ship's lights become misty halos, then pinpoints like stars, then nothing. Adrian seems to have a course charted, but I'm just following along behind him and his rattling cart, not sure how far we're walking or when we're going to start planting our flags. Mostly I'm trying my best to avoid the mud pits that appear from time to time. Not easy to do when you can't see two centimeters in front of your face.

"Any progress?" I say. "In figuring things out?"

"What things?"

I shrug, pointlessly. He can't see me any better than I can see him. "The creatures. Where we are. What went wrong with the mission."

"Who says anything went wrong?"

I almost laugh. But laughter, I'm pretty sure, isn't on tonight's agenda. "What we're going to do, then."

"We're going to travel around a secured perimeter extending several hundred meters outward from Airlock Alpha Eleven," he says. "Make sure the area remains clear of unlicensed life-forms. Expand our range into enemy territory with the additional devices on this trolley. Then go back to base."

"That's it?"

"You questioning my orders?"

"Do you outrank me?"

"I'm acting on behalf of the chief executive officer of JIPOC," he says. "So yeah, I think I outrank you."

We pick up the pace. I splash into sucking mud but keep going. With no warning, Adrian grabs one of the flags from the cart and jams the pole into the ground, then another, then another. At this rate, unless he's got more of the devices tucked away in his pockets, we're going to be finished with our circuit long before daybreak.

"Look, man," I say.

"No, you look," Adrian says, stopping so abruptly I almost collide with him. "This is the mission. You don't like it, go home. Otherwise, keep your mouth shut."

"So that's it," I say. "That's all."

"That's all," he says. "If it was up to me, you wouldn't be here, Cam. I told my dad. I told him you and your Lower-life girlfriend could stay on Earth. Make more dirt rats to shit the place up until the end."

"But he obviously disagreed."

"Maybe he didn't," he says, spitting the words. "Maybe he

meant for your pod to jettison in deep space and float off into a black hole, but that's another thing that went wrong with this lousy mission."

"You saved my life, man."

"I saved a piece of shit that should have died back on Earth," he says. "If I'd known it was you, I'd have let the thing finish you off while I watched."

I'm glad he said it. Glad it's finally out in the open. I realize now why, before I met Sofie, I never said or did anything that might have gotten me on Adrian's bad side. Because I was afraid. Afraid of him, afraid of losing him. You'd think being friends since before either of us could remember would make us safe. But the truth is, being friends that long meant there were some things we could never touch. Things we'd always assumed the other would never say or do. Things that, once they were said and done, neither of us could take back.

"So what happens if we meet another one tonight?" I say.

"We won't," he says. "The sonic devices keep the things at bay."

"And if they don't?"

"They do."

"You've really got this all figured out, don't you?"

"Go to hell, Cam," he says.

"Already there," I say.

And we walk on in silence.

The perimeter devices emit a beep that's too high-pitched for human ears to detect. But the one place the creatures didn't attack the ship was where a geologic team had planted some of the poles. So it stands to reason the monsters have better ears than we do and shy away from the sound.

We think.

Either that or the creatures have retreated for reasons of their own. Or they're regrouping for a new form of attack. Adrian has no idea, and neither does his dad, and neither does anyone else aboard the *Executor*. Adrian doesn't say that, but his confidence has had a false ring to it from the get-go.

The other problem is that the supersonic signal travels from pole to pole, and its range is limited. The poles weren't designed for perimeter defense. They're surveying tools, that's all. They map subsurface fissures and faults, which is why the team planted them in the first place. We haven't reached the outer limit of their effectiveness—probably—but we will soon, and then there will be substantial spans of the ship that remain unsecured. Whether we have the technology to make more, Adrian won't say.

Adrian won't say anything, actually. He communicates in grunts and gestures. So do I. The only sound is the muffled noise of his cart on the soft ground.

We walk the perimeter, wiggling existing poles out of the ground to make sure their tips are flashing, jamming them back in, adding a new pole every so often, though not with any logic or pattern that I can tell. It's tedious, mindless work, and it's all done pretty much blind: Even if our flashlights showed more than a blanket of thick mist, we'd be guessing at how far apart we can place the sensors. I laugh to myself when I remember all the promotional videos we watched back on Earth, which showed colonists capering euphorically across a lush green landscape. That, of course, was based on the assumption not only that we'd be unimpeded by planetary slime and lethal life-forms, but that we'd be able to *see* the landscape. Adrian and I walk slowly, warily. I think I speak for both of us when I say no one feels any desire to caper.

The night wears on. Nothing moves except mist. Bubbles of goop pop around us. My mask fogs, making visibility even tougher. My shoulder's not holding up as well as I'd hoped: It aches from the repetitive pushing and pulling. I want to ask Adrian why I was paired with him on this particular patrol, but I know he won't answer me. Teaching me a lesson, probably. Proving how wise and merciful the commander is, that he'd trust his son with a traitor. Whatever the explanation, I'm sure it's no better than the one Chairman Conroy is preparing for why the Upperworld's little family vacation didn't turn out quite the way he had planned. I just hope the idea isn't to lead me too far from the ship then yank off my oxygen mask. Or nail me in the back with the ion gun my partner is carrying ostentatiously at his hip.

My partner. I laugh. My superior.

We've checked the last fence post. We've placed the few that weren't working on the cart, and we've extended home territory by as much as a hundred meters with the ones we brought. Time to head back.

Adrian steers his cart toward the ship. He's nothing but a

shadow in the mist. The *Executor*, huge as it is, can't be seen at all.

"What's that?" It's the first time he's spoken since cussing me out.

I nearly run into him for the second time tonight. Fog shrouds the sky, and for a second I think he's paused to look for the stars, invisible from our perspective. It's a minute before I realize he's not looking at anything. He's removed his helmet, and his head's cocked, listening.

I hear it too.

A whine, distant and steady. Nothing like the clacking sound of the night creatures. It's barely a tickle inside my ear, but it must be from something big. I take off my helmet, and the whine grows to a howl. It seems to come from everywhere at once, sky and ground. The rock quivers beneath me. My teeth, my throbbing shoulder, the bones in my feet and fingers answer it, and pretty soon my whole body's part of the sound. From the way he's frozen, Adrian feels it too. I can't place it, though something tells me I should.

We both drop to the ground as the sky splits with a scream.

Light is everywhere. The rock shakes against my stomach, pieces of it tearing free and whistling past our ears at a speed that would kill us if they struck home. The mist has arms and legs, but it's not the thing that attacked me. It's tendrils of fog that snake into the sky as if something's pulling them tight while they clutch for a handhold on the ground. With the warring darkness and light, it's impossible to see anything. But I feel as if a mountain, or a cloud, or a moon has collapsed on us, crushing the sky flat. I can't breathe. And then I can, and two words rip out of my chest as if they're attached to the streaming fog.

"The ship!"

In a flash of light, I glimpse Adrian's terrified face. "What ship?"

I see what he's afraid of. In his panic, he thinks his dad somehow got the *Executor* working, then sent his son on patrol before liftoff. There's a grim satisfaction in knowing that, though this is the fate Adrian wanted for 99.9 percent of the world's population, the thought of being left behind scares the crap out of him, too.

"The Lowerworld ship!" I scream, a centimeter from his ear. Which doesn't change his look all that much.

Then again, I'm not sure he hears me. I can't hear myself.

Like a mountain, like a cloud, like a moon cut loose from orbit and plummeting to meet its parent, the Lowerworld ship explodes from the night sky and hangs above us in a mantle of brilliant white light. It must be moving fast, but it's so colossal it seems not to be moving at all, filling the sky from horizon to horizon until for all I can tell it *is* the sky, a daytime sky pulsing with the red-hot veins of atmospheric entry. For a second I think it's going to touch down right on our heads, and I imagine what it would be like to be crushed by something like that, something that dwarfs us the way we dwarf an amoeba. Something so unthinkably big it not only can't see us but can't properly be seen *by* us. But at last I detect an end to its length, a gap where blinding hull meets pitch-black sky, and I watch its tail soar past, its mammoth slipstream pressing us so hard against the ground I think it's not going to matter that it chose not to crush us directly with its weight. I struggle to my feet as it thunders beyond the makeshift perimeter, reverse gravitational thrusters lighting the fog as if it's on fire, nose searching the ground like an insect so mammoth it plans to pollinate an entire planet. When the thrusters die and it settles to its final resting place, so deep in the fog I can't tell where it's touched down, the rocking of its hull throws me and Adrian to the spongy terrain once more. Then it's done and the ground lies still.

I stand, legs quivering, and peer into the night for the place it landed. But it must be kilometers away, and with the bank of fog rising before me like a wall, there's nothing to see. It's traveled a thousand years, crossed star systems and more, and in a matter of seconds caught itself in one final star's pull and found its home.

The *Freefall.*

Prototype for the Upperworld ship, named after the gravitational drive that powered our ship as well. Smaller than ours, more primitive—originally built for storage, not passengers. A backup. The ship that was considered more likely to fail.

Sofie's ship.

Here. On this planet.

I drop my helmet and run in the direction the ship landed, careless of the dark, the steaming mud, the fog. Adrian screams something behind me, but I don't listen. All I can think of is that she wasn't supposed to be here. She was supposed to be somewhere else, a million worlds away. She was supposed to be lost to me forever.

But she's not. She's here. If she's alive, she's here.

I run on, leaving the *Executor* behind, leaving everything behind. Running toward her. Only toward her.

I can't believe the universe can go from so big to so small in a single moment.

Earth, 2150

Upperworld

ew York Central Intercorponational Telecom Interface, the hub of the worldlink, lay less than an hour north of CanAm Capital (formerly CanAm Capital East) by bullet train. Getting there was a breeze. My parents were so busy they didn't know I was gone. Now that Griff and I had our colonization passes and weren't just two stupid kids out for a joyride, we could travel pretty much anywhere we pleased in CanAm, so long as we took a licensed form of transportation and weren't trying to smuggle illegals over the border or anything like that. And Griff had swiped his dad's credit codes, so we went in style—private compartment on the CanAm Capital Line. With something like fifty codes to his name, Griff's dad never noticed when one of them went missing.

I hadn't been on a bullet train since I was a kid, when my parents took me on a tour of the Central territory before the merger. I remembered the excitement of that trip, gazing through the window at a world far bigger than I'd imagined, my mom and dad pointing out features of the landscape while I gobbled junk food courtesy of Universal Comestibles. The great thing about flying at five hundred kilometers per hour is that everything outside your window flashes by too fast to see the chinks in the Upperworld's armor. The buildings gleam, the smog diffusing the sunlight so it looks like you're hovering in a cloud, whereas at ground level you swim in hot, putrid air as thick as a blanket. What used to be the seat of the national government—the Capitol One Building, with its dome and rotunda, the Linked-In Memorial, with its cryptic financial advice from Our Funding Fathers chiseled into the white marble portico—is walled against the intrusion of Lowerworld Terrarists, but even that solid gray barrier has a soothing look when you're rocketing past it too fast to think. The marshy areas where the ocean has nibbled the coastline sparkle in the sunlight, and the river looks clean too, even though you know it's only because of CAPA (CanAm Purification Authority) that you can drink the stuff at all. Riding by bullet train, you forget that the Upperworld is practically as unlivable as the Lowerworld, the only difference being that we can retreat behind walls and afford sewage treatment and Freshen Air Portable Purification Systems and all that. Riding by bullet train is like living in a worldlink video, or a dream.

As soon as we hit the streets of New York CITI, exactly forty-five minutes after we blasted out of the CanAm Capital depot, we were back to a reality check. CanAm shut down most of the metropolitan areas in the past fifty years—too inefficient to run hundreds of cities when you can cram your entire population into three—but it keeps this ancient, crumbling metropolis open for two reasons: historical significance and the CITI itself. Maybe only the second reason. New York used to be the site of political conventions, when there were still politics. Me and Adrian and Griff used to crack up when we'd watch the old campaign videos archived on Two Worlds sites, the Team Party versus the Greed Party, the Plutocrats versus the Publicans, and nothing to show for it at the end of the day except more taxes and gridlock and grandstanding. These days the place is a museum. Filth breathes from the sewer grates, the rivers, the empty doorframes of abandoned warehouses and high-rises. The island's half underwater, with oily craters pockmarking what's left of the streets, some of the holes so deep they show through to where subway cars lie submerged like marine fossils. Girders climb aimlessly into the sky where some development genius had the idea to build another skyscraper then ran out of capital or tenants or dry pavement to build on. I'd never thought of it this way, but now I wondered what all this decay would look like to someone from the Lowerworld viewing us on a worldlink screen. If, that is, they could afford screens down there, where all they seemed to have was mud and trash and disease and Terrarism.

And her.

"Where to?" I asked, looking up and down the street. A corroded sign attached to a leaning metal pole announced that we were standing on what had once been Park Avenue.

"Follow the crowd."

Most days, New York CITI's a ghost town. But today the streets were crawling with privacars on their way to the symposium. They looked important, sleek black limos with tinted windows and corponational logos. There was no foot traffic to speak of, only the few others who'd exited the train with me and Griff, but there were hundreds of Peace Corp. officers in their white uniforms and black visors, guns held stiffly across their chests. They lined the roadways, perched atop buildings, drove alongside the limos in armored transports. Helicars flew overhead. The mutter of the officers' voices speaking into comm devices was far louder than the whispered hum of electric vehicles. Every time we passed one of the soldiers standing at street level, I felt his eyes following me.

In an hour's walk, we arrived at the old United Nations building, a teetering, razor-thin slab of cement overlooking the toxic East River. The burned-out hulk of a skyscraper crouched beside it, fragments of green glass clinging to shattered windowpanes. Gazing at this sad ruin of some twentieth-century dream of international harmony and cooperation—most people in the Upperworld called it the Benighted Nations building—I wished the symposium had been held on the opposite side of the island, at the glistening CITI complex, the only part of old New York that CanAm kept in good repair. But the limos pulled up in front of the UN facade, disgorging their passengers into the waiting ranks of Peace Corp. officers. A far greater number of people were climbing out of privacabs that must have come from the nearby heliport. Griff and I edged closer, and I couldn't help staring at the crowd.

According to Two Worlds History, twenty-first-century CanAm had toyed with the idea that people from incompatible genetic backgrounds could coexist. But that had blown up in their face, especially in the borderlands near MexSanto, where the damage had gotten so bad they'd had to build a wall and then shut down CanAm West for good. For a while they'd tried the half measure of concentrating like-skinned people in separate urban areas, but that had made a serious dent on profits. So in the past fifty years, most people with genetic histories outside designated parameters had been deported by INTERCOLPA to Lowerworld prisons and resettlement camps. You'd see the occasional darker-hued person in CanAm, mostly traveling bigwigs and their servants from the Lowerworld, but nothing like the flood I saw before me now.

There were people in strange clothes and hats, people with all colors of skin, dusty brown and pale gold and near-black, people babbling to each other or themselves in languages that sounded like they were talking through their noses or deep in their throats or, sometimes, with parts of their body that had nothing to do with speech, like their hands or their eyes or their shoulders. Robes flowed, turbans bulged above dark, curly hair. Some of the women had hair practically down to their calves, and sometimes it was twined with beads or small stones that twinkled as their hair swung. Others had their entire bodies wrapped in dark cloaks, black or chocolate brown, only their eyes peeking through a horizontal slit. One of those women wore glasses, with narrow robotic-looking frames, so I wondered if there was a person in there at all. Some men had enormous, bushy beards, while others had hair almost as long as the women's, thick twisted locks that looked none too clean as they burst free from shapeless, braided hats balanced on their heads. Even at the edge of the crowd, the smell of bodies and breath was overpowering. No one paid attention to us, two of the few light-skinned people in the pack, wearing T-shirts and jeans. But I definitely felt like we were the spectacle here, the ones who didn't belong.

If I'd thought the Peace Corp. was out in force when we got off the train, I was unprepared for the solid mass of white uniforms that guarded the entrance to the UN headquarters. They'd set up a cordon right outside, and they were herding the Lowerworld delegates—none too gently, it seemed to me— through a metal detector. Some of the Lowerworlders beeped when they walked through, and the Peace Corp. yanked them from line, swiping their bodies with handheld scanners. The bracelets and necklaces many of the visitors wore seemed to be the worst offenders. But some people without the proper credentials tried to force or slip their way through, and the Peace Corp. weren't having any of that—the gate crashers ended up being marched away under heavy guard. Off to one side, a small group of protestors waved signs I couldn't read and chanted in languages I couldn't understand. But to me, the chants sounded ugly, the unknown words hurled like threats. I guess the Peace Corp. agreed, because they had their guns out where they could use them in a hurry. Taking in the whole setup, I realized there was no way we'd get into the building.

"Griff . . ."

"Relax," he said.

We stood in line, approaching the metal detector. When we got to the front, Griff held up a codebar and the guard scanned it, then nodded us through. He didn't bat an eye at our street clothes or pale faces.

"What the hell?" I whispered.

"My dad's MasterCode," he said. "It's everywhere you need to be."

I shook my head and laughed. I'd never understood exactly what Griff's dad did, other than being involved in top-secret technical operations for the JIPOC starfleet. But apparently the man had access to everything. I wondered if I should have asked him to help me find the girl instead of bothering with his son.

With the motley crowd pushing and shoving at our back, we entered the building. The cracked marble floor of the front lobby echoed the delegates' jabber. Worldlink lenses hovered around the lobby, clicking and whirring—most of them with the familiar logos of Upperworld corporations, but a few with letters that looked like the handwritten signs the crowd had held in that first video I'd seen months before. Peace Corp. officers filled the place, their guns in holsters, but they made no move to stop us as we approached the council chamber.

Wooden doors opened into a large, crowded auditorium, crumbling like everything else. Some seats still existed, lopsided and chewed by time, but most people were standing on what had once been carpet but had worn away almost entirely to bare flooring. A balcony hung overhead, precarious with all the bodies filling it. At the front of the room a long, curved table sat under spotlights, many of them dead or flickering, so there were patches of light and shadow on the people seated at the table. Some of the panelists were dressed like Lowerworlders, while others wore the suits and ties of corponation execs. I was a little surprised—though relieved—to see that Adrian's dad had decided not to attend the symposium. All of the panelists had mikes, but with the roar of the crowd and the condition of the sound system, I couldn't make out what they were saying. Probably most of them weren't speaking English. Throughout the room, I saw hookups for the worldlink, so I knew the event was being streamed live. Still, it seemed to me that the corponational leaders who'd set up this symposium couldn't have had too high an opinion of it, or too much faith in its outcome, if they'd decided to hold it in an old-world tenement like this.

The room stank with bodies. I strained over colorful hats and halos of curly hair, but there was no sign at the speakers' table of Sumati or the girl. Maybe they hadn't come. Maybe they'd only been the ones to set this up, and now other Lowerworld reps had taken their place. Maybe, at that, the whole thing was a sham, a PR move like Griff had said. With all the color and noise and electricity in the room, it sure made great video.

Then there came a loud rustle from the crowd, voices and robes murmuring in confused excitement. Lights flickered above the stage as they struggled to come on. Lenses wheeled to a hidden doorway behind the speakers' table. I caught a flash of white, followed by purple. Sumati's bodyguards trooped in and arranged themselves at the foot of the stage, while the girl led Sumati to a seat at the table.

I could hardly believe it. She was there, not thirty meters from where I stood. She'd been staring at me for months from half a world away, and now, if it hadn't been for the mob between us, I could practically have caught her eye.

The crowd erupted. Cheers, whistles, feet stamping. Some people in the balcony let out what sounded like boos, but when I looked up at their beaming faces I realized that must be their form of applause. Sumati sat heavily, but the girl remained standing for a moment longer, smiling in the spotlights, the fold of her purple robe tucked in one hand while she raised her other to the crowd. The Lowerworld delegates at the table stood and applauded. Some of them bowed, while others performed an elaborate hand gesture I had trouble following and no luck deciphering. The girl acknowledged them with a nod before sitting. Her exotic eyes swept the audience, piercing me where I stood, and the red jewel on her forehead flashed a message I longed to read.

Griff nudged me. I turned to see his smile.

"They sure know how to work a room, don't they?" He raised fingers to his mouth and blew a loud, shrill whistle.

I clapped and cheered, swept up in it, vowing that somehow, before this day was over, I would meet the girl. Talk to her.

And learn what she'd been trying to tell me at last.

Otherworld

Earth Year 3151

Night

I don't know how long I run, but finally the halfway rational part of my brain tells me it's pointless to keep going. The *Freefall* lies out of sight, out of reach. Even if I could find it in the fog, its hull will be white hot from atmospheric entry, and I'll never be able to get inside. By the time it's safe to approach, daytime will have come again, and I'd need radiation gear to make the trek.

We've traveled trillions of kilometers, Sofie and me. I'm far closer to her than I dreamed of being again. But she's still impossibly far away.

Adrian pulls up by my side, panting, sweat pouring from his face. He's ditched his helmet too. The beam of his flashlight shines uselessly against the fog. He glares into the distance as if the invisible ship is an affront to his own abortive colony. His mouth opens, and I hear his distorted voice through the air: "Goddamn Lower-lifes . . ."

Without saying a word, I haul off and punch him in the face.

The punch, a right cross, is strong enough to knock his mask askew and make blood spurt from his nose. He's staggered for a second, but then he straightens, arm reaching back, and at first I think he's grabbing for his gun. Instead, the fist holding the flashlight whips forward and collides with my jaw. My head rings, and I'm knocked to my knees. Adrian was always bigger and stronger than me, a power hitter where I batted for average—and my left arm, much as I've trained it, turns out to be too weak to fend off his fists. For all I know, he's been splurging on nanoroids while I was recovering my strength in the weight room. Before I can regain my feet, he crashes into me and lands straddling my chest, pinning me with his knees so his arms are free to batter my face.

"Let me go!" I yell, blood flying from my mouth, trapped by the plastic mask. My tongue feels swollen double, and the words come thickly, painfully. "Get off of me, you asshole!"

I buck upward with all my strength, and he falls away. I scramble to get my feet under me, but I receive a kick in the temple instead. The world goes up and over and down, and I land with it.

My shoulder throbs. My head aches. I have trouble focusing on Adrian as he stands above me. I think my eyes are swelling shut, too.

"She's here," I say dizzily. "I have to find her."

"You make me sick," he says, and lifts his mask to spit bloody saliva in my face. "You and your Lowerworld lover."

I go for him one last time, but I have no strength in my legs.

He leans down and backhands me so hard I feel like my jaw's been broken.

"I told you, brother," Adrian breathes, pressing the back of his hand against his mask to stanch his bloody nose. "Back on Earth, I told you to let the Lower-lifes alone. But you couldn't keep your hands off that Lowerworld bitch."

I try to curse him, but all that comes from my swollen mouth are blood and spit.

"Now we're all here together," Adrian says. "But you're not going to screw things up anymore. We're going to take what we need from the Lowerworld ship and leave them to rot on this place like they should have on Earth. And you're not going to see your little girlfriend ever again."

He takes a step until he looms above me. My eyesight's blurring badly, but I see something rising behind him out of the mist, something shadowy and much bigger than either of us, with spindly arms that stir the darkness. The shadow splits, or possibly it's another figure appearing behind the first. The arms reach for Adrian, more arms than it seems two creatures should have, and a thought flickers through my hazy mind.

Underground. That's why we couldn't find them. They live underground.

But my mouth won't form the words, and there's no time to warn him. He's leaning toward me, pulling his arm back. Smiling.

The shadows swarm.

I watch his fist coming at me, but I don't remember the impact.

Upperworld

She was telling a story, in her precise, lilting English.

"We have traveled a long way to your city, your world," she said, while worldlink transmitters reeled and TranSpeakers hummed in the air all around me. "We feel like voyagers already, emigrants to a new land, though we know we are only visitors and guests. We know as well that the greater voyage that is here contemplated is full of uncertainty, a leap across the stars. It must seem so to you as well?"

Her voice lifted, making me think she was asking a question. But that might have been her way of speaking.

"We have a belief in my country," she went on. No one used the word "country" anymore, much less "belief." But there was an old-fashioned feel to her words that fit her perfectly. "We believe that this world we inhabit is not the first world to come into being, nor will it be the last. There have been and will be other worlds, more than the drops of rain that fall from the skies, more than the grains of sand that line the seas. These many worlds are nourished by the spirit that rules the cosmos, but they will all be destroyed in their turn, and new worlds will arise from them. Thus we do not mourn things that are no more, for in the end of things we see the same great necessity that has made all that is and ever was."

Members of the audience nodded at her words, clasped their hands, bowed low in that peculiar motion I'd seen months ago on the worldlink. Sumati sat silent and motionless by the girl's side. The corporational reps at the head table frowned and fidgeted in their seats.

The girl went on, smiling, unfazed by their stares. "None of us knows what transpires when an old world is destroyed and a new one created. Some say that nothing is left but a vast and empty sea, others that a seed of the old world is planted in the soil of eternity and becomes the basis for the new. Some say that the spirit that makes and breaks the universe grows lonely in the solitude of the old world's ending, and so splits into two selves, male and female, so as to create again."

"Good story," Griff muttered. I couldn't tell if he was joking.

"But this we believe," she continued. Her voice had quieted, and everyone leaned forward to hear her words. "What is created from the old is not the same as what once was. We cannot say what the new world will hold. Might we find that stars rain from the skies, and sun orbits moon, and the life of each of us glows as brightly as the dawn? We cannot say. We can say only that the cycle must continue, forever and ever, until that one day when the light shines all around us, and the supreme consciousness that rules this vast cosmos pierces us to the soul, and the world is like a dream beyond our imagination. This is the day for which we hope, and pray, and struggle. Thank you."

She finished, lowering her eyes demurely and bowing her head. The crowd, resting back as if her words had suspended them against the force of gravity, exploded in wild cheers, shouting, hooting, laughter. I hadn't understood much of what she'd said, but I felt my body shaking with the energy of the room, the power of her presence.

"Thank you, Miss Patel," the Upperworld moderator broke into the celebration. He tapped his microphone, the sound thudding through the antiquated speaker system. I realized with a shock that this was the first time I'd heard her last name, or any part of her name. "We appreciate your"—he cleared his throat—"little history lesson. The Upperworld so seldom has the opportunity to hear the quaint folktales of your people."

The girl looked up, her face and eyes placid, undisturbed.

"But our purpose here, as you know, is weightier than that," the moderator continued. "We are attempting to determine the basis of the Lowerworld unrest, and to prevent its reoccurrence in the future."

"As are we," the girl said.

"Perhaps you might help us out, then," the rep from Medi-Terri jumped in. "What precisely is your plan for quelling the riots that have convulsed the Lowerworld corponations?"

"*Riots*, Mr. Chevalier?" she asked.

"What would you prefer we call them?" the rep from Sub-Con said in a voice that barely disguised her loathing.

"There are a great many things one might call them," the girl said. "But we call them demonstrations. Lawful demonstrations, such as we know were common in the old world, when *law* was not the forgotten concept it is today. Demonstrations in which not one member of the Upperworld has been threatened or harmed, though I regret that the same cannot be said for the Lowerworlders who have given their lives in the quest for justice."

The final word echoed through the chamber, which then fell silent. The moderator looked up angrily, but his expression shifted when he saw a collection of worldlink lenses aimed directly at him.

"Very well, then, Miss Patel," he said. "Perhaps you can clarify for us the conditions under which we might expect these *demonstrations* to end."

"Grant us passage on the starship fleet when it leaves this planet for worlds unknown at precisely oh-nine-hundred hours on midsummer's day of the calendar year 2151," she answered without missing a beat.

The room stilled. My own breath caught in my throat. Part of me couldn't believe she'd said it, and part of me couldn't see why she shouldn't. By far the biggest part of me, though—the part that spoke through my pounding heart—wondered if it might be possible, if she might actually travel to the new world with me.

"There's insufficient room on the starships for even a fraction of the Lowerworld population," the moderator said, breaking the silence. His splotchy face seemed ready to burst above his too-tight collar. "The *Executor* is already booked to capacity, and the *Freefall* is a supply ship, carrying an array of materials essential to our own colonization. The logistics of such an emigration—"

"We do not ask for wholesale emigration of the Lowerworld populace," she interrupted. "We know that relatively few of our people can hope to make this journey. We are resolved among ourselves to accept the sacrifices that must be made, and we do not request what is beyond anyone's ability to provide."

"What do you want, then?" he asked in a clipped voice.

"We want the opportunity to make those decisions ourselves."

Again, silence.

"Miss Patel," the moderator sighed. "The Otherworld colonization project has been ongoing for much of the present century. You can't honestly believe it's possible to alter our plans at a moment's notice. As it is, Upperworld colonization has been strictly monitored to ensure—"

"Of course," she interrupted again, her voice remaining polite. "We appreciate the magnitude of your own decision-making process. We appreciate that, according to an intercorponational protocol dated 12 December 2145 and signed on behalf of the chief executive officers of the Upperworld corponations of CanAm, ExCon, MediTerri, and UniVers, as well as by Chairman Conroy of JIPOC"—she produced a document from her robe, the first piece of paper I'd seen in years, and began to read—"'the security of our joint financial interests dictates a tightly restricted colonization factoring into account numerous variables, including but not limited to personal wealth, professional and social status, genetic viability, and ideological orthodoxy—'"

"Miss Patel—"

"'—and stringently excluding any cross-world contamination through a rigorous pre-screening process to identify and eliminate applicants expressing Lowerworld tendencies, whether hereditary or acquired—'"

"That is a classified protocol—"

"'—and, needless to say, prohibiting absolutely any applicant from the Lowerworld proper, as determined by genotype, corporation of origin, and/or linguistic, sociocultural, or any other marker of Lowerworld sub-humanity.'"

The room buzzed, most of the audience probably not understanding completely what they'd heard but knowing it was important. The moderator covered his microphone and leaned over to whisper a few words to the reps from ExCon and MediTerri, both of whose eyes bugged with rage. Then he addressed the girl.

"Miss Patel, the information you've illegally obtained—"

"*Contamination*, Mr. Moderator," she interjected. "Lowerworld *sub-humanity*."

"You will surrender any and all data—"

"I will not!" she shouted, rising to her feet. The audience

jerked back as if her small figure filled the cavernous room. "You may believe that we of the Lowerworld will sit by passively while your machinations to rob us of yet another planet proceed in secret. You may believe, because we have never been privy to your executive councils and shareholder meetings, because we have never schemed to deprive the great majority of the world's people of their God-given rights to clean air and food and water, to shelter and decent living and the opportunity to realize their hopes and dreams, that we are mere animals to be kicked and kenneled, petted at your own whim and pleasure then thrown onto the scrap heap when your desires are sated. But we will *not* be so treated. Not today, and not one moment more!"

The moderator sat frozen at the vehemence in her voice. But she wasn't talking to him, if she ever had been.

"We are many billions strong!" she shouted, the mike sitting forgotten, unneeded, on the table. "We are the world's people! We have come to you not as beggars pleading for a handout, but as children of the Almighty, demanding at long last the rights we have been denied. You may hide behind your walls of wealth, walls built by the blood and suffering of our people, but those walls will not hold forever. They will fall, as do all walls founded on injustice, and may God then judge who among us is in the wrong and who in the right!"

The crowd thundered its applause. The room shook as if the Otherworld starships had launched in our midst. Griff and I were jostled by moving bodies, stamping feet. The girl stood in her purple robe under the flickering lights with her arms raised the way I'd seen her in that first video, and I was almost afraid of her, afraid and amazed and struck speechless by her fiery beauty. The only person in the room who seemed unmoved by her speech, whether to anger or jubilation, was Sumati, who remained motionless, staring dully at the cracked water pitcher on the table by her hand.

I looked at Griff. His eyes were fixed on the girl, his freckled face glowing. I felt a pang of jealousy, but I knew what I had to do.

I took a step through the cheering, rocking bodies, toward the stage.

Then I saw blood spatter the girl's robe and, a split second later, I heard the shot.

Otherworld

Earth Year 3151

Night

When I left Earth, the last place I expected to find myself was the ship's brig. I'm not even sure I knew the *Executor* had one.

But it does. And I'm in it.

I can't for the life of me figure out how I got here. My head throbs like it's been squashed between I-beams, and I mean that literally: It feels misshapen, bulging unnaturally around my temples. Dried blood crusts my mouth, hardens the front of my jumpsuit. My left shoulder aches, making it hard to raise my arm above head level. My thoughts swim, and the pool they're swimming in is full of mud. I remember going out on patrol with Adrian, remember sighting the *Freefall*, remember our fight . . .

Adrian.

He's gone. I saw the creatures coming out of the mist, saw them reach for him. Why they didn't attack me, how I made it back to the ship, I have no idea.

But he's gone. The fact that he was trying to kill me when they took him makes it hard for me to summon much sorrow over my former best friend's death. But it doesn't ease the remorse I feel, the train of useless what-ifs that crowd my mind.

Woozily I stand to investigate my prison. It's obviously been rigged up on the spot. No bars, no guards, no slot in the door for them to feed me. Just a boxy room without vents or lights, maybe a meter and a half square. Enough light squeezes under the door for me to conclude it's probably a closet. For cleaning supplies, if the antiseptic smell is any indication. No latrine, though. What I'll do when I need to use the bathroom seems not to have concerned my jailers.

I push against the door. It's locked, and banging on it does nothing except make my knuckles hurt. Kicking it doesn't accomplish much more. Neither does yelling.

I yell anyway. "Hey!" I yell to no one. "Let me out of here!" My voice bounces back at me, but that's the only sound I hear.

There's a gap between door and floor, too tight to accommodate my fingers. I try. The door's solid metal, the walls the same. No doorknob or handle. The ceiling might be made of tiles I could loosen to get at the ductwork, but it's too high for me to reach. When Conroy's goons come for me, to feed me or escort me to a bathroom or put me in front of a firing squad, they'll come armed. I'm sure they blame me for Adrian's death. Probably his dad will be the one to signal the marksmen to shoot.

I sink to the floor, wrap my arms around my ungainly head,

and succumb to despair. In case you were wondering, it feels exactly the same as the emptiness of space.

Sofie's here. On this planet. But she might as well be back on Earth, or floating through the endless reaches of the galaxy. My former best friend's final words of wisdom were right. I'll never see her again.

When we parted on Earth, I told myself I'd never see her again. For all the empty days I've spent on this godforsaken planet, that's what I kept telling myself, as if that could lessen the pain.

But the truth, I realize now, is that I always hoped. Even if I knew my hope was a lie, I held on to it. For the eternity I drifted through the universe aboard the ship that now holds me prisoner, I didn't dream. In deepsleep, you don't dream. But if I had, I would have dreamed of finding her again.

Now I *have* found her. Found her, and lost her. This time forever.

How long I stay down I don't know. Time has no meaning in my cell. But footsteps sound in the corridor outside, and the door swings open, admitting light that blinds me after however long I spent in semidarkness.

"On your feet," a voice says, not one I recognize. Hands grab me and yank me upright.

There are two guards, both armed. Teens I've never seen before, a guy and a girl. Jumpsuits, helmets, the usual costume. Whether they know what I'm in here for, whether they care, doesn't seem relevant. They treat me like a prisoner, which is what I am.

"Move," the one who talked before says, jabbing me in the back with his gun.

I figure there's no harm in asking. "Where are you taking me?"

He grabs my injured arm and spins me around. "I said move."

"I asked you a question."

"Chairman Conroy said to shoot you if you talk."

"You're taking me to see him?"

"You want to get shot?"

"What about the bathroom?" I say. "I need to use it."

"Then take a dump in your pants," he says. "Orders are we don't let you out of our sight."

There's a lot I could say about their orders, but I don't push it. For the moment, I'm out of my cage, which might put me one step closer to freedom, which might put me one step closer to Sofie. So I keep my mouth shut, and hold on to the little bit of hope I've been given.

We walk. Our feet echo on the metal floor. The ship's no labyrinth—the parts of it I'm familiar with are straight, the floors lined with multicolored pathways to direct you where to go—but I don't recognize this hallway, which means we must be in a restricted area. No windows to the outside, like there are in the public sectors. Captain's quarters, maybe. We reach a set of double doors decorated with the JIPOC crest, and unlike all the rest of the doors we've walked through, they're sealed shut. The weak throb of machinery sounds behind them, making me reassess. Could we be near the ship's gravitational drive? What would be the point of bringing me here?

But then, what was the point of bringing me back to the ship in the first place? If these clowns are taking me to see Chairman Conroy, he must need me for something. Information about his son. A public example. Whatever, I'm alive, and while I'm alive, I'm greedy enough to wish for another miracle.

"Hands behind your back," the guard says, and with the other guard's gun to my head, I have no choice but to obey. He cuffs me. The cold metal cuts into my wrists, and the twisting makes my shoulder ache all over again.

The doors slide open automatically. I'm pushed inside. The throbbing sound intensifies, and I take a look around the room.

It's not the drive, I'm sure of that. In fact, I can't tell what's producing the sound, though it pulses all around me. The room we've entered is good sized, easily ten by ten meters, unfurnished except for a single life pod sitting beside a massive metal desk, from which a computer console rears. The screen, though, is blank. Shiny metal walls and floor, ceiling-height windows that show me I was unconscious at least a day, because it's dark outside again. A catwalk runs the perimeter of the room, stairs leading up to it, though what its purpose is I can't say. Maybe to offer a better view of the heavens. Or to look down on anyone entering the room.

Which is what the man on the catwalk is doing to us right now.

He might be chairman of the board of the Joint Inter-corporational Panel on Otherworld Colonization, but Peter Conroy is not an imposing man, which is probably why he prefers the catwalk view of his fellow beings. Adrian was far bigger and broader than his father, who's no better than average height and painfully thin. Adrian used to joke about kicking his old man's ass, and I used to laugh along, never imagining whose ass my dead buddy would end up kicking. Chairman Conroy wears the regulation gray jumpsuit, though his uniform carries the crest of his office, a silver-and-black seal on his breast pocket that might be intended to look like a nebula, the place where stars are born. Either that or a supernova, where they go to die.

He leans over the railing to get a look at us, then descends the stairs. Adrian inherited his dad's sandy-blond hair, though the older man's is thinning. He also inherited his dad's unshakable belief in his own superiority, and one other thing: his dad's dislike of traitors. I never needed to worry about that before.

But I sure as hell do now.

"You can go," he says to the guards, his voice as bland as everything else about him. The two guards trade a look, but with me beaten and cuffed, they must figure there's not much I can do to their leader. They pivot on their heels, and the doors close behind them.

Conroy looks me up and down, the impression that he's inspecting spoiled meat never leaving his face.

"What troubles me most," he says, "is that you used to visit my home."

The thought doesn't exactly fill me with glee either, but I don't say anything. The throbbing of the room hurts my head, makes it hard for me to think. I've gone from the brig to the bridge, and I'm still not sure why I'm here.

Conroy, however, decides to enlighten me.

"Lowerworld tendencies aren't communicable," he says. "But they're transmissible. We've run a supplemental genetic screen on your parents, discovered some unsettling liaisons on your mother's side. Disguised, somehow, prior to liftoff. Your father's part in falsifying her genetic ancestry remains under investigation. Your mother, however . . ."

He lets the word trail off. I'm not sure what I'm supposed to conclude. That she's in lockup too, that she's been shot in the head, that she's been launched into space. If so, it's not much of a threat. Last I heard, my parents were telling me never to darken their door again.

"None of that matters now, though," he says. "Like it or not, you've become necessary to me. And unlike your Lowerworld accomplices, we of the Upperworld do not resort to violence to achieve our objectives."

My head hurts too much to laugh. I consider reminding him that his son beat the crap out of me. But much as I despise this man, I can't throw Adrian's death in his face.

"Come with me," Conroy says, turning to climb the stairs. He grips the metal banister, hunched over, breathing heavily. It occurs to me he's a pretty old man, older than my parents certainly. At the moment, he actually looks a thousand years old.

He pauses to catch his breath when we reach the catwalk, which gives me a chance to look out at the night sky. Our vantage lifts us above the mist that clings to the planet's surface, showing me for the first time the unbelievable congregation of stars that fills the void. Despite my current situation, I can't help staring at them. I never saw the stars aboard ship. I was asleep. I never saw them on Earth, either. Too much light. And I guess I was asleep there, too.

"My son," Conroy says, "is out there."

"Out where?" He can't be talking about the stars.

"He vanished on the night you—well."

On the night I got my ass kicked, he means.

"When his patrol didn't return, we sent a search party and found only you," he says. "There were traces of his blood at the scene, but no further evidence of struggle. It appears he was simply . . . taken."

There was plenty of evidence of struggle from where I sat, but I don't tell him that. "He's gone," I say. "I saw them attack him."

He looks at me sharply. "You watched him die?"

"No," I admit. "But you've seen what one of those things did to me. He can't be alive."

"My son," he says in a weak voice, but then he must remember who he is. And who I am. "We're not as naive as you seem to think. Your own attack has always appeared a trifle convenient to me. *Arranged.* And with the arrival of the Lowerworld ship, we've finally pieced together why."

I say nothing. What can you say to someone who thinks you arranged to be gutted like a fish?

"We know the *Freefall* didn't arrive here by accident," Conroy continues. "And neither did we. There was design behind this from the start. Design we didn't perceive on the day we left Earth a millennium ago."

"And . . . ?"

"And I believe you know what that design was," he says. "We've torn the ship apart looking for what was done to it, and as you can see, we've regained a measure of functionality at the executive level. But we've been unable to discover what caused our gravitational drive to miscarry, our navigational and other operating systems to fail. In light of the past day's events, I can only conclude that you and your Lowerworld cohort were behind this massive act of sabotage. You and the girl—Patel—"

"Sofie."

"You and the girl," he repeats. "Perhaps others. Your association with my son provided you access to information you couldn't have obtained otherwise. Information that enabled you to cripple this vessel."

"I had nothing to do with it," I say. "And neither did she."

He ignores me. "Which leads me to believe further that you've been playing some sort of game since we arrived, biding your time until your appointed rendezvous with the Lowerworld ship. And now you and your . . . conspirators are holding my son. Seeking to gain additional concessions from me. But there will be no such concessions. We of the Upperworld do not submit to Terrarist threats."

He glares at me menacingly, but I'm no longer buying his

bluff. I can see the pain in his eyes. And for the sake of the friendship I once shared with his son, I stop myself from saying the first words that come to my mind.

"If I was in league with those things," I say, "if they're somehow connected to the *Freefall*, don't you think they'd have taken me along with them?"

His pale face reddens, and he raises a fist as if to finish what Adrian started. But then he reins it in.

"I'm not about to bandy words with the likes of you," he says. "A less civilized man would string you up for what you've done. I'm giving you a choice. Find my son and return him to the *Executor* unharmed. Or remain here and suffer the penalty for piracy and high treason."

He's babbling. But he's serious. Either that or crazed with grief. Either way, he genuinely believes Sofie and I sabotaged the ship. He thinks I'm in league with the creatures that attacked Adrian. And he thinks I can broker a deal to get him back alive.

"You leave this ship the minute you say the word," he continues. "I'll take those cuffs off your wrists myself and send you on your way."

"And how do you know I'll come back?"

He smiles for the first time since I entered the room. Maybe for the first time ever. I can't remember seeing him smile on Earth.

"You'll come back," he says.

He leads me down the stairs. Even with my hands bound, I'm surprised he'd turn his back on me. But an anxious feeling is growing in my gut, and he must feel it too. Must know I'm not going to try anything until he's shown me what he plans to.

We walk to a corner of the room hidden beneath the catwalk, pass through another functioning door, into a room much smaller than the first. The throbbing is so strong here I feel it in my injured shoulder, my neck, the bones of my jaw. At first I think we must be in a machine room, but then Conroy touches a button on the wall, and a panel slides aside to show me the source of the vibration.

It's a stasis field, identical to the ones I saw demonstrated on Earth, the ones that hold us in deepsleep. It pulses white, yellow, white, with flickers of red on the edges. It's generated not by a pod but by an upright metal ring, which encloses a single human figure. She stands, upheld by the field, bathed in its energy. Her eyes remain closed in sleep, her face perfectly calm. Her purple robe glows through the white, and on her pure forehead a spot of red winks like a miniature heart.

The aura accentuates the lines in Conroy's face, deepening his smile.

"You'll come back," he says again. "Won't you?"

Earth, 2150

Upperworld

The girl staggered back, her face covered in blood. But it wasn't hers.

It was Sumati's.

The old woman slumped on the table. From where I was standing, I couldn't see where she'd been hit. But even with the crowd in an uproar, diving for cover and stampeding toward the exits, I knew she was dead. She wasn't moving. She wasn't even twitching.

I was moving, though. Moving toward the podium, shoving bodies out of my way.

The next person to go down was one of Sumati's bodyguards, who collapsed in a spray of blood. I glanced up to see where the shots were coming from, thought I saw a flash of white in the balcony. But I was running too fast and there was too much commotion in the room for me to make the shape out clearly. The girl's composed expression had shattered, and she'd ducked beneath the table, the rest of the guards forming a tight phalanx in front of her. Their faces toughened when they saw me coming, and it occurred to me that I'd never be able to fight my way through them.

They weren't armed, not that I could tell. But they were muscled.

The first man to block my way yanked me around so hard I felt as if he'd torn my arm from its socket. Then another shot rang out, and he went limp, pulling me to the ground as he fell. I pushed him away, but not before I saw that the top of his head was gone.

Adrenaline the only thing that kept me from losing my lunch, I scrambled under the table, avoiding the hands that reached for me. The girl, wide-eyed, her face covered in blood, backed away. What I must have looked like, with my flushed skin and wild expression, I didn't want to think. I had only a second to blurt out my first words to her before her bodyguards got a hold of me and beat me to a bloody pulp.

"I want to help—" was all I managed before brawny arms dragged me from under the table.

The biggest of the bunch held me by the throat a half meter off the floor. His fist went back for the knockout punch, but before he completed it, the girl in purple grabbed his arm and yelled at him shrilly in a language I didn't understand. The contest between them was totally unequal, but the instant her hands touched him, he lowered his fist and dropped me to the floor. I was about to get back on my feet when she shouted a few more words to the man, and he wrapped his arms around me and charged after her. The rest of the troop followed, leaving Sumati and the dead bodyguards behind.

"Cam!" I heard Griff yell over the sound of screams and running feet, and then we were gone.

Muffled shots sounded behind us as we burst into the corridor at the rear of the auditorium. The girl led the way, purple robe flying, the five remaining bodyguards storming after her. The one who held me squeezed so tight I could barely breathe. We ran down a maze of identical cement corridors filled with rusting pipes and the rank smell of piss and mildew. The girl darted around corners and pushed through doors as if she'd memorized the place. At the end of one hallway she hurtled through a door with a once-illuminated sign reading FIRE EXIT, and we entered a chilly stairwell. I thought she'd head down to the parking level, but she started up the flight of stairs, speaking rapidly in her own language into a comm device. Pounding feet and the heavy breathing of the guards and the bright swirl of the girl's robe blurred into a fuzz of light and sound as we ran.

We exited the stairwell at roof level, emerging into the relative brightness of a smog-shrouded New York CITI day. Wind whipped the girl's bloody robe and the strands of black hair around her face. She moved to the edge of the roof, her guards right behind, the biggest one maintaining his hold on me. We looked out over a street crammed with the milling, multicolored crowd that had escaped the building. Distantly, I heard sirens screaming. The girl fixed me with her bright, penetrating eyes, and for a single awful moment I imagined her giving her guard the order to drop me to the street below. But she merely scrutinized me carefully, as if she was deciding whether she could trust me. The blood smeared on her cheeks should have made her look frightening, but somehow it didn't. I held still under her gaze and tried to look, well, trustworthy.

I must have passed the test. She spoke a word to the guard, and he let me go.

With the sleeve of her robe, she wiped as much blood from her face as she could. Now that I saw her up close, I saw that she was even more beautiful than video could do justice to. Her skin was flawless, her cheeks flushed after the terror of the auditorium and the run to the roof. Her eyebrows arched sharply, and her lips were naturally pursed, giving her a look of animation I hadn't always seen in the stoic calm of the videos. But what struck me most was the passion in her eyes. Large and lined in black pigment, with a corona of blue-green shimmering around the gold, they jumped from her face with an intensity that made me feel both totally exposed and, in some strange way I couldn't put into words, totally safe. I started to say something, but she cut me off.

"In my country, it is considered impolite to stare," she said in her lilting voice, a bit huskier from the run. A small smile on her lips made me wonder if that was supposed to be a joke, considering she'd also been staring at me.

"I'm sorry," I said, but I didn't look away. "It's considered rude here, too."

"Imagine," she said. "A custom we share."

Before I could respond or decide if she really was joking, her robe and hair rose in a hurricane of wind. I looked up and saw a helicar descending to the roof, the strange red lettering of her language printed on its side, a man leaning out of the open frame. I tensed to run, but I was dragged along by the guards as the car touched down. The girl shouted to the pilot, her words lost in the wind, and he nodded. A moment later we had all tumbled into the car, and it sprang into the sky.

The instant we were airborne, the guards reached beneath their seats and pulled out handguns, which they trained on me. So much for trust. I put my hands in the air while one of them patted me down.

"Our operatives exist throughout the Upperworld," the girl said to me. Despite the roar of the rotors and the rushing wind, I heard each word distinctly, as if it was an arrow delivered to my ears alone. "But we must be cautious, as you have seen."

"I'm sorry about Sumati," I said.

Her eyes widened as if in surprise, and for a second I thought I saw them moisten with tears. But her voice remained precise and businesslike. "She was the first to unite the Lowerworld in the cause of righteousness. But in later years she grew tired and despondent. She continued to travel with us to shield me—to protect me from the violence that follows in the wake of those who seek justice." This time I was sure the tears were going to fall, but they didn't. "Now she has been gathered to her rest, and her wisdom has become ours."

She paused, lowering her eyes briefly, then spoke again.

"'Sumati' means 'wisdom.' We who follow her example take another such name. I am known as Sofie. Another ancient word, adapted from a long-dead language. Among my people, this red bindi"—she pointed to the jewel on her forehead—"represents marriage. But I wear it, as did my teacher, to represent devotion to the truth, to the ideal of wisdom she practiced all the long days of her life."

Again the flicker of sorrow passed over her face, only to be replaced by a calm efficiency.

"So," she said. "Who are you, and how do you propose to help us?"

"I'm Cam," I said. "Cameron Newell. I'm from Can-Do Amortization. In the Upperworld." I blushed. "Obviously."

"Obviously," she said, nodding.

"I saw you on the worldlink," I said. "When all of this started—"

"*All of this* started hundreds of years ago," she interrupted. "When the people of your world determined that the people of mine were pawns to be manipulated in the pursuit of wealth and power."

I had the uncomfortable feeling I'd taken the place of the moderator back in the auditorium. "I know that," I said. "But—"

"Do you?" she cut in again. "Do you know the lives of my people? The centuries of oppression they have suffered in their own lands? The colonies, the slave-labor camps, the factories—only just better than slave-labor camps—where they have lived and worked and died?"

"I mean, I don't *know* all that—"

"Or is this merely another thrilling adventure for you?" she rushed on. "*Slumming*, I believe you call it? An opportunity to soak up some local color, to experience the exotic, before settling into your life of ease on the next interstellar pleasure spot? You do know that the natives there may not prove so tractable as the natives here, do you not?"

I opened my mouth to respond, but she never stopped.

"We get many such pleasure-seekers hanging around us. We have become something of celebrities in the Upperworld, you know. Among the young and disaffected particularly. Those who feel ill at ease about the lives of unearned privilege they have inherited, though never in their darkest dreams would they imagine *actually* living as we do, not for longer than a token moment. *Groupies*, I believe you call them? Camp followers? Oh!" Her hand flew to her mouth, giving me my first look at her long, elaborately painted fingernails. "I believe that expression has another, less genteel meaning?"

Without her seeing, I ran the expression through my selfone, then glanced at the screen. When I looked back at her, my face burning with embarrassment, her lips were set in a mocking smile.

"Look," I said. "I didn't come here to be insulted."

"Heaven forbid!" She spoke rapidly in her language to the guards, and they laughed, deep, throaty laughs that made their broad shoulders shake. "That a trifling girl from the Lowerworld should speak disrespectfully to such an illustrious personage from the great corponation of Canada-America Financial!"

I was taken aback to hear her use the old-fashioned name for CanAm. But more than that, I was seriously starting to doubt everything I'd thought about her. Or, worse, to see myself the way she was making me out to be: as a pampered child from the Upperworld chasing some alluring Lowerworld siren. What did I know about her anyway? About her people? Her struggle? I'd seen her on the worldlink and thought I'd heard her calling out to me. I'd thrown all caution to the wind, alienated and bullied my friends, risked my life to see her in person. Looking into her eyes right now made my heart turn somersaults. But maybe she was right. Maybe there was no way a guy like me and a girl like her could have anything to say to each other. Maybe we didn't belong on the same planet, whether it was this one or one a thousand billion kilometers away.

"I'm sorry," I said. "I guess—maybe this was a mistake. I thought I knew what I was doing. I thought you might . . ." *Need me*, were the words that popped into my head, but they were far too awkward to say out loud, no matter which way she took them. "You can—I mean, if it's possible, you can drop me at the next bullet train station. Not literally drop me, I mean," I added with a weak smile. "I can make it back home from there."

She studied me. The insufferable smile had changed to something else, and her eyes had lost the haughty, belittling look. They'd turned searching, probing, the way they'd always appeared when I'd seen her on the worldlink. Her gaze wasn't gentle or compassionate, in fact it was pretty much the opposite of that. But it was *real*, and as always it made me feel real too.

She leaned forward, and her hand closed over mine. I jerked away, but she gripped me with both hands and wouldn't let go. Her hands were warm, and I felt the blood flowing through them as she lifted our linked hands between us and stared into my eyes.

"So you did not come here to be insulted," she said, her voice softening. "That much I can now see. What did you come here for, Cameron Newell?"

Otherworld

Earth Year 3151

Night

I exit the ship at midnight, when planetary UV is supposed to be at its safest level. I'm decked out in radiation gear, a full-body suit with detachable boots and gloves and hood, but Griff told me weeks ago that the science squad might be down-playing the risk of exposure or the suits might not be working— or both—so who knows. A lifetime or a year or a day from now, when my skin sloughs off or my lungs corrode from cancer, I might find out what counts as safe on this ghost world.

But I don't have a lifetime. The night predators took my former best friend. And they're not going to hesitate to make it a matching set.

My mission is as simple as it is impossible. I'm charged with locating Adrian and returning with him to the *Executor*. Reasoning that his lost son is being held hostage aboard the *Freefall*, Conroy's told me to head directly there. What he won't accept, what he resolutely refuses to believe, is that I'm not part of some grand conspiracy involving Sofie, the Lowerworlders, and the night creatures. If I wanted to spin a good conspiracy theory myself, I might conclude that this whole setup is Conroy's sick idea of punishment—that he knows his son has been slaughtered and is preparing me to suffer the same fate. He's too civilized to splatter my brains all over his nice clean ship, but he doesn't mind sending me out to certain death where the last thought that'll cross my mind is that I found Sofie against all odds, failed her, and lost her again.

But the truth is, his motivations are probably a lot less sinister than that. The strongest likelihood is that the old man's gone nuts with grief and/or the pressure of piloting a shipwreck, and he actually believes I have a chance of surviving out here, bargaining for his son's life, and bringing him back home.

Either way, I have no choice but to go on his suicide mission. He explained to me how they had found Sofie when they went to search for Adrian, found her sleeping in a renegade pod that had ejected like mine. They'd brought the pod back intact, without disturbing its occupant or her thousand-year sleep. But the aura that holds her in suspended, dreamless, timeless forgetfulness could be switched off at any moment, and without the proper reentry she could arrest, stroke out, go into complete systems failure. Griff told me once, though even he admitted it might be no more than a rumor, that if the deepsleep is improperly disengaged, the millennium of suspension attacks the body at once, mummifying it in seconds. At least that's a relatively painless death. He also passed along the theory that people go stark raving mad when the switch is flipped wrong, and their last moments of life are spent trying to tear out their viscera with their fingernails.

My mother, the deepsleep expert, is the one who removed Sofie from her pod, set her up in the mobile stasis-field generator, and advised Conroy on how to handle the situation. I guess I can't blame her, given not only her opinion of me but her fear of what Conroy has on her. Maybe she bought herself some immunity that way. All I know is Conroy's finger is on the switch. And he'll flip it if I return without his son.

What he'll do if I don't return at all I can easily guess. But at least under those circumstances, I won't have to watch Sofie die.

He's given me an hour to prepare, so even if I knew where to find Griff on this city-size starship, I don't have a chance to say good-bye. Most of the time I do have, I've spent cleaning my bloody face and getting my swollen forehead patched by one of Conroy's PMP flacks. I've taken some supplemental oxygen kits, plus the same model of ionizing beam Adrian used against the creature that attacked me. Based on that experience, it works pretty well. I wish I could take a handful of the sonic devices, but they're too awkward to cart around, and they don't work unless they're planted in the rock anyway. I've got binoculars, a couple of electronic flares in case I need to signal the ship for help, a portable homing device to locate the *Freefall* via the pods stored inside. It flashes red to show me direction and distance. I've got enough freeze-dried food and purified water to last me a few days.

I've also got no idea how I'm going to survive if the night creatures come out in force. And no clue what to do if by some miracle I do make it to the ship alive.

I've got practically no chance. And very little hope.

What I've got, and it's enough to get me out the door, is her. I've got my memories of the months I spent with her, memories that have lasted longer than the ages I spent without her. I've got my memories of the plans we made, the world I thought we were building, the dreams I thought we shared.

I've got those dreams, and they'll have to be enough.

Even if, in the end, they weren't the same as hers.

PART TWO

The Sound the Stars Make

Ah, love, let us be true
To one another! for the world, which seems
To lie before us like a land of dreams,
So various, so beautiful, so new,
Hath really neither joy, nor love, nor light,
Nor certitude, nor peace, nor help for pain;
And we are here as on a darkling plain
Swept with confused alarms of struggle and flight,
Where ignorant armies clash by night.

—Matthew Arnold, "Dover Beach"

Earth, 2150

Lowerworld

S ofie told stories every night. During the day she was busy
running from place to place, dealing with the fallout
from the New York CITI fiasco, meeting with her advisory team. But at night, no matter where she was or how crazy
her day had been, she fulfilled a routine Sumati had begun:
telling stories to anyone who would listen.

Actually, Sumati had revived this practice from other story-
tellers, other leaders of revolutions in the past. Back then,
they'd been called lamas, or swamis, or mullahs, or mahatmas,
or priests, or pundits. Or philosophers—the word that had
given Sofie her name. But they didn't exist anymore, at least not
officially. The corponations had done away with them. They
weren't good for business.

The main job of a pundit or priest or philosopher, Sofie
said, was to tell stories. Publicly, where anyone who wanted to
could hear them. Sometimes the stories were called sermons.

Sometimes they were called dialogues. Sometimes they were called parables. Sometimes they were called Vedas. No matter what they were called, their purpose was the same: to lead their audience to the ways of wisdom.

"But the speaker does not *tell* those who listen what wisdom is," she clarified. "The story contains its own wisdom, and those who listen must find it themselves."

"What if they don't?"

She smiled. "Then there will always be another story."

The worldlink, Sofie said, was filled with all kinds of stories that tried to distract people from the ways of wisdom. She rattled off their names: banners, promos, slogans, tabloids, megazines, flicks, techgames, sporting contests—

"Sporting contests?"

"There are no sporting contests in my country," she said. "There have been none for the past hundred years. And why? Because for us, life is contest enough. When to live or to die is a daily struggle, sporting arenas seem a frivolous luxury."

I thought about all the ball games me and Adrian and Griff had watched over the years, all the times I'd sat in the stands or in front of a screen cheering my head off for some costumed superhero, and I felt ashamed, ridiculous. Like a little kid who realized his parents had tricked him for years into believing in Santa Cogs.

Sofie often had that effect on me. Being in her camp was like being in ColPrep all over again—except this time it wasn't my body getting battered and twisted every which way, it was my brain. I'd never gone to school—in the Upperworld we had Classification, not school—but much of the time I spent in the Lowerworld, it felt like I was the *only* guy who'd never gone to school. And everyone else, Sofie most of all, was waiting for the dumb kid in the back of the classroom to finally figure out what the rest of the students had known all their lives.

But that was only half the story. When Sofie came into our mobile camp for the night, her purple robe flying and her face flushed from the day's events, she made my pulse race to learn what had gone on in the world since I'd last seen her. When she gathered everyone around her in the lantern light of the camp—we had electric lights, plus a lot more technology than I expected to find in the Lowerworld, but she liked to keep these meetings low key and traditional—I felt like I was soaring on the music of her voice. I wasn't sure I understood her stories, but at the same time they gave me the feeling I got every time I was around her: the feeling that she knew me better than anyone did, even better than I knew myself. On bad days it was easy to believe she was making me feel like an idiot on purpose, taking out her anger at the Upperworld specifically on me. But on good days it was just as easy to believe that if she *was* being extra hard on me, it was because she wanted something from me she didn't want—or couldn't get—from anyone else.

One night, a month after I'd joined her circle, she told a story that made my head spin with what it said, and what it didn't.

"This is the story of a marriage," she said that night, seated on the ground with her legs tucked beneath her and her robe arranged neatly over her lap. "But it is not the story of a traditional marriage. It is the story of the marriage of two gods. It is a very old story, so old the names are lost. But the story holds true.

"The story tells that one of these gods had grown haughty as the result of his power. He would ride around his kingdom seated on a great beast the height of ten men, and the other gods would bow at his feet and pay obeisance to him. They feared to tell him that he had become a bully, and a nuisance, and a bore—parading around in front of the others rather than coming down to walk among them. But there was nothing they could do, for this god's power was so great that any who stood against him would have suffered a most horrible death."

She looked around the camp, enjoying her story. Some kids laughed and played nearby. Most of the people listening seemed relaxed and happy too, and I tried not to look like I was hanging on her every word.

"But as I have said," she went on after a moment, "this great god was preparing for his marriage. He was riding about, seeking throughout his kingdom an appropriate wedding gift for his betrothed. Now, you must understand that the goddess he had pledged to marry was very beautiful, and also very modest, so modest she had not asked for a gift to be given at her wedding. But this great god believed he must find the most wonderful of gifts for his bride—not truly for love of her, but for love of himself. So he was searching around, mounted on his great beast, for something in his kingdom that no one had seen before, something so marvelous that all who saw it would be reminded of his great power and splendor.

"Now, as he hastened along the main road that passed through his kingdom, he came upon a wise man traveling in the opposite direction. This wise man had lived for so many years and contemplated the things of the hidden world for so long, nothing could remain secret from him. And through his researches, he had discovered the most wonderful flower in all the world, a flower that could make any who inhaled its fragrance weep for joy. He was hurrying along the road, carrying this flower and talking to himself, when he bumped into the great god mounted on his great beast and going the other way.

"Now, at that time, it was considered good manners to dismount before the very old and the very wise so as not to appear to be on higher ground. But this great god, as you can well imagine, would not have thought to show courtesy to any other under the best of circumstances. So he remained seated upon his great beast, glaring at the wise man, even when the poor old fellow was knocked backward and landed on the seat of his pants in the mud.

"This enraged the wise man—who, for all his wisdom, had one sad flaw, which was shortness of temper. And so, rising from the mud, he saluted the god as follows.

"'Oh great one, I see you are in a hurry to wed your beloved, and did not notice me traveling in haste the other way. Forgive me, great one, for my clumsiness.'

"The great god suspected nothing, and was pleased with

the wise man's address, for as you know, the unwary can often be seduced by honeyed words.

"'Take, oh great one, this flower, as a token of my contrition,' the wise man said, holding the flower up to the great god on his lofty perch. 'It is the rarest and most precious of flowers, and will make a suitable adornment for your bridal bower.'

"And without so much as a thank-you, the great god swiped the flower from the wise man's hand and placed it on the head of his great beast. Then he wheeled and was gone, thundering down the road toward the place where he was to be wed.

"'We will see,' the wise man said to himself—for not only did he often talk to himself, but he often predicted the outcomes of his various schemes and machinations—'we will see if he remains so high and mighty after tonight!'"

The audience laughed at this line. I was hearing the story through the TranSpeaker that hummed in my ear, and I wasn't sure what was so funny, but I smiled a little for form's sake.

"Well," Sofie continued once the laughter died down. "You can imagine what the wise man knew but the great god did not. This flower, because its fragrance was so delightful, would make any who inhaled it forget all loves that had come before. Even a woman of such modesty and gentleness as the great god's betrothed could not withstand the power of this fragrance, and once she smelled it, the wise man knew that the great god would find favor in her eyes no longer.

"And so it came to pass. The wedding was held, with all the gods in attendance, and the wise man cackling in the back of the hall. At the conclusion of the ceremony, when the great god and his wife absconded to their bridal bower, and she inhaled the fragrance of the flower with which he had bedecked their bridal bed, her eyes at once lost their luster for her husband, and her heart lost all desire. Suspecting nothing of the wise man's deceit, the great god fell to his knees before his wife, clutching the hem of her garment and pleading for her to return to him. And when the other gods saw him in this pitiable state, his spell was broken, and never again did they fear his wrath. Instead, they laughed at him, calling him a worthless braggart, and vowed to install another god in his place before the sun rose on another day.

"But this is not the story's end," she said, her eyes flashing as they scanned the silent, eager crowd. "Broken and humbled, the great god fled his kingdom, becoming a ragged beggar in lands unknown. For years without end, he wandered the road, his power forgotten by all, even by himself. And then at last, he wandered into the lands of the wise man, who took pity on him, and gathered him to his breast. The once-great god bowed his head and said, 'Forgive me, for I have done wrong.' And tears fell from his eyes as he spoke these words.

"And from those tears sprang the form of a new flower, one that no one, not even the wise man, had seen before. The wise man plucked the flower, and, laying his hands on the great god's head, he said, 'You are forgiven. Return to the lands you once ruled, and rule them now in wisdom.' And when the wise man spoke these words, the great god was restored, and he returned to his wife, who had spent all the long years of his banishment enraptured by the flower from their wedding night. But when the scent of the new flower, the tear flower, washed over her, she too was restored, and she saw her husband as he was now, a wiser and gentler man, and love for him flowed through her heart once more. Their marriage was celebrated again, and in the time to come the wedding couple became the greatest of all gods. And through him her power flowed, and his through her, and the world was made anew. But the wise man . . ."

She paused, her eyes twinkling in the lantern light. I could tell from the breathless silence of the crowd that they knew what was coming.

"The wise man," Sofie said with a smile, "gained nothing, for he risked nothing. He is still out there on the road, trading flowers he will never smell himself. And his temper has not improved one bit!"

She laughed, and the crowd laughed with her. The Tran-Speaker whirred to silence in my ear. I was left with the feeling that there was much more to her words than I'd been able to grasp. But Sofie often had that effect on me too.

"That is the way it is with stories," she said to me once the crowd had dispersed for their tents and bedtime. "If you think tonight's tale was obscure, wait until you hear the legend about the philosopher and the cave."

"I get the great god, and I think I get the bride," I said. "But I'm still working on the flower and the wise man."

"A true-to-life wise man once wrote, 'We murder to dissect,'" she said playfully. "Like a flower or a human being, the life of a story lies in the whole, not in its parts."

"I'll keep that in mind when you do the one about the philosopher and the cave."

Laughing, she laid her fingertips on my arm, before her white-suited bodyguards surrounded her and led her away. They were never far from her, and though I supposed they trusted me by now—or trusted her, which meant they trusted any decision she chose to make—I knew they wouldn't hesitate to take out anyone they believed was a threat to her.

I watched her go. My skin tingled where she'd touched me, and her own fragrance, something made of incense and roses, lingered in the air. It was hard for me to believe that a month ago I'd been as far from her as it was possible to be—and now she was talking to me, teasing me, touching me. I'd never touched her myself, of course, one reason being the presence of her bodyguards—all seven of them, the two who'd died in New York CITI having been replaced by two who looked every bit as intimidating. The other reason was that she'd never given me an invitation.

Unless, that is, she just had.

Otherworld

Earth Year 3151

Night

'**ve** been trudging through the darkness for hours, holding the flashing red beacon the bored commissary clerk insisted would lead me straight to the *Freefall*, when the thought creeps into my mind that I might as well give up.

My radiation gear's heavy as hell. My body's killing me from the beating it took last night. My path's strewn with fissures and mud pits. And though I never noticed this when I was wearing the lightweight jumpsuit, I think this planet's gravitational pull is stronger than Earth's. Not by much, but enough to make a difference with all the garbage I'm lugging around.

Even worse, though, is all the garbage I'm lugging around inside.

I've been hurled halfway across the galaxy. Sampled by a space monster. Beaten within a centimeter of my life by the guy I used to share juice boxes with. And sent on a death march by the guy who used to buy the juice boxes. And all this for a girl who didn't love me, never loved me. Who used me, tricked me, left me.

Who I love nonetheless, and would save in a heartbeat if I could.

I can't wrap my head around it. I'm trying to save a guy I hate to save the girl I love, who's the reason he hates me. If, as I strongly suspect, I can't save him, she'll die. But even if I do save him, he'll personally make sure I never see her again. And even if I do see her again, she won't love me.

Whichever way it works out, I lose.

The sameness of each step, each second, wears on me. Moving makes sense when you can see a purpose to where you're going. Take that away, and it doesn't feel like you're moving. Conroy might think I've got some plan for meeting up with Adrian's captors in our really cool Super Spy bungalow, but I'm close to 100 percent sure his captors are also his killers, and I'm equally certain they're lying in wait underground right now, ready to perform a similar operation on me. I wonder why I'm worried about them, considering the futility of this mission. Maybe, in the end, that's all there is to life: staying alive. High ideals and lofty causes seemed so important when I was living in Sofie's camp. And all they did was land me—and her—here.

The mist clings to me like a web, obscuring everything. I gave up on using my flashlight when I realized all it did was bounce fog back into my eyes through the visor of my suit. An aluminum pole serves as my combined walking stick and probe. I tap it in front of me, swish it from side to side, reassured by the solid if slightly yielding percussion of stick against stone. Though really, is it any worse to get sucked into a steaming geyser than to be devoured? I'm beginning to think the fog comes not just from the pits but from somewhere deep inside the planet, seeping out when the sun's not around to hassle it. Directions are meaningless in this soup. There's no map, no coordinates, no landmarks. There's barely a left or right. There's only the flash of my beacon.

So that's the way I go. Toward the *Freefall*. Toward a ship that's been emptied of the one thing that gave it meaning.

And that's when it hits me.

The *Freefall*.

Okay, I admit it. I'm an idiot. Chalk it up to getting hurled halfway across the galaxy, sampled by a space monster, etc. I've been so focused on what Conroy wants me to find aboard the Lowerworld ship—something I'm almost positive I *won't* find—I never stopped to think what I *might* find.

Supplies. Support. Allies.

The *Freefall*'s jammed to the rafters with equipment for its own journey. Unless someone did a number on the Lowerworld ship as bad as they did on the *Executor*, some of that equipment might be working. Sofie's pod ejected, and maybe others did as well, but there's no reason to think they all did. If Conroy's right that the Lowerworlders sabotaged the *Executor*, he could also be right that they sent the *Freefall* here to finish the job. At the moment, the chairman's holding Sofie hostage to maintain the upper hand. But if I can find a way inside the ship, maybe

I can mobilize my own militia to storm the *Executor* and save her. Conroy thinks I'm working with the *Freefall* anyway, right? Why not give him what he wants?

It's a crazy thought, I know. Probably brought on by the tediousness of the march, the hopelessness of my task. But doing nothing seems worse than doing something. And merely staying alive seems like not enough reason to live.

I head in the direction the beacon shows me, walking far faster than I have since I left the *Executor*. At last I've got a plan, even if it's insane.

There's no sound except my own heavy footsteps. Nothing in sight except, guess what, more fog. It curls like a living thing, rearranging itself according to its own mysterious motives. I wonder if the *Freefall* still bleeds light, if I'll see it before I get there. I wonder, for that matter, if I'm heading in its direction or if I've circled back. The bored clerk showed me how to interpret the homing device's data, but either she didn't explain it very well or her instructions have slipped my mind, because I'm starting to suspect that all I'm reading is the presence of the pods aboard the *Executor*. That would be just my luck, to walk all night and end up back at Conroy's doorstep.

But I don't let doubt work its way from my head to my legs. As long as the ground holds me upright, as long as the homing device flashes any kind of signal, I'm not slowing down.

I walk on. The beacon holds. The red light turns my palm to fire.

Then I'm pitching forward, landing on gloved hands on the

soft, spongy rock. My walking stick flies free and vanishes into the mist. The homing device flashes madly in my hand before switching to a solid, steady red.

I sit up and look around. The beacon's the only light I have, and it shows me nothing except my own glove. What tripped me I can't tell, unless it was a rock formation. Come to think of it, it felt less like I was tripped than like I was shoved. I crawl into the mist, feeling for the stick, but it's not there.

It doesn't take me long to discover why.

The land vanishes beneath my fingers. I flatten myself onto my stomach and reach as far down as I can, but I can't reach bottom. It could be a minor declivity in the ground or a cliff. I vote for a cliff.

If the wind or whatever hadn't knocked me down, I'd have walked right off it.

My excitement from moments ago ebbs considerably. It seems this planet is determined to kill me. But not before it toys with me first.

I can't go on without my probe. But I can't search for it either. I can't walk any farther, knowing I might step off the edge. If I'm reading the beacon right, it's telling me there are other pods in the immediate vicinity, but I can't see them. They could be at the base of the cliff, wrecked. Or intact. It could be the *Freefall* got smashed up on landing or ended up lying at the bottom of a canyon. The people I'm trying to reach might be down there right now, looking around at the invisible land-scape, not knowing and not caring where I am.

So I do the only thing I can do.

I crawl.

With the beacon clutched in one hand and the other hand feeling for a drop-off in the ground, I creep forward on my knees, hoping the pods are on my level, hoping I'm creeping toward them and not away. It's nearly impossible to tell at this point how close they are, with the beacon lit up steadily. Maybe they're all around me and I can't see them. Hopefully, if I move too far away, the beacon will tell me that. Or the sun will come up while I'm knee-walking around, and I'll finally be able to see.

Or this might happen too.

I might hear something rattling right beside my ear.

Apparently, I'm not the only organism with the sense to figure out there's something it wants aboard the Lowerworld ship.

I drop the homing device and stand, reaching for the gun at my belt. The solid wall of night budges, moves. It's got legs. They propel it in a long, elastic spring over my head, land on silent footfalls behind me.

It wasn't wind that knocked me down a moment ago.

The thing paces beyond range of the red beacon, rattling deep in its throat. As with the first time, I can't make the movement resolve into a solid form, my frenzied brain telling me it's shaped of mist and shadows instead of flesh. That'll change, I know only too well, if it manages to lay paws on me. I get the fuzzy impression that it's a quadruped, its shape more horizontal than vertical. The clacking noise it makes might not be vocalization at all but teeth or claws. Its color is a thing of uncertainty too, but I'm going to go with yellow or gray. An unhealthy color, a queasy color. Maybe that's the mist.

It stops moving and, I think, sits on its haunches to stare at me. I can definitely see eyes, or two faintly glowing yellow circles where eyes should be. Its strange wariness makes me wonder if this is the same one that attacked me the first time, the one that got scared away by Adrian's gun. Maybe the terrain between our two ships is its home range. Or maybe this particular specimen has an affinity for guys who stroll into the mist looking for lost friends and lost loves.

I wave my gun at it, but I have no confidence in my aim. The homing device lies at my feet, its glow too weak to be useful. I need a light source I can point at the thing. I can't hit what I can't see.

Then I remember the flares.

The plan, to the extent that there was a plan, was for me to use the flares as a last resort, if I managed to negotiate for Adrian's release but couldn't bring him back to home base. Realistically, the chance of anyone seeing my flare from the Upperworld ship was nil. And the present situation seems like enough of a last resort to me.

The thing rattles again but doesn't spring. Aiming my gun in the general direction I sense movement, I reach behind me, slide a flare from my pack, hold it in front of me. Turn it on. It sparks bright red in the fog, emitting a minor hum. I wave it at the creature, hoping to scare it off or at least give me a clearer view.

The last thing I'm trying to do is give it something to lock in on.

It's on its feet again. I don't know how I know, but I know. Maybe, as a night predator, it prefers the red end of the spectrum. It's moving fast, faster than the fog, faster than me.

Slower, though, than the speed of light.

I fire blindly at it in midflight, the beam tearing apart the darkness like a flash of lightning. I see a rushing body, reflective enough it could be metallic, with long forelimbs and a wedge-shaped head filled with so many teeth they seem to erupt from its flesh. It screams and twists flexibly in midair, landing on legs I can't see in the ensuing darkness. Its rattle sounds thick with mucus, maybe with pain.

But it doesn't run away. It comes at me again.

I fend it off with the beam once more, but this time it darts away into the darkness without making a sound. Could be it's wounded, or it's realized that my weapon does it no permanent damage. I figure I'll find out by what it does next.

What it does next is spring at me from out of nowhere.

I spin and fire just in time. Its heavy body collides with me, knocking me to the ground and jarring the flare loose. Pain stabs my right shoulder, and the gun drops from my numb hand, spiraling free and vanishing into the mist. I know I won't be able to reach it before the thing springs again.

But it doesn't. It lies on its side, legs curled up to its belly, hide illuminated by the red glow of the dropped flare. It doesn't move, and the rattling sound has ceased. If it's possible to kill something that's more shadow than substance, it's dead.

I grope in the dark, my fingers closing on my weapon. My shoulder hurts where the creature hit me, but nowhere near as bad as the first time. Breathing heavily, I retrieve the flare and go to inspect the thing I killed.

It sprawls on the spongy rock, smaller than I would have guessed when it was in motion, not much more than two meters in length. At first I think its gray skin is hairless, but then I realize its skin isn't skin. It's some kind of metal exoskeleton, smooth and shiny, a matching breastplate and backplate enclosing a liquid shape I can't make out in the bad light. What I took for long, spiderlike limbs are six robotic appendages ending in wicked-looking instruments, spikes and blades and a slim tube tapering to a point like a syringe. The part I assumed was its head is more like a helmet, a jagged slash topped by two flat disks and lined from front to back with sharp points that clamber all over each other in a mad rush. Teeth, or the mechanical equivalent. But there's nothing that looks like a mouth, no opening in the helmet for it to ingest its prey—i.e., me.

I lean closer, thrusting the flare into the body cavity to explore the milky figure inside. Much of this inner being is so sheathed in armor I can't see it, but the parts I can see look distinctly organic: throat, shoulders, stomach. The skin, if it's skin, is pale, almost translucent in the flare's glow. The mixture of biology and technology is so intricate I can't tell if this is a living victim that's been partially digested by a metallic monster or a humanoid operator inside a robotic shell. I stare at the biomechanical thing for long minutes, wishing I could pry it open, knowing I don't have the strength. A whisper at the back of my mind tells me there's something familiar about it, but I'm too exhausted to remember what.

A hissing sound close to my ear cuts through the confusion, making me think the thing's coming back to life. But it takes me only a moment to realize the sound's issuing from me, from my suit. I press a hand against the place where the hood of the radiation suit meets the torso, and the hissing stops, only to resume as soon as I let go. I look closely at the creature's robotic claws and see a scrap of gray material impaled on one of them, like a tiny victory flag my dead assailant is waving in mockery.

I have exactly one thought.

Shit.

My suit's been compromised. I'm leaking oxygen. The supplemental kits I brought should take care of that, but they won't prevent me from being assaulted by the light of the planetary day.

Which, judging from the pale glow on the horizon, is less than an hour from now.

I have a new plan. Forget this thing. The revolution can wait. If I want to live to save Sofie, I have to get somewhere inside.

Fast.

Earth, 2151

Lowerworld

You'd think that, living in Sofie's camp and catching a few words with her nearly every day, I'd have picked up plenty of details about her personal life.

You'd be wrong.

No matter how much time I spent in the Lowerworld, she remained almost a complete mystery to me. I was sure other members of her camp knew things they weren't telling me, but there was no way to ask. I could barely communicate with most of them, and talking through a TranSpeaker didn't seem like the best way to have a heart-to-heart. As the year 2150 turned to 2151—with none of the fanfare that was surely taking place in the Upperworld, considering this was the final year those who'd won seats on the starships would live on planet Earth—I found myself more or less where I'd been since I saw her on the world-link: watching, though from close-up this time, and waiting for her to give me a sign.

I heard rumors around camp, of course. I heard she'd lived part of her life in the Upperworld corponation of ExCon, which was super rare for people who looked like her. But no one talked about her parents, Sofie least of all, so I assumed they were dead or as good as. The story of her meeting with Sumati at age twelve and her rise to the number two position by her current age of sixteen was common knowledge among her followers, so that much I knew. It blew my mind, though, to think that while I was playing ball with Adrian and Griff, watching crappy content on the link, and getting my head stuffed full of corponational bullshit, Sofie was traveling the world with her mentor, preparing to take over the biggest movement for justice the planet had ever seen. The biggest, and whichever way it worked out, the last.

Back home, it would have driven me crazy to know so little about a girl who held my fate in the palm of her hand. But back home, the only girls I met were the ones in my Classification, which meant they were the daughters of my dad's business associates, their heads as full of bullshit as mine. It was a welcome change to find a girl who wasn't a carbon copy of everyone I knew, including me. And there was so much going on—so many opportunities for me to hope, as I'd almost said that day in her helicar, that Sofie might *need* me, take that as you will—I stifled any misgivings and let the movement carry me along in its irresistible current.

We traveled by helicar caravan from place to place, never stopping to set up camp for more than a couple of days before moving on. The Lowerworld I discovered in those months was far different than I'd seen or imagined—a place so huge you couldn't really call it a place, so varied it seemed crazy to lump it all together in a single word. We flew from one sprawling, crumbling city to another, cities whose names I'd never heard but Sofie told me had existed for centuries if not millennia: New Delhi, Riyadh, Cairo, Chongqing, Kigali. I saw styles of architecture so foreign to me I had to be taught a whole new language, spires and minarets and mosques and temples, most of them in ruins, with clay and mud huts mingled among the hollowed-out shells of skyscrapers and the far more ancient ruins that Sofie said had been among the earliest monuments of human civilization. The people I'd first seen at the UN building surrounded me in these ancient places, people with skin shades all across the spectrum and clothing to match and unfamiliar languages that merged into a steady chaos of sound— except here the scale was much larger than it had been on that single day back home, so many people crowding the streets I felt at first as if I couldn't breathe. Some days I literally couldn't breathe, days we were camped near one of the spitting, spewing factories or reeking landfills that dominated many Lowerworld cities. My eyes burned for days after leaving those places.

But even through the sting and blur, I couldn't remain blind to the things I saw around me. I saw children so wasted with hunger they couldn't lift their heads from their straw pallets or swat at the flies that buzzed noisily in their noses and mouths, others with swollen bellies picking through garbage heaps for scraps of spoiled food. I saw men and women who'd worked their entire lives in mines or factories until they got too weak to work and were thrown out to spend their final days coughing pieces of their bloody lungs from toothless mouths. I saw corponation logos plastered on walled fortresses from which the sounds of music and laughter and gushing fountains issued, while in the streets outside, Peace Corp. troops leveled weapons at the crowds of starving people who edged close to these scenes of wanton luxury. I saw truckloads of prisoners or workers—who could tell the difference?—traveling to their next destination, with hollow eyes and manacled hands and rifles trained on any who so much as shifted position. I saw rivers that had turned red from the raw sewage spilling from one Upper-world factory or another, desert plains where the only things that moved were the plastic bags—all of them printed with corponation logos—blowing across the ground like dead leaves. I saw some sights I would have called beautiful, or at least some that spoke of beauty now long gone, graffiti-smeared pyramids and waste-filled gorges and fiery, smoke-dimmed sunsets. But I saw almost nothing that spoke of beauty still alive, still growing, still reaching for the light.

Nothing, that is, except her. Her and the people who followed her, the people who believed she could lead them to a new and better place.

I'd joined her camp, it turned out, at a critical moment, by far the most busy, buoyant, uncertain time anyone could remember. The assassination in New York CITI had barely made a dent in the worldlink. The official story was that a crazed Lowerworlder had fired shots in the old UN building, only to take his own life before he could be apprehended. He showed up on the link for a day or two after the symposium, a swarthy, bearded twenty-something whose tattooed face and body screamed *Terrarist*. Though rumors that Sofie had been the true target in New York forced her to change her routine—most obviously by suspending the large, open, outdoor meetings her mentor had begun—the failed symposium, the death of the revolution's leader, and the activities of Sumati's successor carved a silence so deep the Upperworld could slumber on in almost total ignorance.

Which suited Sofie just fine. She had her own link, her own access to the world, and she used it to make sure people knew the truth. Bootlegged footage of Sumati's death was beamed throughout the Lowerworld, and wherever it aired, spontaneous protests sprang up, all of them clamoring for access to colonization as the first step—not the last—toward restitution. When Sofie's team applied to have Sumati's body returned to her home corponation and the request was denied, that became another rallying cry for the movement. Coupled with Sofie's stolen colonization memo, the image of the old woman's limp, bloody body slumped on a table in a foreign land had an explosive effect. The crowds grew and grew, making me think at times the entire Lowerworld was on the march.

During her life, Sofie's mentor had lit a spark. After Sumati's death, Sofie coaxed it into a fire, and it swept across the Lowerworld in advance of her. She didn't have to keep lighting it. When we arrived, no matter where we arrived, we found it burning.

With the need to maintain a low profile, Sofie's new strategy was to meet privately with the organizers of each demonstration, integrating them into the larger movement and coordinating next steps. Her mobility amazed me. How they'd done it I never understood completely, but for years before the public demonstrations began, Sumati's team had worked to set up a network of secret transportation routes so the teacher and her apprentice could fly from MexSanto to ConGlo, ConGlo to MicroNasia, without the interference or awareness of the corponational authorities. What had seemed like magic on the hacked channels I'd watched with Adrian and Griff was the result of countless people across the Lowerworld working clandestinely to jam worldlink transmissions, bribe low-level corponation officials, spread misinformation about the revolutionary leaders' activities, and when it came time, get the two of them the hell out of there as the noose was pulling tight. A handful of well-placed Upperworld operatives played a role in the intercorponational game of cat and mouse, but it was the nameless thousands, Sofie said, who were the real heroes of the movement. They were the ones who risked everything—their jobs, their families, their lives—to make it possible for her to speak on behalf of the billions who would have had no voice otherwise. And all they asked in return was that Sofie never slow down, never fall silent.

There was only one time during our months together that

it seemed her secret network had failed. That day, we arrived in the former capital of ConGlo—a city once known as Kinshasa—to discover that we'd been ratted out, maybe by someone in the organization, and a trap had been laid for Sofie's arrest. Fortunately, her handlers figured out something was wrong when they couldn't scramble the TranSpeakers—the strategy they'd used to block Upperworlders, me included, from decoding Sofie's words on the link. Her bodyguards hustled her back on board the command ship, and our caravan was in the air before the corporation thugs arrived. Once my heart stopped pounding from the close call—and after she had time to review protocol with her inner circle—I asked her if she realized how much *she* was risking. It was a stupid question, though by no means my stupidest. But she answered in a way that didn't make me feel like a complete moron, even if it did make my blood run cold.

"I risk only what Sumati did," she said. "And should I pay the price she paid, there will be another to take my place."

As the new guy in the movement—and a guy from the Upperworld, no less—my own job was absurdly modest by comparison. While Sofie globe hopped, rallying supporters and dodging death, I sat in a mobile comm tent with twenty other people, monitoring worldlink transmissions for evidence of a change in the Upperworld's position regarding colonization. Important work, I told myself, but pretty tame and, to be honest, dull. The only time it got a little dicey was when I stumbled on a spot featuring my own parents talking to some corporation propagandist about how they'd worried throughout my childhood that I'd get mixed up with the "wrong people," but how they were sure I was "treatable." Fortunately, the feed for that one broke up in about twenty seconds, and after I took a deep breath, I got back to work.

Such as it was. Sofie had put me on this assignment because my background supposedly gave me insight into Upperworld thinking, which meant I might be able to read between the lines of the purposely vague and evasive statements that flowed out of corponational headquarters. Truth was, though, it all sounded like double-talk to me. I'd heard it all my life: *It is in the financial interests of corponational stakeholders and affiliated parties to expedite an orderly, equitable, and secure colonization protocol.* But even now that I saw such mumbo jumbo for what it was, I couldn't see through it to the anxieties that might be driving it. It made me wonder sometimes if the Upperworld *had* any anxieties, if they were so in control of the situation they could safely ignore the protests igniting around the globe. Maybe Sofie and her retinue would wake up one morning, ready to cruise into another powder keg of a rally that would bring the Upperworld to its knees, only to discover that the starships had already lifted off. Which, when I thought about it, filled me with the same mixture of feelings everything did these days: concern that the movement might fail, and hope that no matter what world I ended up on, I'd end up on it with her.

I never said anything like that *to* her, of course. But the more days I spent with her, the more I felt a nervous excitement every time she walked into the room, as if *this* time would be *the* time.

For what, I wasn't sure. I only knew that I desperately wanted to find out.

And that was the other thing that drove me crazy about my mind-numbing job in the comm tent, monitoring chatter from overseas: It kept me on the fringes of the movement, away from the action, away from her. I'd known from the start that I wouldn't be welcomed into Sofie's inner circle right away. I knew people had trust issues with me. Her head bodyguard was the worst, staring at me all the time as if I was the one who'd pulled the trigger in New York CITI—or, at least, as if I should have stood in the path of the bullet. But though I knew it made a certain sense to keep a guy like me at a distance, I also felt I'd earned a heap of trust that day in New York, when I was the one storming the stage while everyone else was scrambling for the exits. If you wanted to talk about risk, I'd risked my spot on an Upperworld starship, risked my friends and family—for what that was worth—and, if a Peace Corp. drone locked onto our camp, risked my life. Was it too much to ask that I get a chance to be with Sofie, to hold her hand like we'd done in the helicar, to feel her fingers on my arm one more time? To tell her what I felt—no, *prove* to her what I felt—before I lost my chance forever?

I couldn't let that chance get away.

Which was why my heart beat like crazy when, one morning three months into my new life as a member of Sofie's camp, she drew aside the screen to my personal tent and slipped inside.

Otherworld

Earth Year 3151

Day

The first light of the planetary day shows me how far I am from shelter, how close I am to death.

The *Freefall*'s here, all right. It lies like a toppled tower spanning a bottomless gulf, the same one that almost swallowed me. I can see it in the pale shimmer of dawn, the gleaming shell rising high above the mist, the thousands of lights twinkling invitingly all along its hull. It beckons to me, a gigantic life-support system just waiting for me to crack into it if I can get there on time.

Which I can't.

I can see it, sure. But I can only see it because a.) I have binoculars, and b.) the *Freefall*'s enormous. So enormous that, viewed from afar, it looks less like an object sitting on the ground than like the curve of the landscape. The binoculars give me a reading on the distance: approximately fifteen kilometers away, or at least an hour if I was a marathoner. But even on my best day, I could never keep up that pace for long. Factoring in my suit's weight and the treacherous terrain and the gravitational pull and my current state of exhaustion, I estimate five hours travel time minimum.

I quickly weigh my options. The sun will break the horizon at any minute. The gully might shield me from its rays for a while, but eventually they'd fall on me. Plus, I don't have the equipment for rock-climbing. I've also got nothing to patch my suit. My only hope is that if I start moving immediately, I'll find my way to the ship's interior—or, failing that, its shadow— before the ambient radiation makes me very sick, if not very dead.

I stoop to pick up the tracker before heading for the ship, then stop.

The red light of the homing device continues to glow steadily on the ground where I dropped it. From what little I remember of the clerk's instructions, that makes no sense—it shouldn't be responding this way if the *Freefall*'s pods are inside the ship, kilometers away. It's acting as if the pods are right here.

But they can't be. There's enough light by now to see the area surrounding me, and I can't see them. All I can see are the remains of the biomechanical creature.

Which, now that I see it in the early light of day, sparks the memory I couldn't quite come up with last night.

I move close, lean down to inspect it. As soon as I do, my heart beats a rhythm of fear and dread.

It's a pod.

Or not exactly a pod. But the way a pod might look if its inhabitant was fused with the machinery. The backplate and breastplate resemble a pod's outer surfaces. The multiple mechanical arms are like a pod's innards, if they were pulled out to expose the devices that deliver nanotechnologies to the sleeping passenger. The helmet is a mystery, but still. I lean closer, squinting through the maze of metallic teeth, and then I see it.

There's a word etched into the helmet. An acronym, actually. JIPOC.

I stand, glancing anxiously around me, convinced a whole squadron of the things is going to appear from underground. Almost hoping they do. If they did, they'd show me a way out of the sun.

I hunt for the way myself, and it's not long before I find it.

A hole in the ground opens onto a diagonal shaft, tunneling downward at a twenty-degree angle. It's more than broad enough to accommodate me. After all, it accommodated them.

I push my hood back and wriggle face-first into the hole, keeping the flare in front of me to provide light. The subsurface stone is cool on my face, even cold, and I know I'll be safe from the UV down here. Whether I'll be safe from other things, I'm less certain.

It's a short crawl before I drop into a larger chamber. The air is downright frigid, but I should be okay in the radiation suit. The flare isn't strong enough to show me much more than a collection of humped shapes like stones or burial mounds. But

I've got my flashlight. I take it out and shine it around the room, and then I see.

They are pods. Not as many as I expected, but other tunnels branch off from this one, so possibly there are other chambers. I count eight pods, looking precisely the way dormant pods should look, their shells folded neatly in a two-meter-long oval. When I shine my flashlight on the nearest one, I can see the hairline seams where the thing is designed to open when the sleeper wakes, the recessed button that operates the opening mechanism from outside. I step closer, tracing the part of the shell that carries the JIPOC crest and acronym. I can easily imagine this part as the shape of the biomechanical monster's helmet, as if the head's been tucked, turtlelike, between the other sections of the shell. The rest of the pods carry precisely the same symbol and lettering.

And the things are asleep. At least, they don't stir when I shine the light on them, touch them, press my ear against them to see if I can hear the living being within. I can't, but I can hear the faint hum and feel the vibration that means the deep-sleep aura is engaged.

Shakily I sit, removing my gloves. I can wait here until nightfall, but I'm going to have to be careful. At the first sign of the things waking up, I have to be gone.

My mind races, and though I can't remember the last time I ate anything, the clenching of my stomach has nothing to do with hunger. I can understand what these things are: the missing pods from the *Executor*. I can understand why the creatures come out at night: They're triggered by darkness, their human components unable to tolerate the radiation of the planetary day. I'm guessing I didn't actually kill the one aboveground, but that I merely crippled it, preventing it from folding back into deepsleep when it sensed the sun rising. I can even understand why they've moved themselves to this remote cavern, far from the *Executor*: The supersonic devices we planted around the ship did upset them, forcing them to find other places to hibernate. It was only because me and Adrian had run well beyond the perimeter that they were able to attack him there.

What I simply can't understand is *how* any of this happened.

The pods were meant to protect us in a state of suspended animation on our journey, allowing us to rise from deepsleep undamaged, unchanged. They weren't supposed to fuse with their occupants, turning sleeping passengers into these grotesque hybrids of human and machine.

Could *this* be what happens when the deepsleep goes bad? Could it be what might happen to Sofie if I don't deliver on my promise to Conroy?

But no. I can't believe this is an accident. It has to be by design. The only question is whose.

I think back to my first encounter with the night creature, the blade that skewered my shoulder, the burning, blinding fluid the PMP extracted from my eyes. He called it an organic compound. Could it have been some kind of nanoserum, accidentally delivered by one of the creature's appendages when it attacked me? Not so much a toxin as a treatment? Maybe the very thing that, administered over the course of the ship's journey, transformed a sleeping human being into a mechanical nightmare?

And if it did, could it be that Conroy knows about this? His PMP was the one who identified the compound. His strategy for scaring the things off with the perimeter devices couldn't have been a lucky guess. His belief that I could negotiate with them, that they weren't brute animals incongruously roaming a barren planet, suggests that he knows or at least suspects what they really are. Could he have been responsible for what happened to them? Unless the nondescript commissary clerk is a criminal mastermind during her lunch break, the chairman of the board of JIPOC would seem the most likely suspect to hatch a swarm of interstellar monsters.

But *why*? And if he *was* responsible for them, how did they get so badly out of his control?

I can't puzzle it out. My brain feels like it's stuck in neutral, and I realize I haven't slept—if you can call this "sleep"—since I got my clock cleaned by Adrian. Who I still don't expect to find aboard the *Freefall*, because whatever produced these creatures, they don't seem like the negotiating type. But the other things I might find aboard the *Freefall* are my main objective now, in fact my only objective. I don't need to solve this mystery to save Sofie. I just need to stay alive long enough to find others who are willing to fight with me.

I take out a food pouch and a sac of water, quickly gobbling and slurping down the unappetizing meal. Then I lean back against the nearest pod, holding the tracker in my hands. My plan is to take a short nap and be up long before they wake, but in case I don't, maybe I'll get lucky and feel this one coming out of hibernation. Why I think I should get lucky at this point is beyond me. Hope springs eternal and all that.

I close my eyes. Darkness enfolds me, shot through with specks of light like stars. The pods purr around me, but I can't help amplifying the purr into a rattle, and sleep's in no hurry to come. I feel totally alone, the entire universe my ocean, and me one small ship in an endless sea.

If I were to dream, I wouldn't dream of them. I'd dream of her.

I don't dream.

Earth, 2151

Lowerworld

When the girl you're dying to be alone with strolls into your tent first thing in the morning, what do you do?

If you're me, you thank your lucky stars you zipped up your pants.

She'd never visited me before. She'd stuck her head into the comm tent from time to time, not looking for me in particular. It was always me tracking her down, grabbing a word with her after her nightly story sessions, passing her my reports and getting a minute or two of her time while she flipped through my linkpad. I was so shocked to hear her voice outside, to see her hand—not her bodyguard's—lifting the tent flap, it's a miracle I had the presence of mind to zip up. I wondered how her face would have reacted if I hadn't.

"Cameron," she said. She was dressed like always, her hair in its usual braid, her lips and eyes made up, but I thought she looked tired and more somber than usual. I was so far out of the loop I couldn't remember what she'd been doing this past week, whether she'd had a particularly brutal travel schedule. "Are you busy?"

"Not especially," I said. In fact my agenda was no different from any other day, which meant I was either insanely busy or wasting my time, take your pick.

She smiled a little, but she still looked distracted. "I would like you to come with me," she said. "There's something I need to show you."

The word "need" was all it took to shove everything out of my mind and get me off my butt. Any thought I might have had that this was more than a business excursion, though, was squashed when I exited the tent and saw her bodyguards standing there like always, the original five plus the two replacements. Still, I didn't hesitate. This was the first time I'd been alone with her since leaving the Upperworld, even if "alone" meant me, her, and seven guys who could kill me with their bare hands.

"Where are we going?" I asked as we hustled to her helicar.

"Not far," she said, and that was all I could get out of her. So I settled in and let the car take us away. We sat in silence as the dusty emptiness of the SubCon countryside flowed beneath us.

In less than an hour we landed on the outskirts of a small village, the mud-hut kind I'd seen many times in the past three months. But the second the helicar door opened, I knew this place was different. For one thing, the huts had been fenced in, surrounded by a two-meter-high barricade of barbed wire. For another, the smell that hit me when I stepped out of the car was like a solid wall: piss and decay and something worse, something I couldn't identify and didn't much want to. There was no one in the mud lanes, no sound of children playing like there always was even in the worst of these places. I hesitated as Sofie and her bodyguards forged ahead, and she saw it, because she held up a hand for them to stop.

"Cameron." Her voice was soft, but her eyes probed me. "Are you coming?"

"What is this place?" I asked.

"Please," she said. "We won't stay long."

She raised a fold of her robe over her nose and mouth. I took out the cloth mask they'd given me when I first joined them and held it over my own face. Then I followed her to the fence, waiting while her bodyguards made an opening with wire cutters and peeled a section aside. With them remaining behind, Sofie and I walked to the closest of the mud huts.

The smell was so bad inside I couldn't breathe even with the mask. It was too dark to make anything out at first, but then I saw, huddled on the floor like piles of wood, the bodies of people reduced to nothing but skin and bones. They weren't moving, and they were clearly dead. The air was completely silent, not even the flies wanting to take part in the feast. When I could finally bring myself to look at the people's faces, I saw that their eyes were open and their noses and mouths were smeared with something black that shouldn't have come from inside human bodies.

I ran from the hut and leaned over, trying not to throw up, afraid that if I did, the same black stuff would come out of me. I don't know how long I stayed like that before I felt Sofie beside me. I looked up at her, watching her through a blur of desert light. Her face was calm, and when she spoke, her words were dispassionate, like she was reading from a report.

"One of the Upperworld transmissions you intercepted yesterday contained directions to the SubCon Central Office, instructing local authorities to place this village under *close supervision*," she said.

"One of the ones *I* intercepted?" I couldn't remember reading anything like that, there'd been so many, all of them blending into uniformity.

"The transmission originated from ExCon," she said. "We have learned to treat all such communications with suspicion."

"What happened to them?" I said.

She looked at me sadly, but instead of answering, she asked another question. "Do you know where ExCon got its name?"

I shook my head. All I knew was that it stood for Exceptional Content, since that was what they did, provided the most popular worldlink games and videos. But Sofie wouldn't have asked if there wasn't more to the story.

"Its original name was Extermination Control," she said. "Its charge was to develop seamless and untraceable means of relieving population pressures. Its video empire was built on the blood of countless victims who died never knowing what poisoned them, or why they were deserving of such a fate."

I stared at her, at a loss for what to say. "How do you know about this?"

"I lived much of my life in ExCon," she said. "I found ways to discover the truth." Her arm swept the circle of silent huts.

"The officials who orchestrated this attack are too cowardly to leave a garrison to defend their handiwork. They think no one will come prying until all of the evidence has been destroyed and their propagandists have had a chance to blame the deaths on a Terrarist attack. But we have been here, and so we know."

I fell to the dusty ground, holding my head in my hands. I'd watched ExCon videos, played ExCon games. The excitement I'd felt when Sofie arrived at my tent this morning had turned into the conviction that if this was supposed to be some kind of date, it was definitely the worst date of all time. "Why'd you have to show me this?"

She squatted beside me. "It was your diligence that led us to this place," she said. "Is it not best that you see?"

I shook my head, unable to answer her. She rose and took a step away from me, then stood there, arms wrapped around her middle. The wind blew her robe as dark clouds gathered overhead, but I knew the stink of the place couldn't be blown or washed away.

"You call us Terrarists," she said, speaking to the wind. "You have been taught to fear people such as myself. But I have learned to do the same. I have learned to fear the ones who look like you."

She turned back to me, and under the power of her eyes, I felt compelled to give some kind of answer.

"That's different," I said. "Terrarists attack—"

"The innocent?" she said sharply.

"No . . ."

"Children? The aged? Those who cannot defend themselves?" Her golden eyes blazed. "How are the atrocities committed in the name of Terra any different from this?"

"I just meant . . ."

But now that her words had started, I couldn't stop them from continuing in an angry torrent.

"You have been with us for months," she said. "Have you learned nothing in all that time? Do you cling to the lies you were fed as a child? Is *that* our return for the risks we have taken, son of the Upperworld?"

I tried to say something, but like that first day in the helicar, she never slowed down.

"I have given you time," she said. "More than we have to spare, and much more than I would have given others. I have watched, and waited, and prayed for a sign that you would join us not only in body but in spirit. But now I find that I have prayed in vain."

"I was waiting too," I managed to sneak in. "Waiting for you to—"

"To send you a personal invitation?" she said. "What more could I have done to awaken you, if the suffering you have seen with your own eyes failed to do so? No, I fear you are like all the Upperworld's people: So long as you believe that outer space awaits you, the Earth and its sorrows can have no real claim on your heart."

Her accusation hit me like a physical blow. "That's not true," I said. "I'm not like that."

"Then *show* me!" she said violently. She gripped my shoulders, her face practically touching mine. "Prove to me that you are one of us. Or leave this place, as you meant to do before we met. The Earth will not mourn your loss."

She released me and fell to the ground, burying her face in her hands. A wail rose from her, a cry of anguish so keen it cut straight through me. Raising her head to the swollen sky, she uttered a string of words in her own language. They might have been a chant, or a curse. Her eyes were dry, but her cheeks glistened with the rain that had begun to fall.

"This was my village," she said. "I was born here, before my parents sold me to the Upperworld. I toiled as a slave in ExCon, and the only thing that kept me alive was the thought that I might one day return to liberate others. And now I am left to tell my people that none survive but me."

With that, she walked back to the fence, holding her robe tightly against her so it wouldn't catch as her chief bodyguard held the wire aside and handed her through. I stayed on the ground, not wanting to risk the wobble I was sure would show in my legs if I tried to stand. I knew I could take all the time I needed to pull myself together. I knew she'd wait for me.

But I also knew she wouldn't wait forever. She'd seen through me the way she always did, seen that deep in my heart I was holding back, expecting *her* to prove something to *me* before I committed fully to her cause. Life's like that in the Upperworld. You learn to believe there's always an out.

The next time she called on me, I knew I wouldn't get another chance.

And I promised myself that when that time came, I would prove to her that I was in.

Otherworld

Earth Year 3151

Day

I wake in time to see the pod things stirring, their shells flexing as they prepare to open for the night. I'm almost stupid enough to stand there and watch the whole process, until I remind myself they aren't about to hatch into cute fluffy ducklings. I suit up and crawl out of the cavern in a hurry, and so far as I can tell, the things don't follow.

The creature from the previous night lies on its stomach, insect legs splayed as if it tried to get up before collapsing again. That gives me an idea, and I close my gloved hand around the final joint of one of its segmented legs. With the help of my ion gun, I heat the metal or living tissue or whatever the joint's composed of until it sizzles and snaps, and I've got myself a new walking stick, heavier and shorter than the old one but better than nothing. It creeps me out to think where it came from, but the alternative, I tell myself, is much worse.

Now that I've seen the orientation of the gulf that lies under the *Freefall*, I stay well to the right of it, using my macabre walking stick to make sure I don't deviate from my course. Still, the going's much slower than I calculated—the one thing I didn't take into account was fear of losing my way in the ever-present mist, which blocks my view of the terrain as well as the ship. The whole time I'm walking, the rasp of my oxygen kit makes it impossible to hear if anything's following. I take a couple of breaks to rest and watch for stalkers in the night, but to my immense relief, there's nothing to see.

I'm a good kilometer from my goal when the lights of the *Freefall* finally fight their way through the mist. I pick up the pace now that I've got a visible target, but even so, it's near daybreak before I stand by the ship at last, the first dribbles of sunlight bleeding the fog into a million fuzzy halos. The tracking device has been flashing merrily away during my walk, but now it gives off a steady red glow, so I know at least some of the pods are inside.

The only question is, how do I get at them?

I tuck the homing device into my supply pouch and walk alongside the ship, keeping one hand on its flank for anything that might suggest a way in. Not surprisingly, the hull appears impregnable, which it would have to be to survive an interstellar voyage. If the *Freefall*'s configured anything like the Executor, there should be a cluster of airlocks by the forward command center. But that's half a ship's length from me, lost in a gleam of fog twenty football fields away, and requiring me to cross a gulch with no discernible bottom. Plus I'm not authorized to open the airlocks. I've got no way to communicate with the ship's passengers, whose absence worries me—they should have woken up when they landed, and if they didn't, that's going to put a major kink in my plan to rescue Sofie. But before I can worry about the details, I need to get inside.

Continued inspection of the ship reveals a series of small curved shapes protruding from the hull, which my hand confirms are the rungs of a ladder, one of many laid for construction and upkeep when the ship was preparing for departure. The ladders should lead to maintenance shafts sprinkled along the hull. The shafts will be sealed, but maybe with my gun I can unseal one the same way I melted the monster's leg. The larger problem is that the shafts don't start until halfway up the massive hulk's side. But if I can shinny up a ladder and find my footing where the curve of the hull flattens three hundred meters overhead, I'll be able to work without fear of falling. And if the shafts have twin doors like the airlocks, I'll be able to get into the ship without compromising its pressure or atmosphere.

It's a risky plan, I know. But the mist is leeching away with the spread of the sunlight, and if I don't get in soon, I'll be the proud owner of an extra-special, bone-deep tan.

I'll take my chances.

I grab the nearest rung and climb. I move as fast as caution and my weakened shoulder allow, never forgetting the bottomless crater that lies beneath the hull. The ship's endless. I never saw it up close, only catching glimpses on the worldlink. We'd all lapsed into deepsleep before the pods were loaded. Now that

I'm climbing it, I have serious doubts I'll be able to make it to the top. I haven't gone a hundred meters before both of my arms are shaking, my gloved hands throbbing. The day's brightening, working its way through the mist. Bad news for me, since the side I'm on lies directly in the rising sun's path. It could take hours to find a way in. I could end up frying before I discover there *is* no way in.

Before I've made it halfway, I stop, my head adjacent to a maintenance tunnel. My left shoulder is in open rebellion against my brain, and it occurs to me that even if it was physically possible, it's too late to climb back down and seek shade. Hooking my (relatively) good arm around the ladder so that I hang there like some hapless fly stuck in a spider's web, I pull out my pistol, press it against the exit and dial up the heat setting, only to have it sputter and die. I guess that's what happens when you use your ion gun to liquefy space monsters' limbs. Banging on the exit does nothing but threaten my precarious grip. And cause me to drop the gun. I wrench my eyes away from its falling form before dizziness drags me right after it.

I am so screwed, they're going to have to come up with new adverbs. As in, I am Newelly screwed.

My fingers loosen on the ladder. I can't think of anything else to try.

The only thing I can think of is how I failed.

"Sofie," I say. It sounds like I'm saying good-bye.

Something beeps.

I nearly lose my hold. Sweat beads on my forehead, and my

stomach tries out the drop my body almost did. After taking a deep breath to calm myself, I tighten my shaking grip on the ladder and turn my attention to what made the sound.

It's the homing device. I'm sure of it. Its red light shines through the supply pouch, except now the light's flashing again, not steady.

With a hiss of air, the exit pops open.

It's so unexpected I just about take a tumble. Or I do take a tumble: inside the circular opening, landing against the inner door of the shaft. I let out a breath of relief as my quivering arms get a much needed break. Only when I'm lying on solid metal does it occur to me that if the shaft didn't have double doors, I'd have plummeted to the floor of the *Freefall*.

I have just enough time to grab the ladder inside the shaft before the outer door closes and the inner one drops open, my legs dangling over an abyss as unfathomable as the one beneath the ship.

Newelly screwed.

I'm really starting to think I'm onto something.

Lowerworld

That day in Sofie's village changed everything.

If I'd thought she was pulling out all the stops before, it turned out she had some reserve of energy she'd never shown me. She was everywhere. The public meetings resumed all around the Lowerworld, the crowds pouring in to hear her, the words she spoke burning with anger and anguish as she described what had become of her home. The massacre, it seems, was a tactical error on the Upperworld's part, an attempt to intimidate her that had the exact opposite effect. It was possible they'd gotten their hands on misinformation spread by Sofie's team and thought they were killing the revolution's leader when they dropped the poisons that killed her village. Her handlers spun that possibility, beaming videos that suggested Sofie had been targeted to share the villagers' fate—and then cutting to shots of her alive, speaking on behalf of her murdered people. When those videos aired, you could feel the movement's momentum shift. When Sofie appeared publicly, you could feel it not only shift but explode.

And this time, I was there to watch it happen.

Maybe it was because I was the one who'd intercepted the transmission. Or maybe she was giving me a final chance to prove myself. All I knew was that the day after we returned from her village, Sofie came to my tent again and offered me a seat in her helicar as she traveled to her next public demonstration, the first since Sumati's death. I didn't think twice. I flew to the rally with her, standing with the other members of her team in a packed SubCon square while she exhorted the crowd. From that point on, she no longer had to invite me: Every morning, my tent would be opened by one of her bodyguards, and I'd make my way at a run to her waiting helicar. From the speaker's platform—whether a former gallows, the front steps of a temple, or, once, the base of a pyramid—I'd watch the crowds stream in, watch as they grew so large the Peace Corp. gave up and stopped coming. I'd watch Sofie's small figure whirl across the stage, commanding everyone's attention no matter how big the crowds got, her arms raised as if she was daring the Upperworld to finish what they'd failed to do before. I'd listen to her voice boom from the speakers, sometimes in my own language but more often not, and even when I didn't understand a word of what she said, I knew exactly what she was saying. It was the same message I'd thought I heard that first time in Adrian's room. I couldn't believe it had taken me so long to figure it out.

Sumati, bringer of wisdom, speaks to the world's people.

We do not fear the power of CanAm.

We call for justice.

At the end of her speeches, while the crowd cheered like crazy, she'd turn to her team and smile, and her golden eyes would fall on me the way they had before I met her. Piercing me, challenging me. Offering to take me to a better place, if I'd let her show me the way.

And then there was the time, a month after the massacre, when Sofie didn't merely look at me but beckoned for me to join her. At first I thought she meant someone else, because I mouthed, *Me?* But she mouthed back, *Yes.* I felt like I was in the zero-G gym as I crossed the platform, legs shaking. When she gripped my hand and raised it in the gesture Sumati had first used, her energy was so strong it was as if she'd granted me an extra life. She held my hand all the way to the helicar, and when we boarded, she gave it one last squeeze before entering another compartment to debrief with her team. I watched her until the moment the door closed.

That night, back in camp, she came to my tent once more.

This time she called my name before entering, and I let her in. She looked excited. Not necessarily to see me. Just excited. Her cheeks were flushed in the electric lamplight, and her eyes shone. A full smile shaped her lips, showing off her very un-Lowerworld gleaming white teeth. I smiled back, heart beating, remembering the promise I'd made, the feel of her hand in mine.

"Cam," she said, unusual in itself. She always addressed

me, whether in company or in private, as Cameron. "I hope I'm not disturbing you."

"Never," I said.

"Good." She sat on the cot beside me, which was a first too. We were so close the heat of her body leaped the tiny gap between us. "I have news, and I wanted to share it with you before anyone else."

"Great," I said. "What's up?"

It sounded ridiculously casual, and she smiled.

"What's up is that the licensed corponational channel for ExCon wishes to interview us," she said. "Tomorrow. For live broadcast."

"Us?" Exciting as that sounded, it didn't make sense. "Why us?"

She laughed, a trill that ran higher than the norm. "You mean, why us and not myself alone."

"I'm just saying . . ."

"The station wishes to examine the question of a mutual colonization from a variety of viewpoints. As one of the few Upperworlders among us, you represent a unique perspective on that question."

A token, in other words. "So they talk to us. And then what?"

"Cam." For the second time in a single day, and only the third time in my entire life, the girl I longed to touch reached for my hand. "You do not appreciate the importance of this interview. It is . . . unprecedented. Bigger in its own way than the affair in New York CITI."

I nodded, my heart hitching at the word "affair."

"The losses of the past several months have become our greatest victories," she said. "The death of Sumati and the massacre in my village have opened the eyes of the world to the justice of our cause, as they have opened *your* eyes too."

She looked at me closely, seeking an answer to her unasked question. I nodded again, and she squeezed my hand tight.

"I knew it. You have seen that a new world is possible, and now you will see our dreams come true. All of them."

"All of them?"

"*All* of them," she repeated with absolute conviction. "This interview is the moment we have waited for, the moment we have struggled for. Oh, Cam!"

I stared at her. The Sofie I knew didn't say things like "Oh, Cam!"

"So what do I need to do?" I asked.

"They have not provided us a script," she said. "But they will surely ask about your experience with us. When they do, all you need to do is answer honestly."

Her voice was breathless, her eyes probing. Something about the whole thing made me uneasy, but I couldn't put my finger on why.

"Maybe it's a trick," I said at last. "They get you alone, put you in front of the worldlink lenses, and then . . ."

"They would not dare," she said fiercely. "They know the entire world is watching us, and its eyes can never be closed again. If they should take my life, they know that another will rise to fill my place, and the movement for justice will grow so great it will sweep their petty starships into the sea."

Her eyes burned with passion. Her fingers wrapped mine as if she was physically trying to drag me to the place she envisioned. I was about to tell her I was already there when she spoke again.

"And besides," she said softly. "I will not be alone. I will be with you."

And with that, all the doubts fled from my mind, and I was barely able to respond when she flung her arms around me and squeezed.

Otherworld

Earth Year 3151

Day

Vertigo doesn't begin to describe what I feel as I scramble to plant my legs onto something solid. My vision blurs, and the thought of my body going splat releases a trickle of what I ate last night. If the trickle goes splat, the floor of the *Freefall* is too far below for the sound to reach my ears.

Clutching my right wrist with my left hand to lock myself onto the ladder, I feel for the next rung beneath my feet. When I find it, I squeeze my eyes shut until the world stops spinning. Then slowly, very slowly, I climb down.

It's another endless trip, and my arms and legs tremble so badly the ladder feels as if it's shaking loose from the interior of the hull. But somehow I hang on, my feet finally touching bottom. My body celebrates by collapsing onto the cold titanium floor.

It feels like forever before I have the strength to stand. When I do, I look up and down the hallway, expecting to be greeted by the person who opened the door and saved my sorry ass. But I'm alone.

I'm in. The ship will protect me from radiation. For the moment, I'm safe.

What to do now?

I take out the tracker, find it flashing away. I'm too shaken to be sure what just happened, but evidently, when I said Sofie's name, the homing device from the *Executor* signaled the *Freefall* to open the hatch. That would make sense only if it was programmed to do so, which would make sense only if both ships were programmed to arrive at this destination. Reluctant as I am to endorse Conroy's cuckoo theories, it really does look as if the whole thing was set up beforehand, and by someone who *wanted* me to get into the Lowerworld ship. Someone other than Conroy himself, who would have simply told me if that was the way things were supposed to work. Someone aboard the *Executor* who chose the name of the Lowerworld revolution's leader as the key to open the vault.

But other than me, who in hell would do that?

I hold the tracker at arm's length. It's not flashing merely for the sake of flashing, I decide. It gave me the steady signal when I reached the ship, but now it's indicating that I have to search for the rest of the pods. That's part of its programming too. It wants me to find them. And if I'm reading it right, it's showing me the way.

I don't know this ship. But if its basic layout is the same as the *Executor*'s, the cargo bay will be forward, the drive astern. The tracker's pointing me forward. I shuck the radiation suit, do a few quick squats and stretches in shorts and T-shirt to limber up cramped muscles. Then I strap the supply pouch back on and set off in the direction the tracker's telling me to go.

It's a long walk. My bare feet ping on the metal floor, but the hull's far too big for the ping to carry any authority. The hallway's littered with random boxes and pieces of machinery, stuff that must not have fit into any of the standard storage areas. There are practically no windows, and the few that exist are nothing but small circular portholes, completely different from the soaring, tourist-friendly viewing panels of the *Executor*. The doors leading to the front of the ship slide open at my approach, so it seems the *Freefall's* hospitality systems have come alive to welcome me. I detect a hum, a vibration, just below the threshold of hearing, which supports my theory. I slip the valve of my oxygen kit from between my teeth and take a tentative breath. My lungs fill obligingly, so that clinches it. The *Freefall* has no commuter monorail system, no plasma cannons, no rec rooms—it wasn't designed for passenger use, and it's lucky there's a place to eat—but it's woken up all the same. And though I can't understand how or why, it's starting to look as if it's woken up specifically for *me*.

A good hour has passed before I pull up in front of the cargo bay, which sits where I expect it to, right behind the nose. But as with the rest of the ship, it doesn't look anything like the bay from the *Executor*, with its orderly rows of docked pods. The *Freefall* was originally built as a test model, then repurposed for storage and supply, a backup to follow the *Executor* to its destination and to support us once we got there. In the frantic months between the signing of the Joint Otherworld Colonization Amity Pact (JOCAP) and the loading of the passengers, the ship was turned upside down to make space for hundreds of thousands of human beings. A lot of the materiel that formerly occupied this ship was moved to the *Executor*, but plenty was left behind for the Lowerworlders' own use, or merely by mistake. What that means is that in the dingy, unfinished cavity of the *Freefall's* main bay, life-carrying pods share space with supply crates and the equipment designed to unload them on arrival. And when I say "share space," I mean there *is* no space to share: Pods are stacked on other pods or on boxes full of supplies, and what with the addition of cranes and loaders, everything is crammed together more tightly than the most crowded street in the most crowded Lowerworld city. It's not immediately apparent how I'll manage to squirm into the area, much less open any of the pods. Nor is it apparent how Sofie's pod found its way out of this chaos, a heap of living containers and inert machinery packed together with no room to spare and no exits in sight.

An even bigger question is why, if the ship's woken up in response to my presence, it hasn't tried to rouse the other pods the way it was supposed to on touchdown. So many things have gone wrong with this mission, I worry that all of the Lowerworld passengers might have died in deepsleep. But I'll never know unless I can open a pod.

The bay is four kilometers square if it's a centimeter. It

doesn't seem to matter where I start. I squeeze into the pile of pods nearest to the door, searching for one not completely surrounded or weighted down by junk. To my surprise and gratitude, as soon as I enter the sea of pods, the ship helps me by shining a spotlight from above. I move through pods like a rock climber, grappling for hand- and footholds, sucking my stomach in to wiggle through crevices. Everywhere I go, the light tags along, illuminating the dark crannies between stacked crates and pods. Unfortunately, all it shows me is what I already suspected: Everything's so buried under everything else, there's nothing I can access without shoving loads of equipment out of the way.

I extricate myself from the pods and step back into the hallway to take in as much of the area as I can, but all I see are pods stretching for hundreds of meters in every direction and heaped to the rafters above my head. The crazy thought flits through my mind of scaling the pile to see if I'll have better luck higher up, but the vision of teetering atop a mountain of haphazardly balanced pods makes me decide against it. It seems ridiculous that with this many pods lying untended in front of me, I can't find a single one whose door or controls I'm able to reach. I'm about to give in to the childish impulse to kick the nearest stack of crap when I remember my trusty tracker.

I hold it to my mouth as if it's a comm device. Now that I'm doing this on purpose and not by pure accident, I get that embarrassed feeling that happens even when you know no one could possibly be watching. But I say it anyway.

"Sofie," I say to the tracker.

It beeps.

And, from somewhere far away, something else beeps in answer.

It's faint, buried deep in the pile, and I can't pinpoint its location. I repeat Sofie's name, then hold my breath and listen. There's no sound for such a long time I convince myself I must have imagined it.

But then I hear it again. Closer this time, louder. As if it's moving toward me.

I step back, say her name to the tracker one more time. I feel like I'm playing a game of hot and cold with a piece of technology. When the beep comes again, more faintly than before, I realize the player on the other end must be having trouble finding its way to me. I talk to the tracker again, listen for the response.

There it is. A tiny bit louder, stronger. It's getting hot.

A minute later a wave passes through the pods in front of me. Metal shifts against the floor with a screeching sound that makes my shoulders clench. Something's nudging the logjam out of its way.

The wall of pods parts, and the one I've been calling to floats free of the bay.

It drifts to my feet before settling, a red light flashing on its nose. I set my hands on the smooth white metal, feeling its coldness against my palms, then rest an ear on the curved door in hopes of picking up signs of life. The hum of the deepsleep mingles with the rush of blood in my own ear, turned slightly metallic by its contact with the pod. The source of the flashing light is the release button, which lies flush with the pod's body, beneath the JIPOC lettering and logo. My spotlight friend hovers cheerfully on the pod while I inspect it, as if urging me to give it a try.

I reach out, hesitate. What if this pod is like the ones in the cavern? What if it *was* Conroy who set this whole thing up, and the point of sending me here was to unleash a new plague of mechanical monsters?

What if I'm giving in to paranoid delusions?

I press the button.

And nothing happens.

I'm disappointed, but not entirely surprised. I don't know the programming of the pods, but it would make sense if not just anyone could open them. Probably there's thumbprint recognition on the outside same as on the inside, and only people with the right clearances can pop the top. Still, it's annoying to be this close and not be able to get in.

I set the tracker on the floor and walk around the pod, looking for something I might have missed. But there's nothing: The rest of the pod is all smooth, spotless metal.

It's only when I complete my circuit that I realize the thing I missed is right in front of me.

The pod's release button isn't just flashing. It's flashing in time with my tracker.

I pick up the homing device, press its screen randomly, knowing the commissary clerk never told me anything about this. I say Sofie's name again, without success. I try pointing the tracker at the pod like a worldlink controller, but that works about as well as the random-screen-pressing approach. Then, in a rare spasm of inspiration, I touch the flashing light of the tracker to the flashing light of the pod.

Instantly the twin lights stop flashing. I guess I should be thankful I didn't try this with the creatures in the cave.

The pod hums, whines, and opens.

I stand back and watch warily, simultaneously fascinated and, truth be told, a bit freaked by the process. The components shimmer like a reflection in water, then take on a liquid quality and peel back from the pod's shell, leaving a glowing aperture where solid metal had been. Once opened, the components solidify again, which makes me wonder if that's what it looked like from the outside when I exited my own pod.

But this pod bears one notable difference from mine: The deepsleep field is engaged, and the body of the sleeper lies within.

The yellow aura pulses and crackles, so thick it seems like a liquid, a current bathing the sleeping figure. My eyes take a minute to adjust to the light, but I can see enough to tell that the misty blob is no monster but a human being. When I'm able to make out the figure's face and clothes, I take another step back in disbelief.

The white-garbed man lies on his side, arms and legs curled in a fetal position. But there's no doubt in my mind he's one of Sofie's bodyguards.

Earth, 2151

Lowerworld

T he ExCon interview took place as planned, at a safe
location chosen by Sofie's team. Her bodyguards were
there, though she assured me that was only because they
wouldn't let her go anywhere without them. I remained on edge
during the entire trip to the interview site, the prep for the interview itself. There were lights, microphones, lenses everywhere.
Sofie and I sat side by side, in matching canvas seats, while
a young blond woman in heels and a tailored suit sat across
from us, smiling and chatting and trying to put us at ease. A
corponation propagandist, of course, the kind Griff used to call
an adjournalist, master of phony news. As soon as the link went
live, she was all business. Her voice deepened, her eyes riveted
us. Worldlink lenses whirred while she did her intro, monitors
over her head showing us miniature versions of ourselves. It was
hard not to be distracted by our own images, by the realization
that whatever we said was about to be beamed worldwide.

The adjournalist rattled off a slew of questions without waiting for an answer. She asked Sofie how she responded to accusations that her organization was nothing but a Terrarist front. She asked why the Upperworld should make room on its own multi-trillion-dollar starships for Lowerworlders who had done nothing to plan, prepare, or finance the colonization. She asked whether what had happened in New York CITI didn't prove that Lowerworlders were not to be trusted. She said nothing about the village massacre, and my heart lifted when she didn't. I knew enough by now about how the news worked to know that the adjournalist was hoping the topic wouldn't come up.

She was good, but Sofie was better.

When the woman finally paused for breath, Sofie jumped in, asking whether the babies who'd been slaughtered in their huts were Terrarists.

The adjournalist opened her mouth to answer, but Sofie talked right over her. Calmly, with a restrained passion that thrilled me by its nearness, she reviewed the history of Sumati's movement, the wrongs we were fighting, the ideals we were fighting for. She explained that the Lowerworld would gladly have devoted itself to the colonization had it been allowed — that, in a very real sense, the sweat and blood of its people had been poured into the Upperworld starships in the form of wealth gained at the Lowerworld's expense. Returning to the unasked question about her village, she admitted that, yes, the Lowerworld had given rise to Terrarists, who had killed wantonly in the misguided belief that further violence could heal the planet's wounds. But the vast majority of her people, she insisted, were peaceful, and the Lowerworld shouldn't be made to suffer death and disinheritance for the actions of a few. She defied anyone to portray the movement she headed as a movement of violence when it was, in both its principles and practices, founded in love. When the adjournalist's eyebrows arched at that answer, Sofie silenced the response I could see forming on the woman's lips.

"We have with us today a resident of the Upperworld who has willingly married his fate with our own," Sofie said. "Perhaps you should ask him what he thinks of the rightness of our cause."

The woman turned to me, her perfect teeth fixed in a hungry smile. I got the feeling this was the moment she'd been waiting for, the whole staged event leading up to this point.

It was the moment I'd been waiting for too.

"Cameron Newell," she said. "Son of the Upperworld. Is that what this movement means to you? Did you join it, as Miss Patel insists, for *love*?"

My heart thumped so hard I was sure the worldlink lenses would spot it. The word Sofie had used to describe my place in her movement was "married," not "joined." But I smiled back—at Sofie, not at her—and responded in what I hoped was a steady voice.

"I've lived in the Lowerworld for months now," I said. "I've seen what it's really like. And yeah, I guess you could say I've fallen in love. But not the way you think. There's one thing I've learned to love more than anything else."

"And what is that?" she asked.

Sofie and I shared a look.

"Justice," I said, smiling.

"Justice," Sofie agreed, and the adjournalist smiled back, her teeth as white as those of the girl beside me.

When it was finally over and the lenses shut down, Sofie squeezed my hand and the interviewer smiled again—but a natural smile this time, like I was seeing the person and not the propagandist at long last.

The flight back to camp was celebratory. Initial projections indicated that we'd been seen by hundreds of millions world-wide. And, thanks to our team's hacking into the feed, what viewers had seen was the real thing, not the expurgated stories that typically got broadcast in the Upperworld. The interview, it turned out, *had* been a trick—but a trick orchestrated by Sofie's team to take control of an Upperworld transmission. Her communications director said it had been the most watched world-cast in history. While he went on and on about the numbers, I savored the memory, the moment Sofie had squeezed my hand.

Someone on the helicar popped open a bottle, then two, then three, some overly sweet, syrupy stuff that burned bad when it went down and left a glow from my stomach to my fingertips. Sofie laughed throatily, telling me it was rice wine. She shook her hair free from her braid and gaily offered a toast. Her chief bodyguard glowered as she raised the glass, but she ignored him. I couldn't take my eyes off her, her lips moistened by the drink and her hair spilling over her shoulders. I'd never seen her like this, and the combination of booze in my belly and her flushed cheeks and the scent of her skin, all on top of the wildly successful interview, made me feel bold and invincible. I wasn't totally drunk, but I was drunk enough that all the feelings I'd kept tamped down for months bubbled up inside and made their way to the back of my throat, where they sat waiting for an opportunity to spill out. Not much of an opportunity. Just enough.

My opportunity came when Sofie stood to make another toast and stumbled, falling into my arms. Her smell and warmth and beauty enveloped me, and I whispered in her ear the first thing that came to my dizzy mind.

"You're my flower," I said. "My fragrance."

She smiled, disentangling herself from my arms.

"I would do anything for you," I whispered before she danced away, purple robe fluttering.

I followed her. My steps felt like they weighed ten kilos each. I found her in one of the helicar's private rooms, alone for once, her clutch of advisors celebrating outside. She sat on a bench that looked like a couch. At the sound of my footsteps, she looked up.

I wasn't too drunk to stop in shock. Tears stood in her eyes.

"Cam." She sniffled, wiped at her cheeks. "You should not enter a lady's room without knocking."

"I'm sorry," I said, starting to close the door and withdraw.

"No," she said quickly. "I did not mean that. Stay with me for a minute?"

I entered, closing the door partway. I wondered whether I'd ever figure out if she was asking a question or if that was just her voice.

I sat beside her. Her eyes searched mine, wobbling a little. The heat from her oh-so-close body set a fire inside me. The words I'd said on the worldlink seemed to come from another lifetime. The words I'd said to her moments ago sounded both impossibly stupid and incredibly right. I thought of saying them again. I couldn't think of anything better to say.

Instead, I leaned toward her, my mouth nearing hers.

"Cam," she said huskily. It wasn't a question.

My lips met hers. Their softness, their taste flooded my senses. I felt her hair brush my face, drew her scent into my lungs. My head swam as I brought my hand up to her cheek, touching her, lost in the softness and silkiness of her skin. She gasped and pressed my hand against her.

Then she moved away. I saw a face at the door, the dark, glittering eyes of her head bodyguard fixed on me. Three had never been more of a crowd than at that exact moment. My heart roaring in my ears, I sat up straight, tried to catch Sofie's glance, hoping to see in her eyes her promise for later in the night.

But she looked away. Gathering her robe around her, she floated to the door and was gone, her guard staring at me before closing the door behind them.

I didn't remember much after that. I stayed in the room for a minute, collected myself, rejoined the party. In the brief time

I'd been gone, Sofie had composed her face, wiping away tears and fixing smeared lipstick, capturing her hair in its usual braid. She wouldn't look at me. I got more drunk, waited for another chance to be alone with her, but the man who'd interrupted our kiss stayed glued to her side from that point on. Later she disappeared into another anteroom with her closest advisors. Her guards stood by the door, arms crossed. The sounds of carousing from the main cabin drowned whatever words were spoken inside.

Eventually I slept.

I woke in my tent, head pounding, throat raw. For a second I couldn't figure out where I was or how I'd gotten there, but then I remembered a drunken stumble off the plane, Sofie's chief bodyguard holding me up until I got to the tent, then dropping me like a load of wet towels. My last words to Sofie came back, along with a mixed sense of giddy pleasure and embarrassed regret for saying them. My head was stuffed with cotton, but my gut burned with a bright blade of desire that felt like guilt. I wondered why it was so quiet outside.

I stuck my head from the tent, and then I saw.

I was alone. The camp was gone. No other tents, no equipment, no vehicles. Garbage blew in the wind.

Sofie was gone.

Otherworld

Earth Year 3151

Day

step closer to the open pod, leaning in to stare at its sleeping inhabitant.

I don't know the man's name. No one, not Sofie and not the bodyguards themselves, ever told me their names. I always got the idea they were supposed to be anonymous, symbols of the revolution's strength, so that when one or more of them went down like they did in New York CITI, another could always step in. Or maybe having their identities wiped made it easier for them to evade corponational authorities. But this man, I'm 100 percent certain, was the leader of Sofie's guards on Earth, the one who grabbed me when I fled the old UN building with her, the same one who interrupted us that night in her heli-car. Bigger than the rest, broader, a bit darker skinned. Bearded and sharp-eyed, though his eyes are closed now. Seeing him motionless, defenseless, is disorienting.

But it's nowhere near as disorienting as the thought that, of all the pods that could have chosen to come awake and answer my tracker's call, it happened to be his.

If I wasn't convinced before, I am now.

None of this can be coincidence. Too much has happened to let me believe I wasn't supposed to be here. But that makes exactly zero sense, because the *Freefall* wasn't supposed to be here. It was supposed to be on another world, across an unbridgeable chasm of space.

Maybe, I think, Sofie's bodyguard has the answer. Maybe he knows why his ship's here, why he was the one chosen to wake up at my command. If so, all I have to do is wake him up.

Which I have no idea how to do.

I can't see any controls to shut the aura down. My mother knew everything there was to know about deepsleep, but she never explained any of it to me, not that I'd have understood her if she had. And at the moment, she's too busy helping Conroy rule the galaxy to show me the tricks of the trade.

I reach toward the energy field, but I can tell before I come anywhere close that it would be a very bad idea to put my hand into the shining plasma of deepsleep. My fingers tingle, going numb at the tips, leaving no doubt that if they touch the field I'll be returned to a state of living death, this time with no chance of awakening. I wonder if there's a way to short-circuit the energy, but remembering Griff's warnings about what happens when you wake up improperly from deepsleep, I can't risk it. The man could die, or turn on me, in which case we could both die. There's got to be another way.

I press more random buttons on the tracker, with as much success as the previous time I tried that tactic. I stop pressing when it occurs to me I might stumble across a self-destruct function. Having exhausted my day's supply of genius ideas, I step back, letting out a hard breath in frustration.

The energy field flickers.

It's a momentary thing, a wave passing through the yellow globe of light, so fast I'd have missed it if I had blinked. Luckily, I'm staring too hard to blink.

I try my voice this time.

"Shut down," I say.

Again the field flickers. But other than that, there's no change.

"Turn off," I try. "Release. Come out of deepsleep. Wake up. Get your ass out of there. Double-time, worm." That last one always worked when our ColPrep trainers wanted us to shift into high gear to avoid a beating. Plus, given my history with the guy, it's kind of fun to say.

But with this corpse, nothing.

I breathe deeply, try to rein in my mounting annoyance. What good is having a magic word if you don't know what the magic word is?

Then I remember.

Did I mention that I'm a complete idiot? There's a magic word, all right, and I've known it all along.

I take another breath. Step right up to the pod. And say her name.

"Sofie."

The light quivers. Another wave rolls through it, deeper this time, firmer, like an invisible hand smoothing the energy out of the way. Yellow light turns to white, then slowly dims to gray, then to nothing. Wisps of energy curl from the pod, dissipating on contact with the surrounding air. In a matter of seconds, the field is gone, and Sofie's bodyguard lies before me, eyes closed and body unmoving.

His chest heaves a breath, and his eyelids flutter.

He's groggy, rising clumsily on an elbow, trying to lower his legs to the floor without stepping out of the pod first. I reach for his hand and grip, and he recoils instinctively, throwing his other hand up in a motion that would be threatening if it weren't so uncoordinated. Moments later, though, he returns my hand's pressure, his grasp much stronger than mine. He squints at me through the blear of departing deepsleep, but then his eyes sharpen, and I know he knows me. With my assistance, he swings his legs over the lip of the pod and rests there, head in hands, broad chest expanding as he draws increasingly deep breaths. Minutes pass like that, tens of minutes, an hour. I wonder if he'll move again.

Then, without warning, he slides his sandaled feet to the floor of the ship, and with one strong arm over my shoulder, he stands.

He stumbles, but I catch him. His full weight's probably more than I can bear for long, which makes it fortunate that he quickly gets his legs under him. I reach around his waist to steady him, but he waves me off and takes a step on his own. He wobbles, nearly falls on top of me, then rights himself and cranes his neck around the pod bay, taking in the chaos that surrounds us.

"Where are we?" he asks, the first time he's spoken directly to me. His English is only lightly accented, his voice softer and higher pitched than I expected.

"I don't know," I say. "We're on the *Freefall*. But it's landed on an unknown planet." *An unlivable planet,* I think but don't say. "The Upperworld ship's here too."

"How can this be?"

"I don't know," I say again. I feel like I'm the one who just came out of deepsleep. "But your pod made its way to me. When I said Sofie's name. I think I was supposed to find you."

He nods, but I can't tell whether he's agreeing or as bewildered as I am. "Where is Sofie?"

I wish I could say *I don't know* to this one.

"She's not here," I say. "Her pod ejected before touchdown. She's . . ." I pick my words carefully. He's freshly out of deepsleep, woozy and disoriented. I'm afraid too much information will upset him, damage him. Or convince him to damage me. "She's on the Upperworld ship," I say at last.

"Then we must go to her."

"Right." He stands before me, arms crossed, waiting. This is not the kind of guy I want to disappoint. On the other hand, he's not the kind of guy I want to help, either. He must have been in on the whole plan back on Earth, from the first unknown words

Sofie spoke to him at the United Nations building to the last moment he dumped my drunken carcass in the Lowerworld tent. I don't owe him anything. He'll tear me apart if I tell him that, but I don't owe him a damn thing.

Except Sofie's life.

How many times has he saved her in the past? How far would he go to save her now? I'm not sure I can trust him, but I'm not sure I can find a more trustworthy person I'm not sure I can trust, either.

"All right," I say. "But give me a minute. There are a few things I need to catch you up on."

Earth, 2151

Upperworld

G riff met me at the heliport. He looked happy to see me. Happy, impressed, amazed. The story of where I'd gone hadn't sounded promising, but it had turned into the talk of the Upperworld in the past couple of days.

"Saw you on the link," he said as we sat on the bullet train, speeding back home. "You and that girl. Way to go, dude."

I looked up sharply, anticipating sarcasm in his voice. But there was none. This was Griff.

"She left me, man," I said.

"I know," Griff said.

I didn't expect my parents to welcome me back with open arms. But I didn't expect them to throw me out on my ass, either. Turned out I'd become something of an expert at not expecting crappy things to happen to me. Fearing they'd be implicated in what I'd done—or, more likely, being as disgusted by me as everyone else in the Upperworld was—they reprogrammed their doors and sent me a text suggesting I find another place to live.

If this had been six months ago, I would have moved in with Adrian. But six months and everything that had happened in between had put an end to that.

The only friend I could turn to, the only person in all of CanAm who didn't seem to hate my guts, was Griff. His dad had a place he made Griff stay when he needed his son out of the house. Right now, with three months left to do the final coding on the starships before liftoff, Griff's dad needed him out of the house. So I stayed with him at his separate apartment.

Sofie's interview—I couldn't think of it as *our* interview without getting a sick feeling in my stomach—worked exactly as she had planned. For the first time since the rise of Sumati, the child of Upperworld VIPs and the leader of the Lowerworld revolution had faced the worldlink lenses and declared the same dream: One World not Two, an opportunity Earth had missed but space might make possible. It didn't hurt that sympathy for Sofie's cause had been growing ever since the true account of what had happened in her home village leaked, or that there was genuine concern among the Upperworld corporations that Lowerworld unrest might overwhelm the colonization effort entirely. It didn't hurt either that the request Sofie announced after the interview—no greater than forty percent Lowerworld representation among the Otherworld colonists, with the specific percentage to be worked out at a later date—

helped stave off Upperworld fears of another revolution on the world we traveled to. When she and her team met the following week with Chairman Conroy, the board of JIPOC, and the CEOs of the two most powerful Upperworld corporations—CanAm and ExCon—two additional concessions emerged: The Lowerworld was willing to allow its chosen passengers to be sequestered on the *Freefall* during the starships' flight, and to delay negotiations concerning planetary cohabitation until arrival. Though it obviously incensed Adrian's dad to have his pet project waylaid at this late date by Lowerworld agitators—one of them his son's former best friend—those two final concessions made a joint Upperworld-Lowerworld colonization a virtual certainty. With the Lowerworld a minority on the far distant world, the chances of their being able to force a situation unfavorable to the Upperworld seemed remote.

I watched it all on the link. That had been as close as I could get to her when I first saw her, and though I'd stood beside her since then, worked beside her, touched her, kissed her—*kissed her*—it was as close as I could get to her now.

It wasn't a neat process, this march toward reconciliation. For me there was personal blowback, not only my parents' rejection but the battery of supplemental genetic screens and psychometrics I was forced to take to ensure I remained suitable material for the colonization. Why I didn't get thrown off the passenger list altogether I had no idea. I clung to the fantasy that Sofie had pled my case behind the scenes, but chances are it was some brilliant PR move to show how magnanimous

Chairman Conroy was. Even after I passed the tests, propaganda surfaced portraying me as the dupe of Lowerworld masterminds. The ugliest was a piece that showed me, unshaven and with a wild glint in my eyes, underneath a splashy banner that read: *Kidnapped. Tortured. Brainwashed. Betrayed.* In that one, they'd taken footage from the interview but edited it in such a way as to make me look like a clueless, aimless kid who wasn't trying to change the world so much as he was trying to get his hands on a prime piece of Lowerworld ass. This kid babbled things like, "I've lived in the Lowerworld for months now. I've seen what it's really like. And yeah, I guess you could say I've fallen in love." I remembered saying that—how could I forget, when I'd repeated it over and over in my mind every day since?—though I could hardly believe I had. But when they intercut my words with clips of me exchanging glances with Sofie, headshots of adjournalists winking at the worldlink lenses, and jittery footage of Terrarist bombings, the clear implication was that Cameron Newell was one sick puppy.

Sofie was subjected to more attacks than me, of course. According to one scandalous report, she was the daughter of minor ExCon officials, a wild kid who'd been a worldlink star in her youth but had fled her parents' home as a preteen to mingle with the criminal elements of the Lowerworld. In that report she was charged with everything they could think of: crystal-death smuggling, human trafficking, illegal weapons shipping. The report stopped short of saying that she herself had participated in the flesh trade, but what else were you supposed to conclude? Some seriously disturbing images made the rounds of a precocious little girl they claimed was Sofie, staring straight into the lens with pale green eyes that looked nothing like hers and reciting an oath of allegiance to "the happy lands of the Upperworld." Another equally unbelievable report surfaced saying that she'd been responsible for Sumati's assassination, that she'd charmed her way into the older woman's confidence before having her gunned down. The same source suggested that the village that had died ("of unknown causes") hadn't been Sofie's birthplace at all, and that—just maybe—she'd had something to do with its mysterious end. Splicing footage from her speech in New York CITI with heavily doctored clips from the interview and scenes of Lowerworld demonstrators pumping their fists outside corporational headquarters, they presented Sofie as a violent fanatic bent on the overthrow of the civilized world, or at least on amassing power for her own vile purposes. I imagined her watching this garbage, sitting with her legs crossed and her hands in her lap, taking deep, calming breaths through her nostrils. She knew better than to respond with a denial. She knew the tide of world opinion would turn, already had turned, her way.

Everything had turned her way. I didn't resent that. It was the way I wanted things to turn too. But I'd thought, hoped, dreamed that I would be with her when it did.

When she'd left me in the middle of nowhere, she'd at least had the decency to leave behind a fully charged selfone. Not that it did me much good in the middle of nowhere. They'd confiscated my personal phone, which pissed me off—it wasn't like I'd spent the past four months running around the Lowerworld taking pictures of classified documents. I hiked for a couple of hours, guessing at the direction by the light of the sun and the pockets of displaced sand left by her helicar convoy, until I finally arrived, footsore and sunburned, at the nearest village. There I discovered that Sofie's team had arranged everything for my departure: I was booked on a shuttle to the corponational capital, booked on a flight from the capital to my home heliport. I landed in CanAm with nothing but the phone and the clothes on my back, but that was all I'd taken with me when I'd left anyway. The only other things I carried back home—and these were big and heavy and wouldn't fit in the overhead rack or under the seat in front of me—were the feelings of anger and hurt that came from knowing she'd tricked me and used me and then unceremoniously dumped me, though not before getting herself drunk enough to make me think I stood a chance with her.

If I could've hated her for everything she'd done, my life would've been ten times easier. But the truth was, no matter what she'd done, I still loved her. More than that, I still believed in her, or at least in what she was trying to do. I even accepted that, in order for her to achieve her objectives, a certain number of starry-eyed dimwits like me were going to have to get screwed. But that didn't make it any easier to deal with the feelings of betrayal and loss.

Griff got that. During the months I'd spent in the Lowerworld, I'd barely thought about him—something else I could feel crummy about, even if I had good reason for my mind to be elsewhere—but the reverse hadn't been true. He'd followed the movement as well as he could on the public channels, hacked into Lowerworld sites when he needed to. He claimed he'd seen me on the link before the interview, and I didn't bother telling him when he showed me the grainy, handheld shots from some Cons Piracy site that I hadn't been with Sofie in those early days. He was even more critical of the colonization than I remembered him being before I left, totally convinced that there was some worldwide conspiracy behind it having to do with JIPOC and Chairman Conroy and little green men from outer space for all I knew. But he never doubted me. In fact, now that I'd traveled to the Lowerworld—in the company of its revolutionary leader, no less—he'd chilled out about the dangers of getting involved. His faith that I'd been part of something mind-blowing and world-shaking helped me cope with the deeper dangers he'd never suspected.

Like falling in love. And falling off the map. And falling into despair.

Booze helped ease the pain, and Griff was always ready to supply that. We'd sit on the balcony of the high-rise where he'd been banished, soaking up the smog and setting sun, doing shots of whatever fine aged beverage his dad had placed under lock and key and strictly forbidden him to touch. As our tongues loosened, I'd talk about my time with Sofie, starting with the race through the UN building and the ride in her helicar, all the way to the interview and the plane ride afterward and the morning I woke up in my tent. Griff would pump me for details—how many bodyguards had gone down, what Sofie had said about Sumati, the look on the helicar pilot's face when he realized he'd be transporting the infamous Cam Newell—and I'd ramble on, whiskey burning in my belly, thankful I had someone to tell the story to as many times as I needed. Mostly I talked about Sofie: her voice, her eyes, her fire. But I also told him as much as I could about the Lowerworld places I'd visited, the setup of her camp and what little I knew about the operations of her team, my job in the comm tent. He seemed particularly riveted—or maybe repulsed—by what I'd seen that day in her village. But he let me babble on about Upperworld depravity all I wanted—partly, I was sure, because it fit with what he was reading on Cons Piracy, but mostly, I liked to think, because he knew it made me feel better to portray myself as someone who mattered to the movement. As the bull sessions dragged on and I got into minute details of things said and places seen, he'd try to suppress a yawn, try to act interested for my sake. When I woke up the next day, throat dry and head throbbing, I wouldn't remember exactly what we'd talked about. But I'd feel incredibly grateful that no matter what I talked about, no matter how tedious it must have been to be subjected to endless stories about my breakup with some girl who hadn't even been my girlfriend, Griff was always there to listen. If there was one positive that came out of this whole mess, it was that I realized what it meant to have a true friend.

The only thing I never told him about was the time Sofie and I kissed. That was too personal—and too hurtful—to tell anyone, even Griff.

Because no matter how good I might feel when the liquor was flowing and my best pal was listening, when I was alone, in those inevitable moments before sleep came, the hurt would well up again, as cold and boundless as deep space. I'd tell myself it would go away, tell myself I'd forget her. I had close to forever to forget her, right? Half an eternity to float through black emptiness, asleep, without dreaming, where every trace of who I was on Earth and the things I'd seen and the people I'd loved would be erased as completely as the Earth itself. Sofie would be nothing to me when we touched down on our new home: an acquaintance, a memory, less than a memory. I'd probably never see her again, on a planet with almost two million new inhabitants and our lives likely to be as divided there as they'd been here. She certainly wouldn't seek me out, and I wouldn't seek her out either. And if, by pure chance, I did cross her path in some crowded Tower City boulevard of the future, I told myself I'd look right through her, the way I'd always looked through everyone and everything back on Earth.

But even as I told myself that, I knew it was a lie. I knew I'd been blind before, and Sofie had been the one to make me see.

Not just see her. *See*.

And I knew that once you start to see, you can never stop.

Otherworld

Earth Year 3151

Day

The minute with Sofie's bodyguard turns into more like a couple of hours. During that time, I discover his name— Aakash—and not much else. He offers no information on Sofie's activities since we parted, nothing that might help me understand the chain of events that brought us here. His voice is soft, but his words have all the give of steel. From me he learns much more: the unscheduled arrival of our starships on this planet, the crippling of the Upperworld vessel, the attacks by the biomechanical pods, Conroy's ploy to hold Sofie hostage while I bargain for his missing son. He nods brusquely at each piece of data, but he shows surprisingly little curiosity about any of it. He's single-minded in his concern for Sofie. Either he's hiding what he knows, or everything else is of minor importance to him next to the peril of the girl he's pledged to serve.

I find his devotion admirable, even if it's aggravating. In the face of death, he wants to save her as much as I do. He'll be a good ally.

I just hope he never needs to make a choice between me and her.

One of the first things Aakash suggests we do is rouse others. He knows about the integrated system of tracking and voice commands that were added to the pods of Sofie's team members before liftoff to prevent unauthorized tampering, but he claims ignorance as to how my tracker got hooked into the system. He also maintains a stony silence when I ask him how Conroy and my mother could have cracked into Sofie's pod if they didn't have the right tracker. I wish I could believe he's impressed by my figuring out the password, but short of delivering Sofie unharmed to the *Freefall*—or handing over Conroy's head on a stick—I doubt there's anything I could do to impress him. It's more than a little possible, I think, that I'm not the only one with trust issues.

Aakash produces a homing device from within his pod and announces that he can use it to track down and open the other pods he wants, the ones containing the rest of Sofie's inner circle. He's undeterred by the size of the room, the number of pods, the disarray of them all. He'll search until he finds what he's looking for.

"Shouldn't we be more concerned about saving Sofie?" I say.

"If what you tell me is true, Chairman Conroy has no plans to terminate her until you return empty-handed."

"So we're going to take his word now?"

"We will be in a better position to free her once the team is assembled," he says.

"And how long exactly are we going to do this?"

"I will spend the remainder of the day searching," he says. "But yes, by nightfall, regardless of my success, we must be on our way."

So I'm right: He'll fight to save Sofie even if he knows he'll fail.

I leave him to search for the other pods while I try to find some food in the dispensary, which I passed on my way to the pod bay. My throat's parched, my stomach a wrung towel. I realize I haven't eaten since yesterday in the pod creatures' cave, and though Aakash looks like he can go all day on empty, I want to be fortified for the march to Conroy's ship. I've told my brooding companion about the impossibility of traveling during the day without radiation suits, but he's not worried. Something else he's not telling me, no doubt.

The dispensary feeds me a quick meal of Plop-Tarts and SpaceAde, compliments of Uniform Versatility (formerly Universal Comestibles, before they rebranded). I never asked Sofie if UniVers had another name before that. Considering they supplied the entire Upperworld with everything we ate, I preferred not to know.

I rummage through storage bins behind the counter for a few minutes before turning up a spare jumpsuit, too tight but better than nothing. No weapons, though, which is what I was hoping to find. When I return to the bay, I find Aakash standing with hands on hips outside the door, the pod he's freed from the stack resting before him. The top's been popped, and when I step to his side, I see another of Sofie's bodyguards wrapped in his shimmering deepsleep aura. One of the new guys who replaced the two who were downed in New York CITI. When Aakash speaks Sofie's name in his soft voice, the aura breaks up, but the sleeper doesn't stir. Aakash touches him, shakes him, then turns away, a frown creasing his brow. It seems we've hit the first snag in our otherwise seamless plan.

"There are others," Aakash says simply. He closes the pod door on his dead comrade and pushes the cocoon-turned-casket out of the way.

The next pod takes its time responding to Aakash's tracker, but finally it wiggles through a crack of its own making, nosing other pods out of its way and sailing to a stop at the chief bodyguard's feet. This time, when the pod door opens and Aakash speaks Sofie's name, the white-garbed man inside shivers and moans as he returns from semi-eternal sleep. Aakash says a single word after that: the man's name, which is Ranjit. His companion answers by vomiting discreetly into the bed he's slept in for the past millennium. While I tend to Ranjit's deepsleep sickness, Aakash calls more pods from the pile. How they find their way out of the pyramid, why the entire structure doesn't collapse, I have no idea. But all arrive intact, their occupants alive. If I thought Aakash's stoic expression would change as a result, I obviously didn't know the man. He nods grimly, but that's about it for his show of emotion.

One by one I'm reintroduced—in the most visceral of ways—to the members of Sofie's team, helping them stand and using napkins from the dispensary to wipe the spit and puke from their lips. There's Basil, the key architect behind Sofie's worldlink campaign, a balding, middle-aged-businessman type who's constantly touching his head as if to doff a hat, though he's not wearing one. There's Stjepan, who actually is a businessman though his MediTerri good looks make him appear more like a worldlink model, the agent who funneled secret Upperworld contributions into the revolutionary coffers for fifteen years. There's Mingzhu, one of several women on Sofie's advisory team, and one of very few members of the revolutionary cabal from MicroNasia, known for its particularly extensive factory prison system. There are a few more, but nothing to brag about. Other than Aakash, Ranjit, and a man named Zubin, the one other bodyguard whose pod answered the chief guard's summons, it's more the kind of group you'd want by your side to plan a hard-hitting worldlink exposé than to storm a starship.

I include myself in the former category.

But it's all we've got. The pods containing the remaining three bodyguards won't respond, which must mean they're trapped too deep in the pile to find a way free. Aakash tries again and again to call them, but no go. The planetary day wheels to night while we extricate pods, orient their inhabitants, fill their famished, dehydrated bodies with energy bars and SpaceAde. Aakash talks to them in the movement's coded language, a polyglot I never mastered enough to understand more than a few stray words of. I'm getting anxious to leave, but the leader of the bodyguard can't be moved, physically or otherwise. Protecting Sumati and then Sofie is what he's done for the past thirty years, give or take a thousand. Though he had no reason to believe the *Freefall* would land here, that Sofie would be captured, that any of this would be necessary, he responds to the situation as if he's spent his entire life preparing for this contingency. And who knows, maybe he has.

My own presence in his handpicked group he doesn't comment on, but I can tell he's working it over, trying to figure out if I'm a lucky find or a liability. Or, worse, a double agent for the Upperworld he'll have to dispose of either before we leave or somewhere along the way to the *Executor*.

As day fades to night outside the ship's windows, he's finally ready to go. The team's fed and steady on its feet, the plan's in place—at least in his mind, because he won't tell me a thing about it—and we've got eight or nine hours of darkness to make our way to the *Executor*. Based on my own expedition, we'll also need at least double that to get there. Aakash has obstinately refused to spend time searching for either radiation suits or guns, and to be perfectly honest, I doubt we could find them in this mess anyway. Not for the first time, I think about the relativity of time and space, how twenty hours and fifty kilometers can seem like an eternity to people who've traveled beyond the stars.

"We'll never make it in a single night," I tell Aakash. "And the sunlight will crush us unless we find someplace to hide."

"You know this," he says gravely, but there's a note of suspicion beneath the unflappable voice.

"I could take us back to the cavern," I say. "Though I'm not sure we want to tangle with those things unarmed."

The others nod anxiously. They're no more warriors than I am. Only Ranjit and Zubin seem unfazed by the prospect of facing the monsters at night, the sun by day.

"So are we going to search for suits?" I ask Aakash one last time.

To my complete surprise, he smiles. "That will not be necessary."

The planetary night falls. There's only one star to guide us all. I can hear her voice calling me, as clearly as I heard it all those years ago. The first time I saw her on the link, the words she spoke showed me a world I'd never known. The last time I saw her, her words tore my world in two.

I speak her name once more, and then it's time to go.

Earth, 2151

Upperworld

The first and only meeting of the Joint Upperworld-Lowerworld Intercorporational Panel on Otherworld Colonization (JULIPOC) took place in New York CITI, a mere two months before the official date of departure. That was an insanely short window, considering the enormity of the task: selection of passengers, transportation to the boarding site, the boarding itself. Under my dad's supervision, the *Executor* and its sister ship, the *Freefall*, had been stocked for departure, and according to Griff, his dad was well ahead of schedule in programming the ships' systems. But those preparations had been made with the *Freefall* as a supply vessel, not a passenger line, and whether it could be reconfigured in such a short time to carry hundreds of thousands of deepsleep pods was anyone's guess. Then there was the whole question of what might happen when the passenger list for the Lowerworld ship was announced. The Upperworld screening and selection had taken place over years and had been tightly controlled to guarantee mission compatibility. Though Sofie's team had agreed to 40 percent representation on the starships as their upper limit, they had yet to declare the specific number they had in mind, much less how they were going to go about making their picks. But it was clear that there'd be no time for prescreening, which meant who knew what kind of people would end up on board, what kind of bribes and threats and other forms of chaos would win them a seat off-planet. And that wasn't counting the chaos that might ensue when the billions who were denied a place on the ship discovered that they were the ones being left behind.

The world was going up in flames as it was, which was exactly why we were leaving. But it might go up in flames a whole lot faster before we had a chance to leave.

I considered going back to New York CITI, back to the old UN building, where the council was being held due to the now symbolic significance of the site. Griff didn't say anything, but I knew he'd swipe his dad's security clearances and hop the first bullet train with me if I asked. I didn't, though. In the end, I decided I didn't want to be there, just another face in the crowd, listening and watching like I'd done before this all started. I didn't want to see her and not have her see me. Or, worse, have her see me and not care.

But I did watch it on the link, with Griff. Whatever my feelings for Sofie might be, I wasn't about to miss something this important.

All the public channels aired the council. In fact, you

couldn't find a worldlink site where anything else was going on. Déjà vu set in as I watched the crowd assembling on the street outside the UN building, the officials passing through the security checkpoint, the panel members seated at the table in front. I saw Adrian's dad in his gray JIPOC uniform, the other JIPOC board members and CEOs of the world's corponations in their dark blue or gray suits, the many-hued delegates from the Lowerworld. Something much stronger than déjà vu gripped me when I saw the white-garbed bodyguards, then Sofie's purple robe and black hair, the jewel on her forehead flashing in the dingy room's spotlights. The lenses focused on her, showing me endless close-ups of her smiling, chatting, leaning over to have something whispered in her ear by other Lowerworld delegates, some of them people I'd met. She seemed as relaxed and confident as she'd ever been. And why not? This was her moment, the thing she'd fought for years to bring into existence. This was the vindication of her struggle, the consummation of her dreams. This was who she was.

This was her without me. This was what had drawn me to her in the first place. But it had drawn thousands of others as well, millions of others. Billions of others. She was a bright light in a dark world, and anyone who'd lost their way would be drawn to her. I'd been a fool to think a light that brilliant could shine for me alone.

My heart leaped to my throat when I heard her speak.

"Mr. Chairman," she said, her voice exactly the same as the one I'd been hearing on the link and in my dreams for the past month, "on behalf of the Lowerworld people, I thank you for welcoming us to your celebrated city. I am sure this council will forever be remembered as a defining moment in human history, the time when the Upperworld and the Lowerworld put aside their differences in the name of justice and the future of our race."

The lenses showed Chairman Conroy's reaction. Griff suppressed a laugh at the sight of him. I had to admit, it was pretty funny to see our old friend's dad looking like a man forced to gag down a snake sandwich. The poisonous kind.

Sofie, either not noticing or not caring, continued. "I know we have much business to attend to, and I know time is short. But if the chair will indulge me, I would like to begin with a few words as an expression of our people's goodwill. A prayer, if that old-fashioned term still holds meaning. It will not be long. With eternity stretching before us, we may perhaps spare a moment for such a thing?"

Adrian's dad nodded, his Adam's apple bobbing as if he'd just swallowed the snake sandwich.

"Thank you," Sofie said, inclining her head slightly. "It is said among my people that a time once existed when men and women were much more intimate with the stars than we are now. Oh, we can view them through our telescopes, trap their rays with our instruments, even—as today's council attests—pursue them through endless space aboard our mighty starships. But I speak of a time when we could not only *see* the stars but *hear* them speaking to us. For all our technology, we of the modern world do not listen much to the stars these days. What, then, must it have been like for the people of that time? What must it have been like when the sound the stars make surrounded us always, and we listened, and heard them speaking to us in a language that filled our souls with an aching joy?"

Chairman Conroy had succeeded in swallowing the snake sandwich, but it appeared he was about to puke it back up. Me, all I could hear was the music of her voice. My throat tightened, and tears sprang to my eyes.

In Sofie's words, I heard the sound the stars make.

"We who dream of traveling beyond the stars would do well to remember that time," she concluded. "To remember it, and hold it close to our hearts. The void will be less empty, the nights less long, if we will but listen."

She bowed her head and was silent. Griff looked away as I wiped the tears that had fallen down my cheeks.

Chairman Conroy wasted no time getting the proceedings back on track—his track, anyway. Banging his gavel, he spat out the words. "We will now hear the Lowerworld petition for a percentage share of the Otherworld Colonization initiative."

The room buzzed. The Lowerworld reps, Sofie included, put their heads together. I watched the screen, waiting with the rest of the world.

Then Sofie leaned into her microphone and spoke again. "The Lowerworld requests that the *Freefall* be commissioned to carry the selected representatives of our people to a planet of our own choosing."

I sat forward, staring at the screen.

"We've already heard this petition," Chairman Conroy said crossly. "The Upperworld has expressed its intention to approve a limited joint venture—"

"You did not listen carefully, Mr. Chairman," Sofie cut in. "The Lowerworld is not asking to accompany you as a minority partner to the planet of *your* choosing. We ask to sail in our own starship to a planet of *our* choosing."

"You're asking"—Chairman Conroy spluttered—"you're asking to be *separated* from the Upperworld?"

"That is correct," Sofie said.

"And where do you intend to find this alternative planet?"

"We have consulted our own astronomers," she answered. "They assure us that the Earth-like planet Kapteyn b, long dismissed by your calculations as lying beyond gravitational range of the starship *Executor*, is in fact accessible by the starship *Freefall*."

Chairman Conroy sat back, looking as surprised as you could look when you'd gotten what you wanted but hadn't gotten it the way you wanted to. He'd been expecting a fight. He'd figured he would win it. Now that he didn't have to fight, did that mean he'd lost?

"Let me be perfectly clear about this," he spoke slowly into his microphone. "The Lowerworld is in complete agreement on this course of action?"

"We are," Sofie said.

"And may I ask why?"

"We are realists," she said. "Pragmatists. We in the Lower-world have always been so. We know that we have won a great gift in these past several months. We know what it has cost the Upperworld to concede to our requests, and we hope in our hearts that the giving of the gift signifies a change in yours."

I couldn't take my eyes off the screen. I felt my own heart changing as I watched her. Changing . . . or breaking.

"But we know too that the history of distrust between our peoples is long, and not to be altered in a matter of months," Sofie continued. "Perhaps not to be altered in the course of a hundred lifetimes. The massacre of innocents in the SubCon village proves, if nothing else does, that it is easier to fight injustice than hatred."

"The unexplained deaths in the village—" Conroy began, his face furious.

"Please, Mr. Chairman," she said politely if wearily. "Let us not waste our precious time debating this sad calamity. The fact remains—we know that in the hearts of many among us, there is distrust of the Upperworld still, and that the same distrust exists in many of your hearts as well. We do not wish to travel into the deepest reaches of space, leaving all behind and risking all that lies ahead, only to become on our new home what we have become on Earth. We wish to claim our own world at last, a world in which there is no longer Upperworld and Lower-world, but one world, united. We wish we could imagine such a world existing between us. But we no longer believe such a world is possible."

The room sat silent. Sofie's statements always produced noise: cheering, chanting, feet stomping, whistles, jeers. Her latest bombshell produced only the dry rustle of bodies fidgeting, the dead hum of the worldlink.

"Well, shit," Griff said. I'd forgotten he was there.

I stood and walked away from the screen. "Screw her," I said softly. Then, when Griff raised an eyebrow, I repeated, louder, "Screw her."

"Hey, man . . ."

"I mean it!" I said. "Screw her! I risked my life for her. I played her little game. I could have ended up dead in the goddamn desert. But I believed . . ."

I was crying. I couldn't stop. *I believed in the world I thought we were building.* I believed her when she said her people and mine could live together in peace. I believed it, because if I hadn't believed it, it would have meant I'd left everything behind, followed her halfway around the globe, for nothing. Not for an ideal. Not for the future. Not for her. For *nothing*.

"Screw her," I said, as the tears streamed down my face. "Just screw her."

"It's not her," Griff said. "It's the goddamn Upperworld. They always get what they want."

We watched the rest of the council in silence. Watched Sofie, speaking on behalf of the Lowerworld, arrange for a segregated colonization: her people on their planet, our people on ours. Watched as the council members opened a debate on the massive supply snafu this change would initiate, then decided to hold off that discussion until later. We watched as Sofie smiled and bowed to the leaders of the Upperworld, held Chairman Conroy's hand in both of hers, posed with him for the cheering crowd and the worldlink lenses. We watched her exit the building and stand with her bodyguards outside, the folds of her purple robe draped over one arm, her other hand waving enthusiastically to the crowd. At last, we watched her enter her private helicar and soar away. And I watched my dreams crumble as she vanished like a fallen star into the ashy sky.

I knew three things then.

I knew that even though I'd pretended otherwise, I'd always believed, in the depths of my heart, that I would see her again. That a thousand years from now we'd be together. I knew I'd believed that, because now what I believed was gone.

The second thing I knew was that I would never forgive her for what she'd done.

And the third was that, no matter what she'd done and no matter where she was, I would never stop loving her just the same.

Otherworld

Earth Year 3151

Night

W e drive to the *Executor* in style.

Yes, we drive. Aakash uses his remote to locate a solitary passenger vehicle tucked away in one of the storage areas flanking the main cargo hold, a night-black beauty except for the blue-and-white ExCon logo plastered on its side. It rolls right up to us and opens its doors, giving Ranjit and Zubin time to load an empty pod in case we need to transport Sofie to home base in deepsleep. While Aakash punches our destination into the onboard navigation system and the *Freefall* extends a ramp to let us out into the night, I search the rear of the vehicle, finding a bundle of radiation suits, though not enough for everyone. I slip one over my jumpsuit anyway, since it's what I left the *Executor* in, and I don't want to rouse Conroy's suspicion. Aakash glares at me when I return to the cockpit, but he doesn't say anything. For now, he seems willing to work with me. The second he decides I'm a danger to Sofie or the mission, though, that's the second he puts the finishing touches on what he started back in New York CITI.

Now that we're underway, I think he might relent and let me in on the plan, but no such luck. He remains maddeningly close-lipped, especially considering I'm the one who'll have to carry out most of it. Conroy's expecting me to return with Adrian, so we can't approach the ship in numbers without raising all kinds of alarms. Instead, Aakash informs me that we'll drive to within walking distance, then I'll hop out alone and make the rest of the trip on foot. In the meantime, he and the others will do—I'm not sure what. And what *I'm* supposed to do once Conroy figures out I failed to retrieve his son isn't open for discussion either.

"You will do what you would have done had you returned to the *Executor* without us," Aakash says with a shrug. "Your knowledge of our actions can only put you in jeopardy."

"I've heard that before," I mutter.

He raises an eyebrow.

"After the worldlink interview," I say. "I guess you had to keep your actions secret then, too."

He shrugs again, maybe remembering the night in Sofie's helicar and the morning after, maybe not. Either way, not giving a damn.

"We laid our plans long before you joined us," he says. "You of the Upperworld should understand what it means to be leery of interference from outsiders."

The word "interference" makes me bristle. The word

"outsiders" nearly sends me off the deep end. "And if I'm not up for following your orders?"

"Then it is Sofie's life that will be jeopardized," he says. "But you must make your own choices, as you see fit."

He's got me, and he knows it. I grumble some more, but I agree to carry out my part of the plan. Why should I have expected Sofie's team to keep me any less in the dark here than they did on Earth?

The vehicle rolls smoothly over rocks and mud pits, its eight enormous wheels and floating suspension designed for scientific exploration on rough terrain. Completely automated. Mist doesn't bother it, or monsters: Sensors enable it to dodge obstacles in its way. If we weren't headed where we're headed, I might be able to sit back and enjoy the ride. As it is, I'm jumpy as hell, and it doesn't improve my mood when Aakash and the others drop the polyglot and communicate in glances and gestures, shutting me out entirely. I leave the cockpit and spend some more time poking through the supplies on board, finding a small weapons cache. Nothing that does me any good. Rifles and grenade launchers— the kind of ordnance I can't hide in my suit and can't approach the ship displaying—along with ion pistols, which will have all the effect of rubber bands against the *Executor*'s hull. Once I'm within viewing range, I should be able to talk to Conroy through the microphone in my suit, but whether he'll let me talk my way closer once he sees I'm alone, I highly doubt. More likely, if Griff's dad has managed to get the *Executor*'s plasma cannons working, they'll lock in on me and reduce me to a pile of space dust.

But it's too late to turn back. It was too late a thousand years ago.

When I return from my inspection, I find the majority of our team sprawled in their seats, snoring away. Aakash alone remains upright and awake, staring steadily out a window that shows nothing but night.

"Any luck with the star mapping?" I ask.

He shakes his head. I'd hoped that, with all the other things he's been able to do with his remote, he might be able to coax the vehicle to tell us where in the galaxy we are. But his mind's focused only on our goal. He's not anxious about which world we're on, how we got here, where we're going to go next. Finding Sofie, freeing her from Conroy, is world enough for him.

I sit in the copilot's seat. "How did you meet her? Sumati, I mean."

He answers without turning to face me. "I was imprisoned in my youth. Sumati was there as well. But our paths to that place were very different."

I wait for him to go on. It's a long time before he resumes.

"I had killed a man," he says, speaking without emotion. "In a street fight over drug money. I will not say he did not deserve to die. But it was a grief to me that my life had ended as surely as his. In the Lowerworld, those whom the corporational tribunals consign to the dungeons do not again see the light of day."

In the Upperworld, officially, there is no crime. No deviance. People who commit acts that would have been called crimes disappear, showing up in Lowerworld prisons alongside street thugs and deportees and rebel leaders.

"Sumati came to my cell," Aakash continues, his eyes fixed on the night. "She had won over the jailers not by force of arms but by the power of her words, as she would do to all who encountered her in those days. You who saw her in decline, after sickness and disappointment made her long for an end to her body's suffering, will hardly believe me when I say she lit the dungeon like a thousand suns. When she spoke to me, tears I thought myself too hardened to shed fell from my eyes, and I knew I would follow her anywhere. And when, as it chanced, the intelligence network she had built gave us an opportunity to escape, we took it, and I was at her side until the end finally came."

"And what about Sofie?"

For a long moment he hesitates, and I sense the doubt in his mind. But he answers.

"She came to us as a girl, friendless and alone," he says. "She had heard of Sumati's message, and fled a life of enslavement to seek her out. She became Sumati's daughter, the child she never had."

"And you followed her, too."

"It was a very natural thing, to shift my allegiance from mentor to pupil."

"But the message never changed."

"It cannot change," he says. "It is timeless, though the vessel that carries it may last only a day."

For the first time since I joined him, he looks at me.

"You do not know, you may never know, the greatness of the girl you have pursued across the stars," he says. "Sumati's disciple she may be, but she is greater than her teacher, and her life is a gift to no one man, but to all the world's people. Let her go, Cameron Newell. Let her become here what she was on Earth, what she must be for all time."

I don't know what to say, can't meet his sparkling eyes. When I left the *Executor* in search of Adrian, I told myself I was willing to do anything, to take any risk, for Sofie. Because I loved her. Because I'd be lost without her. Because I couldn't bear to think of a world, a universe, that no longer rang with the sound of her voice.

And yet now, as I sit beside this man who has pledged his life to her, I begin to wonder if I would do the same as he's done. As he'll still do. I'm prepared to take a life. To give my own too, if it comes to that.

But will I do it for Sofie? Or for me?

Aakash looks at me and speaks gently, as if in answer to my unasked questions.

"The fall into love is deep," he says. "But the soul's thirst for freedom is a well without bottom."

Then he turns back to the window, and the vehicle that's taking us to Sofie rolls on through the night.

Earth, 2151

Upperworld

The final two months before launch passed by in a complete blur. I stayed with Griff, but our late-night bull sessions came to an end. He tried to draw me out of my shell, promising to let me in on all the scandalous new revelations about the mission he'd learned in the time since the final council, but I shut him out, wouldn't listen to a word he said. I knew I was being a jerk. I knew Griff was just being Griff, doing his best to cheer me up with some wacky story he'd picked up from Cons Piracy. But all I could think about was the upcoming launch, which would fling my body into space while leaving my heart behind.

Everything came to a dead halt in those months—everything, that is, except the mission. No ColPrep, no worldlink updates, no nothing. It was all one mad scramble to reconfigure and restock the ships before deadline. Whatever Sofie was up to, I couldn't have found out if I'd tried. Griff said—the one time I paid attention to the words coming out of his mouth—that he'd heard her team was busy with the selection process for their starship, working from a top-secret location. When he told me that, the crazy idea flitted through my mind that I could leave CanAm like I'd done before, track her down, beg or bribe my way onto the *Freefall*. But I knew that was impossible. I didn't need Griff to tell me that I was a watched man in the Upperworld. And I didn't need anyone to remind me that even if I did find my way back to Sofie, she'd send me packing the way she had after the night on her helicar.

I'd lived divided all my life. I hadn't known it until I met her. I would have to go on living divided for the rest of my days.

There was one thing that tormented me, though. One thing I couldn't get out of my head, and probably the only thing that motivated me to get up in the morning and make my way through each day. It was as crazy as any of my thoughts in those final months, and I knew it wouldn't change anything. But I longed for the chance anyway.

I couldn't get close to her before the launch. Wherever she was, Griff told me the chatter out there was that the Lowerworld base of operations was a heavily guarded fortress, possibly provided by the Upperworld to ensure the safety of the revolutionary leaders. But he also told me, and I clung to this, that the entire population of colonists would be assembled at the same time prior to boarding. The *Executor* and the *Freefall* were docked together, at the place they'd been constructed, which was itself top secret, though Griff's sources said it was probably in the abandoned and half-flooded landmass that had once been known as Greenland. JIPOC wasn't about to move the ships from there—everyone would be placed in deepsleep together and stored aboard the vessels on-site, right before the gravitational drives engaged and the liftoff occurred. From that point, the starships would exit Earth's atmosphere and travel most of the solar system side by side, before separating to seek their own destinations. No one would be awake to say good-bye at that final parting. But there was a chance, however slight, that people who wanted to say good-bye would have time to do so before we left Earth.

I'd asked Griff for so much already, I hesitated to ask for more. But with me and my parents no longer speaking—and Adrian and his dad no longer able to think about me without cursing—Griff's dad was the only person I knew on the inside, the only one who might be able to make it happen. All I wanted was a few seconds alone with her—or if not alone, then at least alone enough for me to say what I needed to say. Alone the way we'd been on our first helicar ride together, and our last, where, despite everything going on around us, I'd felt for a few moments as if we were the only two people in the universe.

It wasn't much to ask, but it was everything.

So I did.

Griff looked at me. "You sure?"

I nodded. Yes, I was sure.

He eyed me strangely for a second. Maybe he was shocked to hear me say anything after two months of near silence. Then his face broke into a grin. "Yeah, what the hell. I think Big Rich owes me one for cooping me up in this dump the last few months. Don't worry about a thing. I'll take care of it."

I tried to say something, found my heart too full to say it. "Thanks, man," I choked out at last.

"I'll probably live to regret this," Griff said with a laugh. "You stay here. I'll go find him."

It was a week before launch. But I knew Griff wouldn't let me down.

Otherworld

Earth Year 3151

Night

W e reach the perimeter fence by this strange planet's midnight. That's some comfort, since it means I'll be walking the rest of the way through a monster-free zone. The transport knows we've arrived before we do, braking and settling in response to the parameters Aakash entered into its navigational system. He's eager to get me off the vehicle now that we're here, which convinces me that my function in his master plan is pretty much what it was on Earth: I'm a pawn at best, a worm on the hook at worst. An easy target for Conroy to lock in on while Aakash and his team perform their part, whatever that might be.

"Be swift," Aakash says, before practically shoving me out the door. "And go with God." Which, I'm pretty sure, is Lowerworld talk for *It's been nice knowing you.*

The door slams shut, and I'm on my own.

I set off toward the *Executor*, its mammoth bulk invisible from this distance. Within seconds, the vehicle I left is swallowed in the gloom. This is probably only my state of mind, but I could swear the night's darker than usual, so dark I can't see the mist that's preventing me from seeing. I try to compose my speech to Conroy, but I keep stumbling on the spongy stone. Stumbling on the words, too, before they're fully formed. A stray memory of my early life with Adrian flickers through my mind, me and him out on the baseball diamond, the smell of dust and cut grass, the ball snapping and cracking in our gloves. The memory seems to come from much more than a thousand years ago, from some far-off place of pure fantasy, and it's not enough to drive me to guilt that I never made any serious attempt to do what his dad asked me to do. The cold truth is, if our positions had been reversed, Adrian would have done the same thing—namely, nothing—for me.

My solitary walk doesn't last long. A searchlight pierces the fog, gleaming like a chill aurora through the haze. If Conroy's got lenses on the surrounding terrain, he'll see me as soon as I step into the light's orbit, and he'll see I'm by myself. I set my jaw, forget about my half-baked speech, and continue my plodding walk toward the ship.

I can see it now.

It rises out of the fog, a titanic shadow with a single eye sweeping the plain. Of all the things human beings built over all the time we inhabited planet Earth, the *Executor* was one of only two visible from space. The other was a wall stretching across southeastern MicroNasia. According to the lessons we learned in Two Worlds History, that one was built to keep the barbarians out. We tried to build walls like that in the Upperworld, but they didn't work. And so we built the *Executor*: the world's biggest getaway car, an unbelievable piece of machinery designed so we could flee the scene of the crime and never have to worry about the cops catching up to us. After all, the cops died long before we stopped running.

The light from the hull is blinding. I've got to be close enough for them to see me.

I am.

The first warning comes in the form of a cannon blast that arcs over my head, ripping the night mist to tatters for a bright, searing second. Not meant to kill me, obviously—but just as obviously meant to show me that the weapons systems are alive and well.

Message received, I continue toward the ship.

It's shrouded in a silence as deep as it is huge. I wish someone would make an appearance. A diplomatic envoy would be my preference, but at this point I'd take a group of thrill seekers who've come to watch me get vaporized. Anyone to put a human face on this sleeping giant.

Be careful what you wish for.

The second warning is a voice. Conroy's voice. Amplified and mechanical, it squawks through the blinding light and fog.

"Stay where you are, Newell."

I do.

"Where's my son?"

My mind whirls, trying to come up with an answer that will convince him not to blast me into a trillion pieces.

But I've got nothing. I can't see the cannon, but I picture

it wheeling, aperture narrowing, target locking. The silence is absolute. It stretches for minutes, lengthened by the dark.

Then at last his voice comes again. "Drop your weapons."

"I'm unarmed."

"We've apprehended your team," the voice says. "Brazenly approaching the *Executor*, armed with grenade launchers, in an attempt to force ingress. The Upperworld thanks you for delivering them to us."

I hold my tongue. I should have known sending me to the *Freefall* wasn't only about finding Adrian. Maybe it was never about that at all.

"They'll be tried and executed for assaulting a JIPOC starship," the voice continues. "With their death and the girl's, the Lowerworld revolution ends. As it should have ended on the dying planet where it began."

"As opposed to this dying planet," I say, having nothing to lose.

"The only one dying tonight," Conroy's voice blares out of the void, "is you."

An explosion of white fire rocks the night, and I fly backward, blinded, ears ringing. For a crazy moment as I sail through space, I think that death's not so bad. It's actually kind of nice, not to have to hear or see or feel anything anymore.

But I land in one piece, my body smacking the spongy rock, and that brings me back to my senses.

I'm not dead. I'm not even hit. It wasn't the cannon that fired. It couldn't have missed me so badly from such close range.

I lift my head to find the *Executor* belching smoke in the glare of white lights.

I try to stand, lose my balance on the first attempt, get my feet under me on the second. The ringing in my ears has turned to a dull roar: maybe the sound of pressure rushing from the ship, more likely the shock wave that's taken up permanent residence in my head. I can't keep my eyes steady, can't pierce the confusion of light and sound to figure out what's happened to the ship, the cannon, Conroy's voice. I can think of only one thing.

Sofie's in there. And if Conroy survived, he's on his way right now to make sure she doesn't.

I run toward the light and smoke and flickers of flame—there's not enough oxygen to sustain a decent fire—but the ground pitches under me, and I lose my balance again. Nothing's clear. I think I make out voices, not the mechanical bellow of Chairman Conroy, but plain human voices screaming incoherently. Shadows streak the banners of light and dark, dancing shadows with arms as long as ropes and bodies that slide like fog. The pod creatures? Is it possible they're the ones that attacked the ship? I want to run past them, run right into the *Executor* through whatever hole's been opened in its side. But when I get close enough to see what happened, I realize there's no way I can advance any farther.

The *Executor*'s main cannon is a blackened stump protruding from the ship's prow, twisted and smoking like a spent candle. People I can't see clearly enough to identify run through the smoke, casting unnatural shadows as they try either to help or to get out of the way. If I were them, I'd opt for getting out of the way. The massive prow tilts downward, as if it's been partially separated from the main concourse or the ground has collapsed beneath it. And the cannon—one of the few things on this world or any other capable of penetrating the ship's own hide—has been reduced to shrapnel. It took a direct hit. But from what?

It rolls to a stop beside me, and I have my answer.

The ExCon vehicle. Fully automated, and now, I see, fully armed. Not an exploratory buggy at all. A private military cruiser. I should have realized that's what it was when I found all the hardware inside, but I guess I never expected the *Freefall* to transport something like this. But here it is, guns jutting, engine growling deep in its mechanical throat. While Conroy and his men were busy tracking Aakash's forces, thinking their puny arsenal was the best the Lowerworld could muster, this mini-tank took out the *Executor*'s main forward cannon.

The cruiser's door opens, and I lift myself inside. Then it slides shut, sealing me off from the smoke and screams. I don't have time to think about that. I have a single objective, and Aakash and the others have risked their lives to give me a chance to fulfill it. The man was right. If I'd known what his team was up to, I could never have played my part so well.

He trusted me after all. Now it's up to me.

"Take me to Sofie," I tell the cruiser, and it glides across the battlefield, its treads rolling over the smoking rubble from the Upperworld starship.

Earth, 2151

Upperworld

I told Sofie I loved her the day we boarded the ships.

I sidled close to her in the loading bay. She was easy to spot, even with the massive crowd, thanks to the worldlink lenses that surrounded her. The Peace Corp. stood on alert, but they let me be. "There's something I have to tell you."

She stiffened. Her black braid curled down her back. The jewel on her forehead flashed red. We hadn't seen each other since that night, months ago, when she'd lied to me and led me to believe she might one day be mine.

"I love you," I said. "I know that doesn't matter anymore. I just needed to tell you."

She wouldn't look at me. Her pod stood ready to receive her. Across the bay, separated by a distance infinitely smaller than the one that would soon divide us, I knew mine waited for me, too.

"Cameron," she said. "You did not need to tell me that."

"Actually," I said, "I really kind of think I did."

She looked at me then, and smiled. I tried to hold on to that smile, knowing I'd never see her again.

Not in a thousand years.

PART THREE

Freefall

Love is metaphysical gravity.
—R. Buckminster Fuller, *Critical Path*

Otherworld

Earth Year 3151

Night

The battle cruiser knows where to go. It stops before a ramp, does something I can't see that overrides the controls, and rolls into the loading bay. Then it does the same thing to the airlock's interior door, and we enter the *Executor*.

Inside, lights flash red up and down the sterile white corridor—a bit of a surprise, since last I heard from Griff, the emergency warning system was another casualty of the ship's sabotage. But if his dad got the executive chambers and the guns working, maybe he's restored other systems as well. Guards in their gray jumpsuits and helmets, blast visors lowered, stream toward the site of the explosion, but they ignore the cruiser, either thinking it's one of their own or knowing better than to mess with it. I sit back and let it take me where it will. Though I don't remember how to reach Conroy's quarters, I know now that Sofie is the lodestar that guides all our actions. The cruiser's locked onto her, and it'll take me there, no matter what stands in its way.

As it turns out, the only things that stand in its way are time and distance. But time and distance might be all it takes to defeat me now.

We roll through corridors, past housing cubicles, infirmary, dispensary. The few people we see shy from our approach. The hallway lights are working, as are most of the doors—and the ones that refuse to cooperate end up lying in a crumpled heap beneath the cruiser's wheels. The ship shudders unnaturally as we advance, periodic spasms passing through its kilometers-long spine, but whether they're from explosions or something else I can't tell. We're moving deeper into the ship's innards, close to Conroy's stateroom. When we get there, my gut tells me, he'll be waiting for me, holding his trump card. He won't have been at the blast site—why man the cannon when he could supervise everything from the safety of his chambers? Maybe I'm fooling myself, but I have to believe Sofie's alive. And so long as she's alive, I have hope.

The cruiser glides to a stop in front of the double doors I visited once before, the JIPOC crest emblazoned on their shining surface. "Let me out," I say, and the vehicle's door opens with a hiss. The absolute silence of the cockpit yields to the throbbing I heard the last time I was here—the throbbing that comes from Sofie's deepsleep. Or maybe it's a residual effect of the blast, the muted roar of the explosion in my ears.

Please let it be her, I say silently. *Please let me have one more chance.*

I shed the bulky outer suit, grab a pistol from the stash, and hop down to the floor. The doors to Conroy's chambers slide open when my hand nears them, and over the amplified throbbing, I hear a voice.

"Time's wasting, Newell," it says. "Why don't you come join us?"

Us. I cling to the word.

I slip inside. The first thing to meet my eyes is Aakash, lying facedown, his head twisted painfully to the side so I can see the blood streaming from his mouth and caked in his beard. He glances at me, the one eye that's visible glittering like a jewel in his dark face. There's no sign of the other members of his team. I take a step toward him, my hand held out as if to help him up. Then something else comes into view from beneath the catwalk, a gliding shadow, and I jump back, aiming my gun as it enters the light.

It moves like a giant crab, lumbering forward on spindly legs. Now that I see it in full light, it seems much clumsier, less agile, than the ones that attacked me during the night. Maybe it's slowed by the small space. The carapace opens and closes with a clacking sound, the humanoid figure inside concealed by metal valves. On a helmet lined with razor teeth, yellow optic lights glow as they swivel to face me.

A pod.

"Good to have our merchandise back up and running," Chairman Conroy says, emerging from the shadows behind the biomechanical horror. I wish I could get a clean shot at him, but he stays to the rear of the pod creature. He presses a finger against the JIPOC crest on his uniform, and the living pod spears Aakash with one of its metal blades and jerks him from the floor, a splotch of blood spreading across the front of his white jacket.

"'Centurions' is our branding," Conroy says. "A hundred private mechanical mercenaries, all operating under JIPOC authority, manufactured from the bodies of Upperworld passengers whose genetic histories lay outside licensed parameters. A value-added line, with the ability to think and react like human soldiers but without the inefficiencies of flesh and blood. Test models proved much more cost-effective than the Peace Corp. Even more so when we realized the *Freefall* provided a vast pool of raw materials for the taking."

Hearing my suspicions confirmed doesn't make me feel any less like I'm the one squirming on the monster's blade. "Raw materials? You're talking about human beings, you son of a bitch!"

Conroy shrugs. "You didn't honestly expect us to hand over one of our prohibitively costly starships without a return on our investment, did you? The *Freefall* was originally programmed to follow the *Executor*. It was only a matter of reprogramming the Lowerworld pods to monetize our line."

I've been subjected to corponational doublespeak all my life, but it sickens me to hear Conroy's pitch. And it sickens me even more when I realize he couldn't have created this army on his own. JIPOC approved it, leveraged it, commissioned the people who made it happen. Griff's dad must have programmed the *Freefall* to stick with the *Executor* instead of following the Lowerworlders' desired course. My own dad oversaw the stocking of the ships, so he had to be in on it too. And my mom—she was the deepsleep expert, the one who would have known how to turn sleeping voyagers into corporational soldiers.

But it still doesn't make sense. The metamorphosis didn't work on any of the Lowerworlders Aakash and I freed from their pods. And the pods that escaped the *Executor* turned *against* the ship. Whatever Conroy's plan was, it backfired on him. So far as I know, the creature holding Aakash is the only evidence of his success.

I have to admit, though, it's pretty convincing evidence. The chief bodyguard writhes on the pod's metal skewer, his face contorted in pain, his blood dripping on the floor. I could try shooting the monster, but the beam would kill Aakash with no guarantee of disabling the thing that holds him. My heavy artillery sits outside, and even if I could reach it in time, its firepower would destroy everyone in the room, Sofie included. Conroy's got me, and the smile that spreads across his face proves he knows it.

"You'll watch him die first," he says.

The creature's blade drives deeper into its victim's back, the tip bursting from the area around his heart. With a flick of its mechanical arm, it flings him aside, and he crashes to the floor, lying motionless in a pool of his own blood.

"And now the girl," Conroy says. He touches the crest on his uniform once more.

I try to run, but it's no contest.

I'm grabbed by the ankle, lifted into the air, shaken until my pistol flies free. Another of the creature's appendages clutches me by the throat. Conroy strides toward the room where I last saw Sofie, his mechanical pet following with me in its grip. I realize he never had any intention of shooting me out in the dark. That would have deprived him of the satisfaction of watching me held utterly helpless while he flips the switch that ends Sofie's life.

She's there, standing within the ring that generates the deep-sleep field, looking exactly as she did when I left her. Exactly as she did on Earth, with one exception. Sofie was never this still on Earth. Even in meditation or prayer, even in moments of reflection before she acted, she bristled with an energy all her own. I know what Aakash meant when he described Sumati's visit to his jail cell. I wish I could see Sofie as she was. I wish I could bask in her life force, feel it flow through me one more time before the end.

Conroy taps his badge, and the vise around my throat constricts. My brain sends a frantic message to my hands to claw the noose free, but my hands are held by another of the creature's arms. Lights dance before my eyes, and through them I see him smile.

For a moment he looks exactly like his son.

"Deepsleep is an amazing product, don't you think?" he says. "It can keep a body alive for a thousand years, and it can snuff that same life out in a matter of seconds."

I almost rise to his bait, but I manage to hold my tongue. Sofie wouldn't want me to beg for her life.

"A death for a death," Conroy says. "You took my son from me. Now I take her from you."

He presses a button on the mechanism that produces Sofie's deepsleep field. I want to scream. The aura wavers. There's the whine of dying machinery. The aura blinks once, twice, like a bad bulb. Then it goes out, and Sofie slides to the floor in a sea of purple.

Just like that. It's over.

"Tomorrow at dawn," Conroy says, "you die as well. A public execution for a traitor to the Upperworld."

He dismisses me with a wave of his hand, and his machine wheels to follow him back to the main room. I jerk my head, the only part of me that can move, trying to wrestle free. But it's useless. I'm suspended above the ground like a puppet in my metal rack.

Then I'm not.

Feeling rushes into my arms and legs as I hit the floor. Conroy's back is turned to me, and I push up onto my knees, dizzy from lack of breath. I don't know why the pod creature's freed me, and I sure as hell don't care.

I had one purpose when I entered this ship. Now I have another.

But I'm too weak to carry it out. I lunge clumsily for my fallen pistol, my legs tangling. Conroy spins, his own gun in hand.

I look back at the room where Sofie lies. I'm glad we're about to die together.

Then the machine that held me lashes out, grabbing Conroy's neck with its claw, lifting him from the floor above the body of its last victim. The gun falls as his hands scrabble at his throat. His legs kick spasmodically, his eyes bulging in panic.

I can't understand what's happening. The pod ascends the staircase, legs clicking against the metal. When it reaches the catwalk, it freezes, standing like a sentinel against the night window, its shell rimmed in stars. The only movement comes from the frantically kicking legs of Chairman Conroy. They're starting to slow when the creature releases him, his limp body tumbling down the staircase to land in a heap beside Aakash. I can tell he's still breathing, in shallow gasps.

I let him lie there. Sofie remains where she fell, nearly buried beneath her robe and my own tears. I hurry to her side and touch her wrist.

But there's nothing to feel. No pulse, and when I lower my ear to her mouth, no breath. She's gone.

I lift her in my arms. She's lighter than I expected. Almost weightless, as if her spirit was the only thing that gave gravity a claim on her body.

I don't look at Conroy or the thing that stands on the catwalk. I clasp Sofie to my heart as I walk from the chamber to the waiting cruiser, which accepts us like weary voyagers who've lost their way home.

Otherworld

Earth Year 3151

Night

O uter darkness seals in the light as the cruiser carries me and Sofie back to the *Freefall*. I try to revive her, using the techniques we learned in ColPrep, but there's no flicker of response. If this was one of the stories they used to tell in the Lowerworld, a single kiss on those lush red lips would wake her up. But that would require me to be a prince, and princes haven't existed for hundreds of years.

Plus, I already kissed her once. And we saw how well that worked.

When it's obvious she's dead and I'm exhausted from trying to breathe life back into her, I consider exiting the vehicle, stripping off my jumpsuit, waiting for daylight. Vanishing in a wisp of brightness and ash, now that she's gone. I consider it so strongly my finger presses the button to release the door.

But the cruiser won't let me. The door stays closed. For whatever reason, though Aakash was able to bring the vehicle to life and point it toward the *Executor*, it's been on autopilot ever since.

Numbly I pick up Sofie's body, searching for a place to lay her down. It's a long ride back, and I can't bear to see her looking so alive when I know she's gone. Can't stand to think that in mere hours, she'll be cold and pinched and the processes of death will show themselves on her face.

I stumble into the rear of the cruiser and freeze.

Sitting on the floor is an open pod.

Horror shoots through me, my bleary mind convincing me it's the thing that killed Aakash and attacked me and Conroy. But then I remember: It's a regular pod from the *Freefall*, loaded aboard the cruiser to carry Sofie if we recovered her in deepsleep. The interior of the pod looks intact, none of the hardware removed or tampered with that I can tell.

I don't know what impulse makes me lay Sofie's body inside the pod. Right now I feel as if I don't know anything anymore. All I know is that I'm heartsick and exhausted, and light as Sofie is, I can't carry her any longer.

I arrange her hands on her chest, the way I saw them do in secret Lowerworld burials, where they put people in the ground instead of incinerating them like you were supposed to. The calmness of death sits on her features, but it hasn't destroyed her beauty. Her black hair remains lustrous, her lips slightly parted as if she's about to launch into another story. The jewel on her forehead flashes crimson against her pale brown skin. Yet her chest doesn't rise and fall, her blood doesn't stir. When

I told myself I'd never see her again, I should have added one word.

I'll never see her again *alive*.

Tears well in my eyes. I bow my head and let them fall. I'm not sure if I'm crying for Sofie, for me, or for something else. For Adrian, and the friendship we once had. For Aakash, the last leader of a failed cause. For a civilization, a people, a world coming to an end. For the darkness that will soon cover everything.

I'm crying for her, I decide. Nothing else matters if she's not here.

A whirring sound startles me. I look up to see the door to the pod slide closed, sealing Sofie from me. It happens so fast I can't stop it, even if I knew how. I press the button, but without the tracker to help me, it doesn't respond. I say her name, but nothing doing. In frustration I hammer on the shell, producing only a series of dull echoes. Whatever the pod's up to, it won't let me in. I lay my hands on the cold metal and close my eyes, willing it to unlock its secrets.

Then my fingertips feel a hum, and I open my eyes. Tears blur my vision, but there's no mistaking what I see. At the sight of it, the tears fall harder, and I can't tell if they're tears of wonder or grief.

The sealed door is outlined in light.

The deepsleep has switched back on. It's shining inside the pod, the yellowish-white aura I last saw before Conroy ended Sofie's life. Maybe, when I laid her body in the pod, it responded as it would have if a living body had been placed there. When we gave the pods a trial run on Earth, I remember lying down in my own, the hum of light surrounding me for a split second before sleep descended. Then there was the second time, the time that lasted a thousand years. For those thousand years, I might as well have been dead. For all intents and purposes I was, until I woke up.

But with Sofie it's different. You can wake a dead body that's only sleeping. You can't wake a dead body that's truly dead.

I press my face to the pod, trying to peek through the sealed door. The aperture is far too narrow for me to see anything but a crack of light like a delicate vein beneath the smooth metal skin. I leave my tears on its surface, but with the door closed, I can't hear the throbbing of the deepsleep aura. All I can hear is the faint hum as it rocks Sofie's body in her cradle of death.

I try the release button once more, with the predictable non-result. I could pound on the shell, scream at the pod to stop playing this pointless game, but that would be every bit as pointless. It won't listen, and I've run out of things to say. Exhaustion from the day's events has stolen over me, and I know it's only a matter of seconds before I surrender to sleep.

I lie on my back, hands folded neatly on my chest, the way I left Sofie. Close my eyes. Think of her. Hold the picture firmly in my mind, until the edges blur and darkness carries everything away.

JOSHUA DAVID BELLIN

Otherworld

Earth Year 3151

Day

I wake after a dreamless eternity to find the cockpit flooded with light, the *Freefall* looming out of the mist. I don't feel much like living, but it seems my body refuses to die, at least not permanently.

I rise, stretch stiff joints, place my hand on the pod. It hums the same as last night. I press the button, expecting no reaction, getting what I expect. I speak her name, just to speak her name. Just to feel a tiny bit less unutterably lonely.

The Lowerworld ship opens its arms to welcome us back.

Now that we're inside, the battle cruiser's doors release and I'm free to exit. Unloading Sofie's pod gives me a moment's hesitation, but while I'm standing there trying to muster the strength to push something that weighs well over a hundred kilos, the pod rises on its own and floats to a rest in the loading bay. No sooner have I walked down the ramp to join it than the cruiser backs up, wheels in a tight circle, and opens the airlocks so it can leave the ship. I guess now that its mission has failed, it's got no reason to stay. I watch through a porthole as it drives off into the blinding light. Part of me wishes I could go with it, now that my mission has failed as well. But the much larger part of me knows I belong here, until the end. Whatever and whenever that might be.

First order of business, though, is to revive myself. I don't know if Conroy's dead or alive, but I do know that if he's alive, he'll come after me—and if he isn't, some flunky or another in the chain of command will. The Centurion line's obviously not responding quite the way the chairman planned, but Griff's dad managed to get other weapons systems aboard ship in working order, so I wouldn't be surprised if the *Executor* has some nasty surprises up its sleeve. I need to replenish my body, then get down to arming the *Freefall*'s defenses, if it's got any. I'll be damned if I'm going to let Conroy or some other licensed hit man from the Upperworld—say, my dad—waltz in here without a fight.

Why I'm determined to fight when there's nothing left to fight for, I can't say. I guess hope is just another of those things. It refuses to die. At least not permanently.

"I'll be right back," I say to the closed pod, the first complete sentence I've spoken since last night. "My love," I add, and my heart swells as I say the words, before folding back into grief and shame that I can't say them to her living face.

The dispensary supplies my needs. My throat's sore, my muscles weak. But I'm as fresh as I'm going to get.

I'm also dismayed when I discover the state of the *Freefall*'s defenses.

Basically, it has none. Or none that I can figure out, anyway. The command center that sits forward of the cargo bay lets me in, and I scan the consoles, looking for something I can use. But there are no external cannons, no energy shields. No robotic weapons systems. That makes perfect sense, from a corporational point of view: You don't waste high-tech artillery on a supply barge. Probably the single battle cruiser Aakash located was meant for the *Executor*, a mistake in someone's procurement order or shipping manifest rather than an intentional passenger. The hull's sturdy enough to withstand all but a direct hit from an asteroid, but I saw what happened when the cruiser took out the *Executor*'s cannon. If Griff's dad has gotten any of the ship's military vehicles into fighting trim, the *Freefall* doesn't stand a chance.

On Earth, the only weapon the Lowerworld had was the old-fashioned kind: people power. With Sumati and then Sofie to lead us, we marched, mobilized, moved mountains. But even if I could rouse the crowds that lie asleep in the pod bay, human bodies aren't going to hold against an armed assault.

I'm on a ship with nearly a million passengers. But I've never felt more alone.

I return to the spot where I left Sofie. To check on her, I tell myself. To delay the inevitable, I know. The moment when I'm going to have to leave her for real, to try to protect the ship that's become her grave, not knowing if I'll be able to come back.

Her pod sits open.

I'm as shocked as I was last night when I found the pod in the cruiser. This time, though, surprise turns instantly to fury. My only thought is that someone from the *Executor* has been here already, that they've forced their way onto the *Freefall* and desecrated Sofie's tomb. Why, I can't imagine. Unless the plan is to hold a mock execution aboard the *Executor* in front of a cheering mob that doesn't know she's already dead.

The Upperworld wouldn't let her live in peace. Now they won't let her die.

Teeth clenched to stop my heart from exploding out of my chest, I rush to the pod, expecting to find it empty.

But it's not.

Sofie lies there, hands folded, eyes closed. The deepsleep aura has switched off, showing me her perfect features, her radiant skin. In the brightly lit bay, the luminescence that swaddled her in deepsleep seems to pour from her, making her hair and nails and parted lips shine. She looks so much like the Sofie I've dreamed of for so long, the Sofie I fell in love with on Earth, it's a second before I realize she shouldn't look this way. Shouldn't look so tranquil and beautiful hours after I witnessed her death.

Her eyelids flutter, and she draws breath in a gasp.

I jerk back instinctively, then lean forward as her breathing steadies, her chest rising and falling in the gentle rhythm of sleep. The sickening thought leaps into my mind that this is one of Conroy's reprogrammed pods, that I'm about to watch her transform into a twisted slave of metal. I tell myself I'll end her life before I let that happen to her. But my will is paralyzed, and my hands won't move. I feel like the *Freefall* itself, tumbling through space, drawn by my soul's utmost gravity.

Then her eyes open. Golden, focused. They tighten in momentary confusion when they see me, but they lose none of the intensity that first spoke to me across worlds.

"Cameron," she says.

She smiles. The red jewel on her forehead flashes.

"How . . . ?" I ask, barely a whisper.

She doesn't answer, other than to lay her hand on mine.

Otherworld

Earth Year 3151

Day

I help Sofie from her pod, offering an arm to steady her. She's less disoriented than most people who've spent countless days asleep—not to mention one day dead—but she does stumble when she takes her first unassisted step in a millennium. I watch her closely, not only because I'm afraid she'll fall. More because I'm afraid she'll vanish before my eyes. I long to hold her, to feel her solidity and warmth. I ache to ask her all the things I've been asking myself, all the things I could never understand: why she left me, whether she felt anything for me on Earth or if I was nothing but a pawn in a game of galactic intrigue she couldn't afford not to win. I'm this close to asking her too.

But I get a hold of myself. The last thing I want to do is pick a fight with the girl I've loved forever the minute she returns from the dead.

The next to last thing I want to do is tell her what I know I have to.

"You're wondering where we are," I say.

She turns to face me. Her eyes are placid, the way they were on Earth even when Upperworld big shots were raining accusations on her.

"We're on the *Freefall*," I say. "It misfired, along with the *Executor*. I don't know the name of this planet. No one does. Somebody sabotaged the ships, and we all wound up here, wherever *here* is."

She nods calmly, as if this is pretty much what she expected to hear. As if I'm the guy she pretty much expected to tell her.

"Conroy had something to do with it," I add. "He was planning to use Lowerworlders as a private army. But that plan fell through too."

Sofie nods again, businesslike. "We had been warned of such a possibility," she says, while I thrill at the sound of her voice. "In the months prior to departure, Cons Piracy uncovered plans to use our people in a pilot program code-named Juggernaut. Apparently the program was delayed on Earth and reserved for outer space."

"You heard about this through Cons Piracy?"

She smiles. "A front group for Lowerworld specialists in information extraction. They operated covertly in the Upperworld, with unparalleled access to JIPOC communications. Much of what we learned about the Otherworld colonization flowed through that channel."

I'm not surprised to discover there's something else she

kept from me on Earth, but I'm not exactly overjoyed, either. "So you knew about this beforehand?"

"It was one of the reasons we attempted to distance ourselves from the *Executor*."

"But the *Freefall* followed the *Executor* after all," I say. "So maybe your Cons Piracy friends were the ones who sabotaged the ships."

She shakes her head. "Cons Piracy had no access to the starships themselves. And their mandate was a peaceful one. It would have been inconsistent with their beliefs to engage in violence."

I look at her, so calm, so sure. I can't read her mind, but my own thoughts are an inferno. I desperately wish I didn't have to tell her the next thing I have to.

"It doesn't matter anyway," I say. "This planet's dead, Sofie. Dead or dying. The atmosphere's a wreck, and the radiation's lethal. Even if we had our terraforming equipment, there's nothing to terraform. We'll never survive here."

She closes her eyes, revealing the glistening black kohl that lines her eyelids. She breathes deeply, lets the air out slowly. When her eyes open, they've lost none of their golden fire. "We of the Lowerworld have survived great odds before."

"Not this time." I'm not sure why I'm so eager to burst her bubble, but the words keep tumbling out. "Conroy had his team working on the *Executor*'s weapons since we got here, and they've restored some of the systems—the cannons, maybe other stuff too. I doubt they're ready to move on the

Freefall yet, but it's only a matter of time. And, Sofie . . ."

She waits. I get the feeling she knows what I'm about to say.

"Aakash is dead," I tell her. "And the rest of the team—the ones we could wake up—are trapped aboard the *Executor*. They might be dead too. Conroy sent me here to look for his missing son, but I think he only did it so I could lure your team onto the *Executor*. We've got no one left who knows how to operate the ship. And even if we did, the *Freefall's* not equipped for combat."

She nods again, smoothes her robe. Something about the way she's reacting—*too* calm, too businesslike—makes me decide to tell her the one thing I least want to say out loud.

"I saw you die too, Sofie. Conroy disengaged your deepsleep, and you died. When I brought you back here, you weren't breathing. No pulse. I don't understand how you . . ." My eyes burn at the memory. I don't want to cry again, but I can't stop the tears from falling. "I thought I'd lost you forever."

Her hands close on mine. I feel her warmth as she leans close, smell her fragrance. Even that hasn't changed.

"No one is greater than death," she says. "I was trained by Sumati to control my heartbeat and breathing as a survival strategy, but this should not have enabled me to withstand an interruption of deepsleep. Some power we do not understand must have thwarted Chairman Conroy. But, Cam . . ."

I look at her. Her voice, her eyes are tender. They always are, before she plunges the knife into my heart.

"If I have been given a second chance at life," she says, "I must live now as I always have. I cannot live the life another would have me live. And I cannot live in fear of death—my own or any other's."

I nod. I know what she's saying. And deep down, I know she's right.

But I still can't stand to hear her say it.

"So basically," I say, "you're determined to get yourself killed."

She cocks her head and looks at me, lips pursed, eyes bright. But not with tears.

"You got lucky the last time," I say. "Next time, they're going to be a lot smarter. Figure out a way to kill you for real. Trust me, the Upperworld's not exactly short on methods of killing people."

"I know the ways of death of the Upperworld," she says flatly. Her tone is measured, but there's an angry light in her eyes.

Ladies and gentlemen, Cam Newell. The guy who decides to pick a fight with the girl he's loved forever the minute she returns from the dead.

"I've never asked you to betray your people," I say. "To stop being who you are. I just don't want to watch you die again. Is that too much to ask?"

She opens her mouth to answer—more than likely something I won't want to hear—but she's cut off when the *Freefall* sends out a loud squawk that echoes through the corridors. The alarm repeats itself, over and over, while red warning lights flash above our heads. Sofie looks at me, and I know we share the same thought.

I was right. It was only a matter of time before the *Executor* came after us. And that time is now.

We're under attack.

Otherworld

Earth Year 3151

Day

The battle cruiser that drove me to the *Executor* with Sofie's team, then back with Sofie herself, rolls toward the *Freefall*'s main forward airlock. Its body gleams in the daylight, stark black against a world cleared of mist.

Another cruiser comes up behind it, different only in the maroon-and-gold CanAm logo on its side. Behind that, ranged in battle formation, are more than fifty mechanical monsters, missiles cocked like antennae above the eyes of monster bugs.

Centurions.

Though I expected some form of assault, I'm stunned by the force that confronts us. Up to this point, I've seen only one of Conroy's robotic beasties aboard the *Executor*, and that one was either malfunctioning or choosing to take matters into its own metal hands. The pods I faced previously had no weapons like they do now—if they had, I'd be dead—and they weren't able to withstand the daylight, either. The only working vehicle

I've seen since landing on this planet gave us a free lift to the *Executor* before blasting the Upperworld ship's cannon to smithereens. Based on that behavior, I kind of assumed it was on our side.

Griff's dad must have been busy this past night.

The ExCon cruiser coasts to a stop before our prow, close enough that from my position at the command center's visualization screen, I can see that its blue-and-white logo is streaked by the fire damage it inflicted on the *Executor*. Its cannon swivels, sniffing the air, locking on our heat signatures through the triple-titanium-reinforced hull of our ship. One shot from that cannon and we'll be on a fast track to another world.

And this time, we won't be waking up.

The second cruiser, the one with the logo of CanAm, edges up beside its partner. Our screen crackles as the CanAm cruiser tries to open a channel with us. I glance at Sofie, who's been uncommunicative since our little spat and won't meet my eyes. I can't think of anything I'm in the mood to talk to the *Executor* about, but I suppose I don't have much choice. I touch the screen to let the cruiser through.

A second later I wish I hadn't.

"Game's up, Newell." Chairman Conroy's voice emerges. "We've got you surrounded."

Technically, he's got about one-thousandth of 1 percent of the *Freefall* surrounded. But I don't quibble. "So, how's your throat feeling?"

He doesn't respond. Unless you count the ExCon cruiser

rolling closer, its gun locked onto us, the Centurions fanning out behind it to show us he means what he says.

"Chairman Conroy," Sofie speaks into the screen. She's been silent so long it surprises me to hear her voice. "Our destruction will not accomplish what you seek. Would it not be wise to work with us to achieve our common goal?"

Conroy says nothing. I assume he's using the lull in the conversation to scan our ship, make sure we don't have any other war machines like his on board. If so, it won't take him long to figure out we don't.

"Earth is behind us," Sofie speaks again. "The future ahead. The fate that brought us to this place might not have been what any of us desired, but could it not have been given to us for a reason? Let us not lose what we have wandered so long, fought so hard, suffered so much to find. Let us work together to survive as we can, as we must, if the universe is to remember us as a people and not forget that we ever were."

Despite our recent argument, I find myself moved by her appeal—or by the mere music of her voice—and it seems to me it would take a heart of stone to resist. But that's exactly what Adrian's dad has rattling around inside his chest. Unless she can speak to him in a language he understands, a merciless language of profit margins and externalities, he's not going to hear her. And though Sofie speaks many languages, I'm pretty sure she doesn't speak that one.

"Cameron tells me you have lost a child," she says, her voice softer than before. "I grieve with you, and I would offer you what comfort I can. Will you not let us board your ship, and join you in mourning your loss?"

It's a nice try. But it doesn't work.

"You will stand down while we board *your* ship," Conroy announces. "Any resistance will be met with deadly force. You have thirty seconds before our soldiers fire. Their first target will be the pod bay."

A look of panic crosses Sofie's face. "What terms are these—"

"You're in no position to negotiate terms," the voice cuts her off. "Twenty seconds until we fire."

I look at Sofie. Her finger hovers over the controls.

"No," I whisper.

"Ten seconds."

She smiles sadly.

"Five seconds."

"I'm sorry, Cam," she says.

She presses the button to open the loading dock. I can't stop her.

Back on Earth, I believed in the future. Sofie was the one who first showed it to me, who convinced me that the centuries before our time didn't have to control our destiny. As the rumble of the cruisers entering the *Freefall* echoes outside the room where we sit, I try to recapture the faith I had back then, when I was sure that people who fought hard enough for their beliefs could create something beautiful and blameless and new.

But then I hear heavy boots in the hallway, and I know the truth.

You can't escape the past. The decisions we make at the beginning put us on a path we can't step off, even at the very end. And those five final seconds are all the future we're going to get.

Otherworld

Earth Year 3151

Day

Four of Conroy's thugs enter the command center, their faces shielded by blast visors, their ion beams leveled at our chests. As if they weren't enough, a pair of Centurions clanks in their rear. Sofie and I barely have time to rise from our seats before the human and inhuman soldiers intrude.

Conroy enters the room. The collar of his uniform covers most of his throat, but purple blotches peek out where the Centurion choked him. The way he looks at us makes me sure his mind is flashing on the same kind of thought his son would have, *Upperworld traitor caught in compromising position with Lowerworld breeder* or something like that. But then his face breaks into a triumphant smile, and as with the first time I saw it, I like that smile even less than his typical look of disgusted superiority.

He signals, and the teen soldiers cuff us. I'm hopeful they'll take us to the *Executor* together, but they immediately separate us, two of them dragging Sofie to Conroy's side and another two blocking me from making a move toward her. A Centurion joins each of the teams, so even if it was possible to overpower their human counterparts with our hands cuffed, we'd have to tangle with these soulless things of metal.

"I'm not sure how you survived, Miss Patel," Conroy says, his voice raspier than normal but the smile never leaving his face. "I can assure you, we won't be so careless again."

Sofie meets his eye but says nothing. I search for something to say, something to show I'm not afraid of him, but I come up empty.

He wheels, addressing one of the flunkies who holds me. "Trainee!"

The teen straightens. "Yes, sir!"

"After securing the prisoners, you will deploy Juggernaut Team A to this ship's cargo hold. Requisition five hundred dormant pods for special handling. The remaining pods are to be disposed of to make room for our own company."

"Yes, sir!"

"No!" Sofie shouts. She struggles for freedom, but her captors hold her fast. "Chairman Conroy, have pity. Take my life if you will, but spare my people."

"Always angling for concessions," Conroy says coldly. "Always trying to outmaneuver us. I've told you, Miss Patel—this is not an intercorporational parley. This is a hostile takeover." He chuckles at his own humor, though the chuckle turns quickly to a cough. "In view of the damage inflicted on our own starship, the *Freefall* currently represents the Upperworld's best hope for securing our interests. We will therefore occupy it, taking possession of its assets and excising its liabilities. You were a fool to surrender your vessel when it was the only bargaining chip you had left."

For the barest instant, Sofie's body sags, and I'm reminded of Sumati, broken and defeated after years of struggle. But then she draws herself up and meets Conroy's smirk with a calm, steady gaze.

"I will pray for you, Chairman Conroy," she says. "For you and your people. I will pray that they outlive the madness of their leader, and come to know wisdom before the end."

Conroy doesn't bother to respond this time. He signals to his goon squad, and they pull me and Sofie toward the twin cruisers that sit idling outside the command center, the Centurions following close behind. I try to fight free of my restraints to reach for Sofie's hand or Conroy's throat—I'm not sure which—but I get neither. Instead, I get the butt of a pistol to the back of my head, and the room swims before my eyes.

They're loading Sofie onto the CanAm cruiser. I'm five meters from where she stands, but I feel farther from her than I've ever been. I focus hard, meet her eyes. They're the first thing I saw for real, and now they're going to be the last.

"I love you," I call out to her.

She returns my gaze. Smiles. And speaks my name. "Farewell, Cameron Newell. There will be other worlds for us."

Then the guards yank me into the ExCon cruiser, the Centurion looms in front of the doorway, and I lose sight of her for good.

Otherworld

Earth Year 3151

Day

'm locked down to the bench in the rear of the ExCon cruiser. The guards sit up front, joking and laughing, while the Centurion remains in the *Freefall*, probably waiting for its handler to give it the signal to remove pods from the hold. My head hurts like hell, but I haven't lost consciousness. I'd kill both of Conroy's stooges without hesitation if I could work myself free.

But I can't. And as soon as Conroy has what he wants from the *Freefall*, the surplus pods will be nothing but a smoldering memory.

All those people, I think. All the people who died on Earth to give this handful a chance to live in space. And now they're as good as dead too.

If they were awake, they could flee the vessel. But they wouldn't get far. The sunlight would stagger them in their tracks, and even if they survived until nightfall, the Centurions would destroy them before the next day's sun had a chance to do its deadly work. I've seen how maneuverable these monsters are out in the night. Unarmed and leaderless, the last survivors of the Lowerworld would be little better than live target practice.

I never learned how to pray, but I try now.

I pray for all those innocent lives. For the waste of their beauty, their unknown futures. For the safe passage of their souls. Guilt pricks me when I realize I never prayed for the victims aboard the *Executor*, the ones killed when the battle cruiser I'm sitting in right now attacked the Upperworld starship. I never prayed for Adrian. I add him to my list of prayers, mourning the friendship we shared, wishing it could have worked out another way.

But I can't bring myself to pray for his dad, or for the faceless guards at his command. Maybe Sofie can find it in her heart to forgive them, but I never will.

I think of the story she told back in New York CITI, the first time I saw her in the flesh: old worlds exiting the stage, new ones waiting in the wings. I wonder if she truly believed her own story, or if she knew all along a time would come when nothing new would survive the death of the old.

I pray for us, too, for the world I wish I could believe awaits us.

The battle cruiser spins in a perfect circle, and, through the visualization screen, I see the *Freefall*. It spans the gulf in all its silent majesty, one of the greatest things we earthlings ever made. A ship that took fifty years and millions of lives and trillions of dollars to build, a ship that sailed for a millennium into black emptiness in the hope of our race's rebirth. Centurions crawl over its prow like spiders. The guard in charge opens a channel to the CanAm cruiser.

"Awaiting your orders, Commander Conroy."

There's a crackle of static. "Is the prisoner secured?"

"Yes, sir."

"Then proceed."

The guard pats his partner on the back and swivels to a separate console I assume to be the Centurion controller. He's punching buttons on the box when I call out to him.

"Hey," I say. "You going to do whatever Conroy tells you?"

He ignores me, pushes more buttons. I press my luck and keep going.

"Back on Earth, there was this little thing called freedom," I say. "We used to think that was a good thing. That we should make our own decisions, instead of running around kissing our boss's ass."

"Shut the hell up," he says, but he's not looking at me. He's looking at the controller, frowning as if he's about to ask it a question.

"Conroy wants to turn you into a mass murderer," I say. "He won't do it himself, but he doesn't mind letting you have all those dead bodies on your hands. How do you feel about that?"

"Shut the hell *up!*" the guard hollers. He spins to face me, his eyes covered by the visor of his blast helmet.

I shrug, or come as close as I can with my hands pinned to the seat. "The truth hurts, my man," I say. "But it's a good pain."

He stands and takes a step toward me, gun drawn.

I should have left the speeches to Sofie.

But before he can come any closer, a flash of light envelops him and he crumples over the top of his seat, his body convulsing before rolling limply to the floor. That's when I see that the other guard's got his gun out too, and I realize what he's done. A moment later he stands, nudges his dead companion with the toe of his boot to make sure, then comes for me.

I tug as violently as I can against the restraints, but they don't give at all. Whatever it was about my little ethics lesson that drove this guy insane, I'm not going to be able to escape him.

He's a step away when he jams his pistol into its holster and slides back his visor.

"You should have seen the look on your face, my friend," he says with a laugh. "Like you were about to poop your pants."

I thought I'd gotten used to accepting the impossible, but I guess I was wrong. Because even though I see the red hair and the face full of freckles that jump out at me from beneath the oversize helmet, I can't believe what I'm seeing.

It's Griff.

Otherworld

Earth Year 3151

Day

He unlocks my shackles and helps me stand, and together we move to the front of the vehicle. The dead guard's body he shoves to the side, but he doesn't look freaked out by it. He keeps cracking up like we're playing some crazy vidgame in his room back on Earth, and my amazement at seeing him here turns to worry that there's something even more seriously wrong than it appears.

"Check this out," he says, sitting in the driver's seat and clicking the commlink back on. "Commander Conroy, do you read? This is Trainee Griffin reporting. Do you read?"

"What is it, Griffin?" Conroy's voice comes over the link.

"Systems malfunction, Commander Conroy," Griff says. "Unable to operate Juggernaut Team A remotely from battle cruiser *Maverick*. Please stand by for diagnostics."

His fingers play over the cruiser's front console, but nothing happens, which I suspect is because the buttons he's pushing are completely random. I notice through the visualization screen that the Centurions have frozen in place on the side of the *Freefall*, their weapons pointing aimlessly at the bright sky. The CanAm cruiser rolls into view, and Conroy's voice sounds again over the link.

"Well, Griffin? What's your report?"

"Remote weapons systems controller aboard battle cruiser *Maverick* reads as nonfunctional, sir," Griff says in a serious voice, though he's smiling like a lunatic the whole time. "It's possible the system matrix overloaded during the previous attack on the *Executor*."

"Goddamn it, Griffin," Conroy's voice snarls through the static. "You told me you had these vehicles up and running. Explain yourself, trainee."

"Running secondary diagnostics, sir," Griff says, with a wink that leads me to believe there is no such thing. A minute later, despite the fact that he's done nothing to the controls and nothing new has popped up on his screen, he continues. "It appears that my original analytics have been confirmed, sir. Complete weapons systems failure aboard battle cruiser *Maverick* due to inadequate matrix reload."

"I'll have your ass for this, Griffin," Conroy snaps.

"Might I suggest, sir, that you activate Juggernaut Team A via the interface aboard the battle cruiser *Imperial?*" Griff says, still in that ultraserious voice. "Your own cruiser, sir?"

"I know bloody well it's my own cruiser," Conroy returns. "Trainee!" he spits, presumably at the guard operating his vehicle. "Prepare to activate Juggernaut Team A."

"What the hell are you doing?" I whisper to Griff.

"Take it easy," he whispers back, though the link is down and there's no need. "Watch the screen."

I do. The Centurions bristle over the *Freefall*'s nose like poison quills on some long-dead sea creature. Conroy's cruiser remains in our sights, and though I can't see inside to whatever the guard's doing, I imagine him diligently pressing the buttons that will send Conroy's biomechanical monsters swarming into the *Freefall*'s pod bay. I can't believe Griff is going to be a part of this, but then, I can't believe Griff is on this cruiser at all. Or that he killed someone. Or that he's bullshitting Conroy into believing he's on his team. I hold my breath, hoping I know my second oldest friend a lot better than I knew my first.

"Pow," Griff whispers, and I flinch as if it's an actual explosion from the Centurions' guns.

But it isn't. The machines do absolutely nothing. Neither does the *Imperial*. In fact, the CanAm battle cruiser does less than nothing.

If, that is, spinning in a wild circle counts as less than nothing.

"Griffin!" Conroy's voice howls over the screen. "What in the hell have you done to my cruiser?"

Griff's laughing so hard tears stream down his face, but he manages to rein in his voice when he answers.

"Apologies, Commander Conroy," he says. "It appears

the *Imperial*'s systems are nonfunctional as well. As you know, I revived your cruiser via the matrix aboard the *Maverick*. It appears that was a mistake on my part."

"You're damn right it was a mistake!" Conroy yells. With his cruiser spinning as wildly as it is, I don't see how he—or anyone—can hold on to his lunch, much less process Griff's increasingly ridiculous responses. I think of Sofie, spinning along with the others, her only advantage—maybe—being her ability to calm her nerves through meditation. "Now shut the damn thing off!"

"Attempting to shut off battle cruiser *Imperial*, sir," Griff says in that deadpan voice. He smiles at me and fingers the controls.

"Listen up," he says in a whisper. "In about two seconds, the *Imperial* is going to fill with methoxypropane. All the cruisers have that as a fail-safe in case the vehicle's taken over by an enemy combatant or the crew just plain loses it." He laughs quietly. "The Prophet will control her breathing to prevent the worst effects of the anesthesia, but the rest of them should be flat on their asses in a couple of minutes."

"The Prophet?" I say. "You mean Sofie?"

"Later," Griff whispers. "Just be ready to move when I give the word."

I watch through the viewscreen as the *Imperial* slows its frantic spinning and finally comes to a stop. There's a pause where I think I should see something happening, but all I see is the cruiser sitting motionless, the way kids do when they've spent too much time on the merry-go-round. Finally, a weak voice—maybe Conroy's, maybe not—comes over the link, but it's slurring its words, making no sense at all. The voice trails into silence, and Griff slams his hand against the control panel with a laugh.

"Let's go," he says, revving the engine and heading for the *Imperial*.

The Centurions spring into motion as our cruiser approaches, clambering off the *Freefall* and lining up in twin ranks in front of Conroy's vehicle. They open a space for us, pivoting neatly like Peace Corp. soldiers while we roll through to the *Imperial* and lock onto its door. The realization that Griff is controlling everything—including the Centurions—sinks in slowly. He must know where my thoughts are headed, because he smiles and taps his jumbo-size helmet, and one of the creatures tips forward and does a headstand.

"I call 'em Terra Tanks," he says. "Much better branding than Centurions, don't you think?"

Griff hands me an oxygen mask, and we enter the CanAm cruiser. We find what he predicted: the bodies of Conroy and one of his guards sprawled in their seats, heads lolling and tongues exposed. The only thing he didn't tell me was that the other guard would figure out what was going on and try to get out, because we find him fallen beside the entrance, fingers swollen and bleeding from his efforts to pry the unresponsive door open. Griff smiles at me as he steps over the inert body, and the feeling that I'm trapped in some kind of trippy tech-game grows stronger. I only hope I can figure out the rules, and fast.

"Where's Sofie?" I say, just before I see her lying on the floor in a corner of the cockpit.

I run to her, falling at her side to cradle her head in my lap. For the second time in a day, I think she's not breathing—but then I see that she is, very slowly and shallowly, her breaths coming at the rate of maybe two a minute. Her pulse feels similarly sluggish, with large gaps between beats. I wonder if this is what I missed last night, when I was so desperate for her to live I overlooked the signs of life. But how she survived having her deepsleep turned off remains as much a mystery to me as it was to her.

I lift her in my arms. Her body's warmth and solidity give me hope. Griff stares at us for a second before nodding and leading the way back to his cruiser.

As soon as we get there and Griff unlocks her cuffs, Sofie takes a deep breath and her chest rises and falls at a normal rate. I place her on the cruiser's rear bench, watching anxiously until her eyelashes flicker and her eyes open. When she looks at me, I find that I'm the one without breath. I tear off my oxygen mask to speak to her, but she silences me with the intensity of her gaze. She reaches up to touch my cheek, the lightest of caresses with the tips of her fingers. I swallow whatever I was going to say and simply look into her golden eyes, vowing never to let her go again.

"All right, you two," Griff says. "We're not out of the woods yet."

I turn to him, smiling like an idiot. Griff's got a strange, distant look on his face, as if he's gazing back over the eons since he last saw her.

The Prophet. He must have known her on Earth. And he never let on.

"Richard," Sofie says, her voice huskier than usual, probably from the gas. "I have no words to thank you."

Griff colors, red under red. "The contract we signed wasn't just for Earth. It was for all time."

I wait for him to say more, or for Sofie to say something else, but they both sit there staring at each other.

Uncomfortable silences. Not so much my thing.

"Griff's with the revolution?" I ask.

"He was one of our Upperworld operatives," Sofie says. "Cons Piracy put us in touch with him, and we were happy to add him to our team. As you can see, he possesses unsurpassed technical skills to go along with his . . . unique personality."

Griff guffaws. "Like I told Her Holiness back on Earth, no one suspects a total screwup like me. These corporation big shots, they figure anyone who's not as well-dressed or well-connected as them must be some kind of moron. So when Conroy tapped me to keep tabs on you, Cam"—and he nods my way—"he thought he was getting a carbon copy of my dutiful old dad. He didn't know he was getting a world-class double agent," he finishes with a laugh.

"Wait a minute," I say. "Was that then, or now?" It sounds stupid right out of my mouth, but space travel can mess up your sense of *then* and *now* in a major way.

Sofie laughs, the trill I first heard in New York. It's electric, being this close to her, the fight we had an hour ago seeming like it's vanished along with the mist. Her hand rests on mine, and when I put my other hand on top of hers, she doesn't pull away.

"It appears I missed quite a bit while I was sleeping," she says to Griff. "When did Chairman Conroy assign you to spy on your best friend?"

To my surprise, Griff doesn't answer. And his laughter, in fact his whole laughing face, goes dead like a light blinking out. He's staring at me and Sofie, and what replaces the laughter is an expression I can't remember seeing on him before, some combination of anger and distrust and malice that doesn't match the Griff I know.

"Hold on a second," he says, and sits at the *Maverick*'s controls. The vehicle springs to life under his touch, backing away from Conroy's cruiser. Griff guns the motor and speeds off as if he's at the wheel of an emergency vehicle, before slamming on the brakes and spinning sharply to face the CanAm cruiser. Through the screen, I see the Centurions scrambling away from the *Imperial,* taking up positions again on the *Freefall.* Griff half turns in his seat and shoots us a grin, but it's got that same ugly tinge to it.

To be honest, it scares the hell out of me.

"Did I mention that methoxypropane is highly flammable?" he says. "That's why it only has military applications these days. Not that it makes much difference. The firepower on this beauty would punch a hole in a starship. But you already knew that, didn't you, Cam?"

Sofie goes rigid at my side. In the second it takes her to leap to her feet, I've picked up on her horror and follow one step behind.

We're both too late.

The *Maverick*'s cannon booms, and Conroy's vehicle explodes in a ball of light. Ordinarily the atmosphere wouldn't hold the blaze for long, but there's enough flammable gas in the CanAm cruiser to produce a towering pillar of fire that shoots from the ground as if the planet is venting flame. Our own vehicle rocks from the blast, and through the *Maverick*'s viewscreen, I see blackened pieces of the *Imperial* raining down on the plateau. When the fire and smoke clear, there's nothing of Conroy's cruiser left to see, nothing but the black scorch mark it deposited on the spongy ground.

Sofie grabs my friend's shoulders and shakes him, hard.

"Richard!" she screams. "There was no need for those men to die!"

For a moment his face looks stricken, like a kid bawled out by his mom. But then he shoves her from him and stands, backing us away with his gun.

"I'm on my own orders now," he says. "Not Sumati's. Not Conroy's. *Mine.*"

His gun swivels, pointing straight at Sofie.

"Such a cozy pair," he says. "Why don't you tell Cam the real reason you let him tag along back on Earth?"

Sofie faces Griff with the same calm expression she showed

Conroy. "You cannot threaten me, Richard," she says. "You know that."

"No?" The gun twitches to the side, so it's on me. "What about now?"

Sofie's face changes. It's like the first time I saw her up close, back in the United Nations building: crouched under the table, her eyes wide, her cheeks covered with her teacher's blood.

"Richard," she says, and her voice shakes.

A searing pain shoots through my leg at the same moment I hear the buzz of Griff's gun. I fall to one knee, the muscles of my thigh cramping and quivering. I bite down on my tongue and taste blood. Through eyelids I can't seem to master, I see that Griff's face remains relentless.

"One shot for each lie," he says. "And that one was at the lowest setting. How many do you think he can take?"

"Richard," Sofie says quietly. "Please."

The next shot hits my other leg, and I'm slammed to the ground by the force of the charged particles. Sofie throws herself between me and Griff, her arms held out as if to protect me.

"If I shoot you at full power, he dies too," Griff says. "Now, why don't you tell him the truth, *Your Holiness*?"

Sofie looks back at me, and there's a haunted quality to her eyes. Then she kneels and bows her head. "Where do you want me to begin?"

"That's more like it," Griff says. "I'm thinking you should begin with the village."

And Sofie speaks, telling a story I've never heard before.

Otherworld

Earth Year 3151

Day

I was born in ExCon," she says. "My parents were high-placed officials there. Though they were native to SubCon, they had been recruited by corponational headhunters seeking local talent to track and apprehend radicals throughout the Lowerworld. Sometimes, when they discovered large pockets of resistance, they adopted more permanent methods to eliminate the threat." Her eyes lower, but not before I see the tears. "The village you visited was not mine. It was one of many similar places, one of many like those my parents ordered to be destroyed. Throughout my childhood, they toured such sites with me to inure me to their horrors. To groom me to take over their work when I came of age."

My body isn't entirely my own, but I force the words past my teeth. "You told me they made you a slave."

"They did," she says fiercely. "From the time I was old enough to speak, my parents arranged for me to be featured in worldlink promos for their campaign against the Lowerworld. Under their hands, I faced lenses and spoke of my hatred for my own kind, my thankfulness that I had been rescued from Terrarists. My mother and father made me a slave to the Upperworld as surely as any who labored in its mines or factories. The only difference was that I did not know what I was until I met Sumati. Until she set me free."

I remember Aakash saying something similar, and I know what Sofie means. I know it because the same thing happened to me when I met *her*. But how could I have been set free by a lie? "Did Aakash know?"

"None but Sumati knew my past," Sofie says. "And she knew how dangerous it could be to the movement if others found out. She gave me a name and an identity that she hoped would shield me from exposure, by my parents or anyone else."

"Are they here?" I say quietly. "Were they chosen for the colonization?"

She shakes her head. "When they failed to recover me, their superiors determined that they were too great a security risk. Sumati offered to help me find them, but by the time we made the attempt, it was too late."

A silence hangs over us, heavy with ghosts. It's only when Griff prods her with his pistol that she speaks again.

"In the second half of the year 2150," she says, "we had put out a call to our Upperworld operatives for a—a recruit. To help us with a new initiative we had developed as the date for the starships' departure approached."

"An 'instrument for accelerating revolutionary imperatives' were your exact words," Griff throws in.

"I know what our words were, Richard," Sofie snaps.

"Careful," he says, flourishing the gun.

Sofie takes a deep breath before resuming. "The revolution's spread had become a matter of great concern to the Upperworld by this time, and there was talk of diplomacy to address the Lowerworld's grievances. But we feared that such talk was little more than a stalling tactic, that the most we could expect was more wrangling and delay. It was our hope that a well-placed Upperworlder, new to the revolution, could help us secure representation on the JIPOC starships in the desperately short time that was left to us. Richard was the first to provide a referral."

"I started by trying to recruit Adrian," Griff says. "Because of his dad. But I realized ten seconds after I conned him into watching the first video that he was a lost cause. Then I saw how you responded to the hacked feed. You were exactly what the revolution was looking for: young, impressionable, extremely well-connected. And it didn't hurt that you were obviously gaga for Sumati's protégé."

The pain in my legs has subsided, but the pain everywhere else in my body, starting with my heart, is growing. "New York CITI was a setup," I say.

Griff grins.

"Was Sumati supposed to die?"

The grin falls. "I had nothing to do with that. You were supposed to meet Sofie, that's all. The Upperworld saw their chance to silence the revolution's leaders and took it. I can program Terra Tanks, but I can't stop bullets."

There's another long silence after that little gem. Sofie smoothes her robe with shaking hands before speaking.

"New York CITI changed everything," she says. "Prior to that point, I had been the public face of the revolution: the one to make speeches, rally the crowds, supply the photo opportunities Sumati no longer possessed the energy to provide—"

"Or the looks," Griff says. "Can't forget that."

Sofie glares at him but goes on. "Because of my childhood experience on the worldlink, managing the symbolic side of the revolution had been my duty from the moment Sumati won me to the Lowerworld cause. I was her disciple and her successor, yes, but in private she confided to me that I must also be her younger self, the image she could no longer project. But with her assassination, I was thrust into the role of revolutionary leader. I did not believe I was ready for such a responsibility, but there was no one else, and there was no time to train another. And when the members of my team complained that you were not progressing rapidly enough, Cam—"

"That you weren't being brainwashed fast enough, she means," Griff adds.

"—it was decided that some more extreme measure was needed to bring you along. I remembered my own first visit to a targeted village when I was a child, before I became hardened to what I saw there. I felt that seeing such a place might have a similar effect on you. But I could not tell you, Cam. If you had known the truth about the village, about me, you would never have agreed to help our cause."

"You don't know that," I say.

"I feared it," she says in a voice that's barely a whisper. "I had promised so much to so many, and I feared what would happen if they felt I had deceived them."

"So you lied to *me* instead."

She nods, huddled in her purple robe. Her face is a mess, cheeks splotchy and eyeliner smudged in black streaks. She looks so unlike the girl who stood up to Peace Corp. soldiers and worldlink adjournalists and corponational CEOs, the girl who shouted defiance from Upperworld stages and Lowerworld scaffolds, who faced death a hundred times a day. Was that Sofie nothing but an act? All the stories, the speeches, the prayers? Could she have been so perfect an actor that her lies felt like they'd opened up a new, truer world for me? And not just me. Could she have been so convincing that she'd dazzled Aakash and the rest of her team and billions of the world's people into throwing their lives into the cause?

And what about the other Sofie? The one who held my hands, touched my face, kissed me the night of the interview? The one who'd smiled at me minutes before Griff pulled out his gun. Was that Sofie an act too? Was she doing what she did only because it made great video, pumped up the crowd, achieved revolutionary imperatives?

Lying there on the floor of the SubCon cruiser, with the girl I thought I knew sobbing beside me and my legs twitching from the ion discharge and my former second-best friend pointing a gun at my head, I find that I can forgive all the lies except one. I don't need to know everything about the revolution and the corners its leaders cut to succeed in a cause I fundamentally believe is right. But there's one thing I do need to know, and I don't give a damn if Griff hears me ask it.

"Did you love me?" I say. "Or was that all in my head too?"

She looks pleadingly at Griff through a face smeared with tears. He waves his gun at me. "No lies, Your Holiness," he says.

Even with the threat of the gun, it's a long time before she answers. When she does, it honestly sounds like she's reading from a script.

"I was not meant for love," she says. "That is what I told myself when I took the bindi as a pledge of my devotion to the Lowerworld. I had given my all in atonement for my sins, and I believed I was meant to preach of love, not to know it myself. To risk my life for the many, not to risk my own heart."

She's quiet for another long spell, and out of the corner of my eye I see that Griff's getting edgy, shifting from foot to foot and adjusting his grip on the gun. But I focus on Sofie, and when she speaks again, it's in a voice so laden with sadness I can't believe she's speaking a lie.

"Love is selfish, Cam," she says. "You say you have never asked me to betray my people, and I know you would not do so willingly. But the night I kissed you, the seeds of betrayal were sown. On that night, I came close to sacrificing the dreams of a whole world to the one tiny dream of an unworthy heart."

She shakes her head, and seems to collapse into herself.

"I thought to love you once," she says. "But I know what it means to live in thrall to hatred, and I cannot allow myself to live in thrall to love. That is why I could not join myself with you on Earth, and why I cannot join myself with you on any other world. I am sorry."

Her head drops to her knees, and her sobs fill the void left by her final words. Griff lets out a mocking laugh, the hand holding the gun waving back and forth in the air as if he's playing a violin.

"You two are breaking my heart," he says. "And now, Your Holiness, you're coming with me."

She rises like a sleepwalker, lets Griff put his hand on her arm to steer her away from me. When I try to stand, he points the gun at me and releases a short burst that sizzles the floor at my feet. "Where are you taking her?" I ask.

"Her Holiness is about to receive a lesson in revolutionary exigency," he says. "She's going to leave you here, and then she's going to come with me so we can watch my Terra Tanks burn the *Executor* to the ground. But not before she gives another of her pretty little speeches to the fat cats cowering inside that luxury liner of a ship."

"Richard," Sofie says, but her voice is so dull it's lost the capacity to plead.

"Or you can stay with Cam, and I can order the Tanks to destroy every pod aboard the *Freefall*, just like Conroy wanted," he says. "How about we do that instead?"

She lowers her head, blinking away tears.

"I thought you'd see it my way," Griff says. He smiles, and I wonder why his smile looks so strange. "Now say good night, lover boy."

His visor lowers over his face. The air I gulp tastes sweet and stale. I fumble to stand, but my motions are slow and uncoordinated. Sofie freezes, her eyes closing, her breath leveling. I assume she's going into hibernation to escape the gas.

My last thought is that I wish she'd taught me that, too.

Otherworld

Earth Year 3151

Night

H ey, buddy."

I'm lying in darkness on something soft. The air's freezing cold, but there's a trace of warmth left from my own body. For a second I'm back in bed on Earth, my dad stooping over me to wake me up for Pre-Classification. That's what he used to say to me when I was a kid: *Hey, buddy.* Before he got too big to pay attention to me. Before I got too big to pay attention to anything.

"Earth to Cam. Do you read me, Cam?"

There's a laugh, not my dad's. A beeping sound. Red light parts the darkness behind my eyelids. The cold makes me shiver.

I open my eyes.

A bright red glow floods my vision. It's too much for me after the darkness, and I squint against the glare. My brain feels like rubber. I try to concentrate and realize I'm lying on spongy rock. In fact, I'm surrounded by rock, top to bottom and all around. My breath rasps, the air on my face feeling hot and sticky. I reach up and find I'm wearing an oxygen mask. The surrounding air is absolutely frigid. The best I can figure is that I'm outside in the planetary night, though why I'm hemmed in by rock doesn't quite compute.

The red light, it dawns on me, has a point of origin: a flare, the electronic kind that needs no oxygen to burn. It waves in front of my eyes, tracing squiggles that make me dizzy. Finally, it stops moving and I'm able to lock in on the one who's holding it.

Griff.

"How're you feeling, buddy?" he says when he sees me looking at him. His words fog the inside of his own mask, and he's wearing the oversize helmet, except the visor's up so I can see his eyes. "You okay?"

"I feel like shit," I say, which is true on many, many levels.

"Just breathe deep," he says. "You walked all the way down here in a semiconscious state. Good thing too, because I sure as hell couldn't haul your fat ass." He laughs. "The oxygen will clear away the effects of the anesthesia in a few minutes."

I do as he says, breathing deeply, the cobwebs thinning. My legs ache, but not so bad I can't move them. When I'm strong enough to sit, I push myself up from the ground to face him.

"Where's Sofie?" I ask.

His face twists. "You don't need to worry about her anymore."

"What did you do with her, Griff?"

He throws himself to his feet. We're in some kind of cavern, not much taller than he is. The red light casts his shadow against the walls, fading in and out as the flare blinks in his hand.

"We all know what *you* did with her," he says. "So let's not talk about me, okay?"

He laughs, though not the laugh of my old friend. The harsh sound echoes in the enclosed space, making my head hurt all over again. I've oriented myself enough to our surroundings to be sure we're underground, which explains the freezing air. For the first time, I notice tunnels branching off from the main cavern, too dark to see down. And I also notice the deep scratches that run through the spongy rock at my feet, their edges illuminated by the red light. Gashes like scratch marks from something heavy and metal dragging itself across the stone.

Like tracks.

"God, Griff," I say. "What have you done?"

He returns to the place where he was sitting. This time he's got his gun out, pointing straight at me. His face is placid again, even friendly.

"It's all right," he says, gesturing toward the rear of the cavern. "It's quick. Adrian went quick."

I take a glance at the dark shape he's pointing at, then look away, bile rising in my throat.

"On the plus side, our good buddy learned some humility before the end," Griff says. "It was quite a breath of fresh air, watching the great Adrian Conroy beg for his life."

He smiles, looking so much like the old Griff I can almost convince myself that everything that happened on the *Maverick*, everything that's happening right now, is a crazy joke, or maybe a nightmare, that the real Griff is going to jump out of this imposter's skin and have a good laugh for scaring the shit out of me. But then he starts talking again, and if I weren't already freezing, his words would chill me to the bone.

"I gained access to the starships by hacking into my dad's program," he says. "Dumped a buttload of extra stuff into the *Executor*'s code while I was at it, made sure it would arrive with all its systems trashed. Reprogrammed its Centurions, too, so they'd go after the *Executor*. That was hard, and I had no idea they'd react to the sunlight and the sonic devices. It's taken me all this time to get them back to where I wanted them. Conroy even managed to regain control of one—temporarily, anyway."

He lets out the ugly laugh, then reaches into the pocket of his jumpsuit and produces what looks like a selfone. He stares at it a long time before raising his eyes to mine. "I ever tell you about my mom?"

I take the phone. The screen shows a woman, late twenties. But if I'm expecting her to look anything like Griff, I'm disappointed. She's got jet-black hair, dark eyes, petite features. "She was—"

"From MicroNasia, yeah."

"I was about to say she was beautiful."

Griff looks at me as if he's momentarily disarmed, then his face hardens into a scowl. "For all the good it did her. I could show you how she died." He points at the phone. "Apparently it was a big hit back in the day. A real crowd-pleaser."

He reaches for the phone, glances at it before shoving it into his pocket. Then he lets out a hard breath that steams his mask.

"She was one of Sumati's earliest supporters," he says. "Helped get the movement off the ground. But thanks to Her Current Holiness's parents, the Peace Corp. tracked her down and tortured her. For names. And when she wouldn't give them what they wanted, they killed her."

"God, Griff," I say. "I never knew."

He looks at me resentfully. "No one did. Not even me. I was too young to realize what was going on, and my dad never told me."

"Was he with Sumati too?"

"That's a laugh," Griff says, making a sound that's anything but. "When my mom was caught, you know what Richie Rich did?"

I don't answer. I'm pretty sure I don't need to.

And I'm right. "I got the whole story from Cons Piracy," Griff says. "Imagine my surprise when I discovered I was born in MicroNasia, but, after my mom was killed, my dad found some guy in the Upperworld who was known for erasing people's pasts. Changing their appearance." He waves a hand around his face. "This guy helped me and my dad move to CanAm, got him a job working on starships. They didn't know about my mom. And when Conroy ordered my dad to reprogram the *Freefall* and turn his dead wife's people into monsters, the son of a bitch did exactly what the chairman wanted."

He swipes at his eyes above the oxygen mask, his motions so violent it's as if he's trying to gouge the tears from his face.

"So, anyway," he says after he's given up trying. "The Upperworld needed to be taught a lesson. That's why, when I programmed the *Executor* to land on this shit hole, I made sure the *Freefall* would arrive right after. Give the filthy-rich bastards a chance to sweat it out, see what it's like to have less than nothing, and then have to go crawling to the Lowerworld, begging for a handout. And on top of that, have the Prophet spit their words back in their face." He laughs, that short, ugly bark. "Exactly the kind of revenge she was talking about back on Earth."

I can't keep quiet any longer. "Were you listening to her, man? She's been talking about *justice*, not revenge."

"Revenge *is* justice," he says. "Turning the tables. Sun orbiting moon. Take what's theirs, leave them to fight over scraps, and then burn the whole goddamn place to the ground. That's what she said."

I try to remember Sofie saying anything like that, but I can't, not in all the time I traveled with her. "She never said—"

"You weren't listening!" Griff shouts, his face contorted with anger. "The *destruction* of the old world. The walls of wealth *falling down*. She laid it all out that day in New York CITI, man, and it was *great*. The top was going to come crashing to the ground, and the bottom was going to rise up and take what was theirs."

He shakes his head, the flame in his face instantly dying. Where a second ago he was raving, now he's breathing heavily, looking old and vulnerable and sad. None of this is like the Griff I knew. The Griff I never knew.

"But she didn't keep her promise," he says. "As soon as you joined up, she started talking about *peaceful reconciliation* between Upperworld and Lowerworld. All that hearts and flowers crap she spouted in the interview. It wasn't bad enough you violated her body. You infected her *mind*, man!" he shouts, the vehemence jumping into his voice again. Then he continues more quietly, as if he's trying to reason with me. "She lost her way when she fell for you, Cam. I knew I had to bring her back to the light. I kept you alive all this time so I could test her. And I think you saw today that she's on her way back."

Even with the numbing cold and my dizziness from the gas, it doesn't take long to put the pieces together. Griff had been tracking me after touchdown as he had on Earth, and when he realized my pod was missing, it was him, not Adrian, who chased off the Centurion that first night. He was the one who programmed the homing device to get me into the *Freefall*, who arranged for the *Maverick* to take me to Conroy's quarters. Could he have been the one who made sure Sofie didn't die when her deepsleep was shut off? Or was his plan almost ruined when Conroy gained temporary control over the single Centurion? But when she did survive, he brought the cruiser back to the *Freefall* so he could see if the girl whose parents had killed his mother was willing to carry out his design. If she was willing to make a choice.

Kill me, along with all the people aboard the *Executor*. Or save me, and watch her own people die.

JOSHUA DAVID BELLIN

I don't blame her for the choice she made.

I think about the times Griff and I used to talk, on Earth and on this planet. The stuff I told him about my days with Sofie, the accusations I leveled at Chairman Conroy and his son. Griff drank it all in, the way he'd drunk in Sofie's speeches back home. And he'd used it to carry us to this cold, lonely place where love and hate and justice and revenge were one and the same, where the only way things could end was with the end of everything.

"I'm sorry, man," I say. "I'm sorry I wasn't there for you."

Griff's eyes widen, and for a second I see my old friend, the goofy kid who made so much fun of himself none of the rest of us noticed how much anger and grief he was carrying around. He stands and reaches out as if he's about to take my hand, but he lets just the tips of his fingers rest for a second on my head, like a blessing or, more likely, a good-bye.

Yes, that's it. A good-bye.

"I'm sorry too, Cam." He holsters the gun, shoves the flare in his belt. "I wish it didn't have to be you."

He's on his way out when I call after him.

"What's going to happen to Sofie?"

He stops and half turns, refusing to look me in the eye. "I told you. She's coming with me to the *Executor*. And she's going to prove to me she meant what she said."

"Don't hurt her, Griff," I say. "I'm asking you as a friend. Please."

I see the tension in his face before he speaks. Anger and

love fighting for the upper hand. And I see which one wins.

"She'll return to the true path, or she'll suffer like the others," he says. "Don't try to follow me."

Then he disappears down one of the stone tunnels, vanishing in a pool of light as red as blood.

As soon as he's gone, I stand, thankful my legs will hold me. In the utter darkness, I quickly review my options. There are exactly two, and they both lead to the same outcome. I could follow Griff, but he'd zap me again and leave me for his Terra Tanks to finish. Or I could stay right here and try to fight them off, but without light and without weapons, I don't stand a chance.

I'm alone. I can hear them clacking and rattling toward me. And there's nowhere to hide.

Otherworld

Earth Year 3151

Night

I see their eyes first.

Yellow disks suspended two meters above the cavern floor, glowing too weakly to reveal the creatures they belong to. Six eyes total. They swivel back and forth as the Centurions approach.

Tracking me. Hunting me.

It's too dark to see anything except the eyes, but I feel along the wall, searching for some means of escape, finding none. Not that it would do me any good. Where would I go? Running from them in their lair would only make me more lost. And reaching the surface would only make me a sitting duck for the light of the planetary day.

Griff had all the time in the world to plan my death. He wasn't about to screw it up.

These thoughts pass through my mind with a strange unreality, as if I'm watching the impending death and dismemberment of someone else. On the worldlink, maybe. As if the real me is some*where* else.

And, in a sense, it is.

I'm with Sofie. In the *Maverick*, the last time I saw her, the last time I ever will. I see her face, hear her voice speaking my name. I guess impending death and dismemberment make you a philosopher, because I've forgiven her everything. How can I blame her for being afraid? My only regret is that I wasted so much time finding out the truth. An eternity without her yawns ahead, and I wish I'd known earlier that she did dream of loving me, even if she couldn't bring herself to let her dream grow. I could have lived in that knowledge. I could have died in it too.

In fact, I'm about to.

But another thought snaps me out of my reverie. Griff's heading back to wherever he left her. In the *Maverick*, probably. Or, worse, down here, somewhere in the labyrinth of tunnels, surrounded by his mechanical pets. He'll free her only when she agrees to preach his message of hate. If she submits, his tanks will tear the *Executor* apart. If she refuses, they'll do the same to the *Freefall*. Now that I think of it, even if she does what he asks, will Griff allow the *Freefall* to survive? If the *Executor's* as bad off as Conroy said, the Lowerworld ship is the only hope for the human race. Leaving it intact would deny Griff what he seems to want, what he's wanted since he discovered the truth about his mom's death: the death of everyone, Sofie included.

I might not survive another day, another hour, another minute. But I've got to try to survive long enough to stop him.

The yellow eyes are a few meters away. I hear the knife sound of their limbs scraping against the rock. My fingers find an opening in the cavern wall, one of the tunnels I saw in the red light of Griff's flare. It's much narrower than the cavern I'm standing in, almost too tight for me to squeeze into. I don't know if it leads anywhere. But it's the only escape route I've got.

I wedge myself inside. My head bumps the ceiling, forcing me to crouch to back up any farther. I can't see anything, can't tell if the tunnel's about to come to an end. I wriggle backward, rock tightening around me, adding claustrophobia to the list of things that make my head hurt. I'm sure the creatures know where I've gone. All I can do is hope they won't be able to follow.

The tunnel bends, and I barely squeeze through by sucking in my stomach and turning my face sideways. But not before I see the first pair of yellow eyes hovering outside.

There's the scraping sound. The shriek of metal against stone. The tunnel shudders, dust and flakes of rock falling from the ceiling. I'm crammed inside so tightly, my whole body vibrates as the creature hammers against the rock, determining if it can break through. There's a pause when it must realize it can't.

Then something else.

A whistling sound reaches me, followed by an explosion of light and noise. I'm thrown backward, my head slamming the floor. I can't see anything, but I can hear the tunnel collapsing, rock scraping and squealing against rock, fragments flying loose to strike my face. I crab-walk away from the falling debris, so afraid of being crushed it doesn't instantly register that I'm no longer squeezed between narrow walls. When the floor stops shaking and the noise subsides, I stand and find myself free to move.

I still can't see anything. But I must have made my way through to a larger cavern or tunnel. Just in time. Just before the Centurions under Griff's command decided to save energy and expensive biomechanical appendages by bringing the tunnel down on my head.

I touch the wall of collapsed stone in front of me. It'll take them forever to force their way through. If their human leader even thinks I'm alive. Which, if he was watching the cave-in through their optic lenses, he'd have to be a fool to.

For now, I'm safe.

But I still have no idea where I am.

And I have no idea how to find Sofie.

Otherworld

Earth Year 3151

Night

stumble through the tunnels in utter darkness. That's pretty much the state of my soul, too.

How Griff learned so much about this planet is one more thing I'll never know about my former second-best friend. He didn't know everything, didn't expect the high level of radiation to affect his Terra Tanks. But he knew enough. He knew about the tunnels that snake beneath the unstable crust, knew the route to walk me down here, knew the way out. And he must also have known I'd never find Sofie without him.

The place is a maze. I walk with my fingers against the spongy rock, but without any source of light, I can't tell where I'm going. And without any weapon, I've got nothing to fight with if another of the creatures happens to find me.

Which it does.

I hear its rattle before I feel its presence. Its yellow eyes blink into being out of darkness. I have no clue if this is one of the creatures I thought I escaped or a new one. But it makes no difference. I can't determine the tunnel's circumference at this point, but with my luck, the thing will be able to follow wherever I go.

I run anyway.

The tunnel's apparently not quite wide enough for my pursuer to move with its unearthly surface speed, which is all that saves me from being instant lunch meat. But it's right behind me, rattling in my ear. I can't risk a look back, not that there's anything to see. I'm running blind, in danger of slamming into a wall or cracking my head on the ceiling. But I keep running, because Sofie's somewhere up ahead and the beast is behind. If I slow for a second, the death of the human race is about to begin, starting with me and her.

All at once the pitch-black tunnel explodes with white light, and the creature behind me screams. In the momentary brightness I see one of its six arms flailing toward a startled face, a face covered with freckles, topped by a helmet like a giant gray mushroom. A face I've known all my life.

Griff's face.

Our tunnels must have intersected, but in the darkness and confusion he didn't realize how close we were. When he fired at me, he hit his own creature instead. And the last time he used the gun, it was set to stun a human being, not kill a metal monster.

From the sounds it's making, it's none too happy to be fired at anyway.

The Centurion's metallic claws scrabble against stone. It's on its feet. But it doesn't go for me.

It goes for the one who shot it.

The gun flashes again, and I see Griff's face illuminated in the brief glow, his eyes wide in terror, his mouth open in a scream. Spit glistens inside his oxygen mask, but the helmet that controls his creatures must have been knocked loose. I catch a glimpse of red hair before the monster slams into him, its body invisible as a gust of wind in the blackness. Griff screams again, and I think he's calling my name.

If I could find him, put my hands on his gun, would I save him? Would the gun let me use it, or is it another of the toys Griff programmed to serve only him?

I think I'd save him, if I could.

But I can't. There's a final, choked scream and a wet ripping sound, and then silence except for the heavy rattle of the victor. A wave of nausea washes over me, replaced by an unspeakable sadness at the loss of a friend I knew for over a thousand years. I can still remember the day I met Griff, practically the first memory I have.

Come to think of it, it might also be the last.

The creature wheels to face me. Yellow eyes glow. There's the sound of knives scraping. The chatter of the machinery that drives it.

I've nearly used up all my prayers, but I send out a quick one for Sofie's life. Maybe she can find a way out. With Griff dead, maybe the Centurions won't be able to attack. If she can make it to the *Freefall*, she'll live as long as anyone can on this planet—long enough, I hope, to figure out a way to deal with whoever takes Conroy's place. She'll never know what I tried to do—she'll never find my body if she looks for it—but I'll know. For the last few seconds of my life, I'll know.

"What are you waiting for?" I say to the thing.

Bad question.

It leans in close, rattling. My eyes burn from whatever drips from its syringe.

They burn so bad they play tricks on me.

A red light appears in the absolute darkness behind the optic disks, a concentrated dot hovering a meter and a half above the floor. It's not a flare, not strong enough to illuminate anything around it. It's more like the point of a laser scope on its target. With one exception: It pulses slowly, as if responding to the beat of a heart.

The creature's optic disks swivel toward the red light. Its rattle softens, lowering into something like a purr. I can tell it's about to spring.

Then white light envelops it, showing me its poised claws, its pale humanoid innards. It shrieks and spins to escape the beam, but there's not enough room for it to get away. The light hits it again, and it staggers, one of its legs collapsing under it. Another shot and I can see the creature inside the metal shell bubbling with the power of the beam. The Centurion lurches to its feet, tries to lunge at its attacker, falls again. This time, it doesn't rise. The heat of the ion discharge pervades the icy darkness of the chamber.

I stare into the gloom, trying to see. The after-effects of the light make shadows jump unnaturally before my eyes, and I can't tell if I'm seeing anything real or only the visions in my own head. Then hands touch my shoulders, and the red light shines right in front of me. I'm surrounded by the fragrance of incense and roses.

Soft lips press against my cheek, and the hum of her voice sounds in my ear.

"Cam," Sofie whispers. "Let us leave this place of death."

Otherworld

Earth Year 3151

Day

Hours pass without a glimpse of light. But Sofie's hand never leaves mine, so I'm not complaining.

There's no sign of Griff's Terra Tanks as we make our way through the underground lair. Either the surviving ones can't find their way around now that their operator's dead, or they got buried in the cave-in they caused. Whatever, we're alone, which I'm thankful for. I was really starting to get tired of my best friends trying to kill me.

Sofie has one major advantage over me down here in the dark: Her biofeedback techniques prevented the gas from muddying her mind, so she remained fully alert when Griff walked her into his trap. But he doesn't seem to have known that, because he used a flashlight to guide himself and made no effort to disguise his trail by doubling back or anything. Her memory's sharp enough that she can remember the paces and turns she took from the *Maverick* to the place Griff left her, the place Griff died.

I let her guide me. That feels as natural now as it did on Earth.

Light eventually appears, glowing faintly from a great distance. We've been belowground all night. We pick up the pace now that both of us can see where we're going. Sofie's anxious to get to the ship, to see if anyone's woken up or if Griff's army has acted in its leader's absence. I'm with her, though without radiation suits, I'm not sure how we're going to make the hike to the *Freefall* in daylight.

As usual, I'm worried about the wrong thing.

We reach the end of the tunnel to discover that the exit sits directly beneath the *Freefall*'s prow, blanketing us in shadow. That makes sense: Why would Griff waste time driving or walking us to another of his creatures' hiding places if he had one nearby? The problem is, the *Freefall*'s not the only thing at the end of the tunnel.

The Centurions are there too.

Fifty of them at least, all but the few that went into the tunnels with us. If I was wondering whether they could function without Griff, I have my answer: They crawl across the ship, moving in a rigid pattern of straight lines and sharp turns that makes me think they're on some kind of auto-program. Whether that program includes the command to shoot anything that moves, I can't say. The one in the tunnel was about to attack me and Sofie before she used Griff's gun against it, so it seems they can respond to threats without a human operator. But the gun won't work against fifty of them. And the only way

I have of finding out the limits of their programming doesn't exactly thrill me.

Still, it is the only way.

I face Sofie. In the half-light beneath the ship, I can see what a toll the night has taken on her. Her robe's torn and dirtied, her cheeks grimed, her eyes red with exhaustion. She's wearing the oxygen mask Griff supplied to keep her alive belowground, and through the fogged plastic, I see her smile.

Maybe it's her smile that makes time freeze, then reverse. I'm back in the Lowerworld, listening to her tell her stories. I hear the murmur of the audience, see the flicker of the lamplight. The girl beside me might not be everything I thought she was, but she's still the girl who showed me what it means to live.

And I think I understand the part of the story I didn't get then. Not the great god. Not his bride. Not the flower.

The wise man.

I know what I have to do.

"I'm going out there," I say. "If the Centurions attack, you stay put. I'll try to draw some of them off so you can make it to the ship."

"Much has changed in the past thousand years," she says, "if I must hide in the shadows while others risk their lives for the cause."

She's still smiling. But I decide to go for broke.

"Some things haven't changed in the past thousand years," I say. "I love you, Sofie. I've loved you from the moment I saw you. You have to let me do this."

"Cam." Her voice is husky, a whisper. A single tear brightens in the corner of her eye, but she makes no move to wipe it away. "You would do this for me? After everything I told you?"

"I would do anything for you," I say. I remember saying it before, that drunken night in her helicar, and I don't know if I meant it then, but I know I mean it now. "The revolution needs you, Sofie. More than ever. If you die, who'll lead them?"

"Cam," she says again. Her hand rises to touch my cheek. I assume it's a parting gesture, and I'm about to say something to acknowledge my appreciation, though I'm not sure what. Maybe only her name. But then her fingers gently pull my mask down, and before I can ask her what in the world(s) she's doing, she tilts her face upward, and her mask is gone too and her lips melt into mine.

We haven't kissed in a millennium, but it feels as if no time at all has passed since the first time, as if everything that's brought us closer or driven us apart in the eons that stand between then and now doesn't matter anymore. Never mattered to begin with. The kiss lasts approximately another millennium, and I'm thinking this is one hell of a parting gesture and trying to figure out whether I should be the one to end it when she pulls me closer, pressing herself against me as if she could fuse our two bodies into one. I'm starving for oxygen but deciding that no matter how long this lasts, the warmth of her breath is much better than breathing, and I've resigned myself to never taking another breath in my life when I realize she's crying for real, the taste of her tears tangy on my lips. I pull back to see her golden eyes, fixed on me with the look I remember so well. She can't have any breath left either, but she smiles at me and speaks.

"We will go together," she says. "And whatever happens, we will face it as one."

I'm about to object when she closes my mouth with a final kiss and then lifts the mask to my face. I breathe in, and I was right: There's no comparison between the thing that keeps you alive and the thing that gives you a reason to live. Trust me, even if it's only for a few seconds, you should choose the latter.

We step out into the shadow of the *Freefall*. The Centurions react instantly to our presence, halting in their tracks and scuttling off the ship. A thin squealing reaches my ears, far less noise than they'd produce in Earth's atmosphere, as their missiles lock onto the two human beings foolish enough to confront them.

I guess I have my answer to that question too.

Sofie doesn't budge, doesn't try to run. Instead, she calmly raises her hands in the gesture she used in all the videos and all the rallies on Earth. Only this time her left hand is linked with my right, and the two of us stand there, hands held high. I feel her life force flow into me the instant before both of us die. Personally, I could care less about that. I'd rather die now, holding the hand of the girl I love, than live long enough for her to let go.

The Centurions prepare to fire.

I'm about to get my wish.

There's a brief burst of flame, doused instantly as it con-
sumes the scant supply of oxygen. It's followed by another
explosion, and another. I throw myself in front of Sofie, as if
I could block a missile. But we're still alive, our hands linked,
our bodies untouched. It takes me a minute to realize what's
going on.

Three of the Centurions have been reduced to scrap.

They're firing on each other.

"What's happening?" I shout above the roar of another
explosion. Sofie shakes her head, her eyes wide with wonder.

The Centurions are firing nonstop, their missiles aimed at
whichever of their number is the closest target, each machine
consuming one or more of its companions before disappearing
in its own ball of flame. Several of the creatures retreat from
the field of battle, but not to go after us—instead, they fling
themselves into the abyss beneath the *Freefall*, too deep for
me to hear them hit bottom. Some go up in flames without
anything striking them, which must mean they've got an auto-
destruct. Others plunge claws into their own bodies, toppling
to the ground with their biomechanical innards torn free. It's
a totally bloodless battle, though the ones who've eviscerated
themselves ooze a dark fluid that soaks into the spongy stone.
And it's over in a matter of minutes, the field entirely cleared of
everything except scorched remains and broken bodies.

Sofie and I step out into the carnage. We're still holding
hands—clutching them as tightly as possible, to be exact—
though we're no longer raising them in the victory gesture.

Maybe, with the Centurions decimated, we should be.

Or, then again, maybe we should keep them right where they are.

A military cruiser rolls into the shadow of the *Freefall*. Its logo has been painted over, leaving a gray square on its night-black side. I'm half-convinced my eyes deceived me before and the cruiser was the one that fired on the Centurions. Except its cannon is retracted, and something waves from the space where the muzzle would be.

A white flag.

"Surrender," Sofie says. "They surrender."

"To who?"

The cruiser stops a few paces in front of us. Its door opens, and two people climb out, wearing oxygen masks but not the JIPOC uniforms and military-style helmets of Conroy's goon squad. Grown-ups, not the teenage guards I expected. They take a step forward, and I see that their hands are linked like Sofie's and mine.

I know them.

I've known them all my life.

The tall man with salt-and-pepper bristles and a dark gray business suit looks a lot like me, or so everyone says. There's one picture of us playing catch where, if you took away the suit, he could even pass for an older version of the renowned Cam Newell. Except in that picture I must have been all of four, with my oversize plastic mitt and my maroon-and-gold CanAm Clippers T-shirt reaching practically to my knees.

The other person is a woman, small and with long blond hair pulled back in a loose bun. Like her husband, she's wearing the attire that never left her body on Earth: a white lab coat with her name stitched on the pocket, a pair of glasses strung around her neck. Her eyes are brown like mine, and thanks to medical nanotechnologies, they don't need the glasses. I always assumed she wore them because they made her look like the total brainiac she is.

I haven't seen either of them since I left Earth. I barely saw them the final year I lived there. They were busy, like all the grown-ups in my life. Busy in their office and lab, spending days and nights outfitting the ships and perfecting the technologies that were supposed to save us for the long years of our interstellar flight. Our most recent communication made it pretty clear they wished they'd never wasted their time saving me.

You can call them Samantha and Robert. Sam and Bob among friends, if they have any.

Me, I called them Mom and Dad.

Otherworld

Earth Year 3151

Day

I consider all the things I could say to them. Beginning with *Any luck renting out my room?* And *So what's it like helping an evil corponational dictator kill innocent people to save your own useless necks?* You know, conversation starters.

But my impeccable Upperworld grooming takes over. That and the fact that I don't want to come across as too much of a jerk in front of Sofie. And that I genuinely want to know what the two of them are doing here, driving a surrendered military cruiser onto a battlefield littered with the bodies of dead monsters.

So I go with something neutral. "Hi, Mom and Dad."

"Cam," my mom says in her soft voice. "How are you?"

Why do grown-ups always ask questions it would take a novel to answer? "I'm okay." Sofie gives my hand a squeeze, which reminds me of the required etiquette. "Mom, Dad, this is—"

"Sofie Patel," my dad says. "It's a pleasure to meet you at last."

That throws me. It throws Sofie, too, if her silence is any indication. All of a sudden I feel self-conscious holding her hand in front of my parents, which is fairly ridiculous considering what they've put me through. But Sofie picks up on the awkward vibe and, giving my hand one more squeeze, lets go. "Mr. and Mrs. Newell—"

"It's Park," my mom says, deciding to increase the awkwardness. "Data Recruitment Specialist Samantha Park. I prepped you for deepsleep, Sofie. So I suppose you could say we've already been introduced."

That's met with another silence. My mom was always much better with unconscious people.

"I'd like to suggest we continue this conversation inside," my dad cuts in. "Before the sun gets too high."

He leads us to the *Freefall*. An airlock's open. Old Bobbo does the thing corporational wheeler-dealers get really good at doing, ushering us ahead with one arm while he corrals us with the other. Kind of like a hug, except without the warmth, and with the primary purpose of showing who's in control. My dad, the smooth operator. What he and my mom ever had in common—other than helping out evil corporational dictators—is a mystery likely to outlast the ages.

"Let's find someplace quiet," he says. "We've got a lot to talk about."

Last time I was inside the Lowerworld starship, every place was someplace quiet. But not anymore. In the time we've been gone, the passengers of the *Freefall* have finally come out of deepsleep.

All half million of them.

Well, okay, I'm not actually counting. But for whatever reason—maybe something having to do with Griff's death, maybe nothing but random luck—the pods are behaving the way they were supposed to, and those who woke up first are busy clearing out the bay and waking up others. No sooner have we entered the ship than we walk smack into a crowd that spills from the pod bay into the corridors, multihued clothing and jewelry and skin colors swirling all around us. I'm not surprised by the attention Sofie gets, but I'm blown away to find that some of it spills over on me. People smile, pat my arm, touch their fingers to their foreheads in greeting or salute. Some smother me in hugs. One or two even bow, which is totally embarrassing, though not so embarrassing that I ask them to stop. I walk through the masses of the Lowerworld like a hero returning from war.

Sofie never leaves my side.

It takes a while, what with everyone wanting to touch us and chatter a few words I can't understand in our faces, but eventually we make our way through the mob and escape to the command center, the place where Conroy and Griff put us in chains. My dad acts like he's holding one of his infamous staff meetings, smiling at everyone as we settle into chairs and making small talk about nothing in particular. The man would probably comment on the weather if it wasn't the kind that can kill us. There's no conference table, so we end up sitting in a circle with our knees practically touching. The last thing he does before planting himself next to my mom is give my shoulder a fatherly squeeze. My good shoulder, fortunately.

Then he gets down to business.

"This isn't going to be easy," he says, leaning back and finding a way to look both me and Sofie in the eye at the same time. "With Chairman Conroy's decease, the chain of command has been broken, and the JIPOC board of directors hasn't authorized anyone to conduct business on behalf of the citizen-shareholders of the Otherworld Colonization Limited Partnership. In that respect, any decisions we arrive at today and moving forward aren't likely to be considered binding."

I shrug. Judging from this gobbledygook, our centuries-long voyage hasn't changed my dad one bit.

"Moreover," he says, "there are many aboard the *Executor* who would prefer to have nothing to do with the Lowerworld—"

"There's a shock," I cut in.

"Cam," Sofie says. My mom tilts her head and looks at the two of us, smiling faintly.

"And in the absence of clear guidelines"—my dad goes on as if I didn't say a word—"it's going to take some time to figure out how best to represent the interests of all parties. Everything's been thrown out of joint by the events of the past several weeks."

"Not to mention the past several hundred years," I say.

My dad looks blank.

"On Earth," I add. "You remember that place?"

"Cam," Sofie says again, and this time she sounds peeved. But frankly, so am I.

"You can go on talking like this is some kind of deep-space team-building retreat," I say to my dad. "But there are plenty of people on the *Freefall* who want nothing to do with the Upperworld, either. And with much better reason. Even if we had a rat's chance of surviving on this dump, whose *interests* do you think are going to win in the end?"

My mom's smile shifts. My dad clears his throat.

"It's not quite as dire as all that, Cam," he says. "Yes, we're still a world divided to a great extent. And yes, there's much work to do. But we're not the same people we were on Earth. The instinct to survive generally trumps ideology, and the passengers aboard the *Executor* are finally starting to realize that we're going to need to band together if we're to survive."

"Not according to their esteemed leader," I say.

"Pete Conroy was losing support before his decease," my dad says. "Which probably explains his ill-advised attempt to take the *Freefall*. The *Executor* is dying, Cam. Leave aside the loss of functionality in-flight, it was critically compromised in the assault that recovered Miss Patel. That attack not only inflicted severe damage on the vessel itself, but destabilized the underlying terrain to the point where the entire ship might simply be swallowed. For the Upperworld right now, it's literally a matter of life and death." He smiles, and for once it doesn't look like he's pretending to make nice with his peons. "And no, it wouldn't surprise me at all to learn of the Lowerworld's distrust of Upperworld motivations."

He nods at my mom, who reaches into the pocket of her lab coat and takes out a small object. When she holds it up between her thumb and forefinger, I realize it's a red jewel, the same kind Sofie's wearing. My heart lurches sideways as the gem catches the light.

"We were followers of Sumati's in the early days of her movement," my mom says to me, and the hunk of muscle thumping inside my chest lurches even more. "I grew up in MicroNasia, before my parents were transferred to SubCon. That's where I met your father, Cam."

I lean forward in my seat, eyeing the jewel as calmly as my out-of-control heart will allow. This is all news to me.

"I accepted my first corporational post working for the SubCon Division of Data Recruitment," my mom continues. "It's where I did the basic research for deepsleep, which had become a top priority as the colonization effort picked up steam. Everyone in the Upperworld was looking exclusively to modifications and enhancements of bodily processes, but I'd discovered mystics in SubCon with the ability to enter dreamstates where the brain effectively convinced the body to shut down, and I thought we might start there before turning to nanotechnologies. My research led me to Sumati. She became my teacher, and I became a recruit to her cause."

I feel like I'm hearing the voice of a ghost, or of someone who died a millennium ago and was reborn as this complete stranger in front of me. "You didn't think I should know any of this?"

"We felt the knowledge could put you at risk," my dad says. "After your mother was recruited to complete her research in the Upperworld, I relocated with her to CanAm, where we were married. My job as vice president of operations for Otherworld Colonization put me in a perfect position to work for Sumati behind the scenes, placing members of the revolutionary movement in sensitive areas within JIPOC. I helped them emigrate to the Upperworld, cloaked their genetic histories, altered their identities when necessary. It was dangerous work, and we thought you'd be safer if you knew nothing about it."

"Griff's dad," I say. "You were the one who brought him and Griff here."

My dad nods. "I also arranged for the work that was done on Sofie's personal file. Sumati knew by then that she had few years to live, and she considered it her top priority to find a replacement." He smiles at Sofie. "She was quite insistent that it be you."

Sofie sits silently by my side, tears painting trails down her dirty cheeks. I grip her hand and turn to my dad. "Did you know Griff's mom, too?"

He nods again.

"And so you know what Griff did to the ships."

He takes a heavy breath. "His father suspected. But Griff covered his tracks too well for us to pinpoint him as the source. It was only last night, when we unexpectedly recovered control of Peter Conroy's creations and were able to watch a video feed from one of the Centurions operating beneath the planet's surface, that we knew what Griff had done—and what had become of him."

I shove down the image of Griff's dad watching his son's death on a video screen. "Griff said his dad was working for Conroy. That's why he sabotaged the ships."

"It's understandable that Griff would believe that, given the need to convince the chairman of our loyalty to JIPOC," my dad says. "But I can assure you he was wrong. When Griff's father received his orders to reset the Lowerworld ship's gravitational drive and institute the Juggernaut programming for its pods, he came to us for help. Together, we developed a plan to protect the *Freefall*, its passengers—and its leader."

Once more, my mom holds the jewel up to the light. Maybe it's an effect of my own pounding heart, but I can swear the gem pulses between her fingers.

"Griff's father defied the chairman's orders," my mom says. "Had Griff not intervened, the *Freefall* would have carried out its planned route to Kapteyn b. But as an extra precaution in case we were found out, I implanted a chip similar to this one when I prepped Sofie for deepsleep. It's a homing beacon, and much more. Most important, except in the case of severe bodily injury, it provides a form of life support to her."

"So when Conroy disengaged her deepsleep—"

"I'd visited her beforehand, under the chairman's orders," my mom says. "He'd been digging into my past, and he thought he could blackmail me. Once I'd determined that her implant was functional, I supplied him with the means to power off her stasis field. What he didn't know was that I'd equipped Sofie with a backup, one that prolonged her deepsleep until she could be restored through the normal pod technology."

The whole time we've been talking, Sofie has kept quiet, as if she's taking it all in. Or maybe she's been reluctant to interrupt the Newell family reunion. But now she speaks, touching two fingers to her own jewel. "You did this—for me?"

"We did it for the revolution," my mom says. "For Sumati, and the Lowerworld, and all who fought and died in the name of justice. But yes, Sofie, we did it for you, too. For you, and for our son. Our people are going to need both of you in the days ahead."

I sit back, staring not at the technology that saved Sofie's life but at the woman who developed it. Everything I thought I knew about her just went out the window, and I feel like a little kid again, with a whole world to learn from scratch. It makes me wonder if, all those years ago, she was spending time cooped up in her lab not for people like Conroy, not for the salvation of the planet, but for *me*. To give me a chance to live a life, even if it meant a life lived a thousand years too late.

But it is too late. Too late for this planet, too late for us. There are no days ahead. As a scientist, she has to know that.

"Thanks for trying, Mom," I say, and I do mean it.

She smiles, brushing away what I think is a tear. When she reaches out to touch my cheek, I flash back to the time when I really was a little kid, before the colonization heated up and she and my dad were never home, or—I realize now—before

JOSHUA DAVID BELLIN

they got worried that I was old enough to catch on to what they were up to. I remember the two of them coming into my room, just before I went to sleep, and sitting on either side of me to tell stories. I don't remember their exact words. I don't even remember what the stories were about. But I do remember the warm echo of their voices as they traded back and forth, filling in each other's silences, turning the tales into a single tale that included me. My heart aches, though it's different from the ache of things lost: my two best friendships, my two best friends' lives. It's more the kind of ache you get when you're out on the road and you think you forgot something back home.

And then you find it again.

Sofie lets us have our moment, then she slips an arm through mine. "What is it that you need us to do, Dr. Park?"

My mom smiles, but there's definitely moisture in her eyes. My mom, I tell you. Her mad science skills are matched only by her ability to embarrass the hell out of me.

"I don't think you have to ask me that, Sofie," she says. "I think you and Cam already know."

Tau Ceti d

Earth Year 3151

Day

We stand in the corridor outside the pod bay of the *Freefall*. The sharp light of the planetary day floods the ship, washing out the sky so we can't see the other heavenly bodies that hang above us. With his son no longer blocking his efforts, Griff's dad finally got the *Executor* to yield the secret of where we are: not on Tower City, but on the fourth planet in the same system, the one labeled *d*. Comparable to Mars in climate and atmosphere, a place we couldn't have survived for long. We'll never know why Griff chose to send us here when he had the whole universe to play with. Maybe it was nothing but accident, or malice, him finding the worst place he could imagine just shy of the place we wanted to go. But I like to think he selected this place because, even at the end, there was more to him than the cruel lesson he wanted to teach. Because he knew that here, so close to our original destination, we stood a chance.

I like to think that, even when he'd lost so much of himself, my second oldest friend held on to hope.

A huge crowd—as many as could cram themselves into the corridor—surrounds me and Sofie as we take our place on the storage boxes that serve as our makeshift stage. It reminds me of the crowd I saw that first day in Adrian's room, except this time it contains not only Lowerworlders but Upperworlders as well. Though they're pretty much segregated into distinct groupings—a patch of dark faces here, a cluster of light faces there—at least they're closer to each other than they were on Earth. In the case of my parents, they're standing among the members of Sofie's team who were imprisoned on the *Executor*, Basil and Zubin and all the others, a bit dinged up but alive and well. The parents I thought I knew on Earth would have called this decision to mingle with the Lowerworld "engaging in acts of corporational charity." The parents I'm getting to know out here in space call it "breaking down the barriers of injustice."

I like these parents a lot better.

I stand on the stage, looking out at the buzzing crowd. It's been weeks since Griff's death, weeks for us to move people and equipment from the *Executor* to the *Freefall*, weeks for Sofie to reassemble the team she headed on Earth, the major difference being that I'm now a member of it. As an advisor, mostly. But it's still weird to me, the idea that I'm some kind of public figure. Ever since she was a little girl, Sofie's been used to people following and watching her all the time, every word she speaks getting beamed around the world for listeners to clothe with their own particular meaning. Me, I'd prefer to retreat from the spotlight so we can work on the private part, the part about me and her. In the rare moments we have alone, Sofie tells me she needs time to figure that part out: time to heal, time to grow. I know we have time now. I'm just impatient for it to begin.

I also know, though, that this is where we need to be right now. The *Executor* is one tremor short of sinking into oblivion, and the *Freefall*, though Griff's dad has assured Sofie's technical crew that it's fully operational, is also stuffed to the gills with people not accustomed to playing fair. Defeated as the Upperworld is, someone might get the idea to start a revolution of their own. My parents have been working feverishly with me and Sofie to make sure that doesn't happen, to broker a new articulation agreement, but we're not there yet. Maybe we never will be. Still, we have to try.

I look at the girl I accompanied across the stars. Her jewel flashes in the corridor's light. Red for marriage, she told me back on Earth. I consider reaching for her hand. What would be the harm? But something holds me back. Something tells me that if I can stay cool for once in my life, it'll be worth the wait.

Something is right. She returns my look, and her lips part in a dazzling smile.

I smile back, my traitor heart going haywire. My face is probably as red as the jewel. Then she nods, and we step to the front of the stage. The Lowerworlders cheer. There's a smattering of applause from some of the Upperworlders, led by my mom and dad. No boos, at least. Once everyone's settled down, Sofie raises her arms to the crowd.

"People of Earth," she says, her precise, lilting voice carrying through the corridor without need of a microphone. "We have traveled much farther than any people of the past have dreamed. And we have suffered much since our arrival—much loss, much sorrow, much that has challenged and changed us as a people. But we are gathered here now because we have not lost faith. We recognize that we have all been given a second chance at life. And if we are wise, we know that we must prove ourselves worthy of this great gift. We must leave behind all that shackles us to the past. Two Worlds were our history. One world must be our future."

She pauses, dropping her eyes as if in prayer. I scan the crowd to see how they're receiving her speech so far. The Lowerworlders seem to be listening intently, but the majority of the Upperworlders are fidgeting, looking embarrassed or uncomfortable. I glimpse a splash of red hair and my heart freezes. But of course it's not him. It's his dad. I haven't seen Mr. Griffin since before we left Earth. I try to catch his eye, but he's looking away.

Sofie must see him too.

"People of the Upperworld," she says, her voice softer but no less powerful. "We mourn with you for all you have lost. We mourn the death of your leader, Chairman Conroy, and his son, and all who have given their lives on a world far from home. We mourn as well for the one who brought us here, a child of both Lowerworld and Upperworld who had lost his way in all the distance we traveled. We mourn for him, but we do not accept the path he followed. We know that there is another end to our common history than the way of violence and death."

There's absolute silence, not even the sound of uniforms rustling. The Lowerworlders seem unwilling to risk an outburst. I can't be sure if this means people are listening to Sofie or tuning her out. I can't be sure how any of this will end.

All I can be sure of is the girl I love.

"People of Earth!" she cries, lifting her voice so loud it makes my body sing. "Soon to be people of another world. I am a child of the Lowerworld, as he who stands at my side is a child of the Upperworld. At one time we were divided by walls so high we could not think to overcome them. Chance, or fate, brought us together. But the path we have now chosen is of our making alone. The walls of ignorance and hatred have fallen in our hearts, as they must fall in all hearts, across all lands, across the very stars! We stand before you united in spirit, united in purpose, and united in the struggle for justice!"

Her voice ends, the ship catching its echo and letting her final word hang there for a moment before it fades. There's a jostling in the bodies closest to the stage, people pushing against their neighbors as if a scuffle is about to break out, the Lowerworld portions of the crowd and the Upperworld portions shoving for space they can't or won't share. *When will we stop fighting each other?* I think. *Killing each other?* Billions of people have died already, along with the two brothers I loved back home. Haven't we learned anything in a thousand years?

But then, to my amazement, I realize it's not a fight breaking out. It's something I never thought I'd see: Lowerworlders and Upperworlders falling to their knees together, bowing their heads. Not everyone, but enough. Some of them link arms, while others clasp their hands or spread their palms on the floor in front of them. A few surge forward and reach up to where Sofie and I stand on the podium, eager to receive our touch. We do what they want, my head spinning as I look into faces alight with smiles and tears. Then Sofie grips my hand and raises it before the crowd, and her voice rings out again, as clear and strong as the first time I heard it. I hold her hand as tightly as I can, and I lift my voice with hers.

"Justice!"

"Justice!"

The members of our team stand, join hands, and hold them high, crying the word over and over. The rest of the Lowerworlders follow their example, thundering the refrain in a hundred different languages, much louder, I think, than they did on Earth. Slowly the Upperworlders lift themselves from the floor and stand unsteadily, unsure what to do, as bewildered by the noise as I was that day in New York CITI. But then a few take up the chant, my mom and dad and Griff's father all by themselves at first, then more and more, still not everyone but enough to rock the corridors of the *Freefall*. I feel tears on my cheeks, tears for Adrian and Griff, for all the ones we've lost on this planet and the planet we left so long ago. We can't go back and save them from a world that's ceased to exist. But we can go forward and try to lead those who remain to a world that's yet to be.

Not Sofie's world. Not my world.

Our world.

At last I think I can see a way there.

Earth Year 3151

Freefall

S ofie tells me she loves me the day we launch the ship.

Actually, she tells me that a lot these days. There's a guarded quality to her words sometimes, a sense that she's feeling her way. But there's no doubt in my mind that what she feels is real. Though we spend practically every waking minute together, we haven't kissed since that morning in the tunnels. She tells me that even a prophet has many things to learn. I tell her I'll always love her, no matter what, and we leave it at that for now.

There's so much we need to work on. Not only me and her, but all of us. Healing old wounds. Building a new society. We'll arrive on Tau Ceti e as passengers of a single ship, united by our determination to survive. But it'll be up to us to decide if we can live that way. We might end up falling into old patterns, divided by history and suspicion and resentment. Or we might make the effort to live in peace, the first pioneers of a truly new world. That's the hope, anyway. It's what Sofie and I have pledged ourselves to work toward for the rest of our lives.

Together. As friends, allies—or something more.

That's my hope too.

And there's one thing, more than anything else, that makes me think it's all going to work out. I've talked with Griff's dad—cried with him too, but that was only part of it—and he told me that everywhere he looked in the *Executor*'s code, he saw signs of how hastily Griff had done his damage. In some ways, that explains why the problems were so hard to fix, because everything was random and unorthodox. It probably also explains why the *Freefall* was so glitchy, why no one woke up when the ship touched down. But it doesn't explain why, when both of the starships went astray, the only pods to eject—other than the Centurions under Griff's control—were mine and Sofie's. You could say that was Griff's doing too, but it's hard to see how casting us into space could have served his designs. No, I think there was something else going on, something that can't be explained by science or technology. The best I can put it is that it was *meant* to happen that way. When we needed each other most, we both called out, and the other answered.

If that can happen, isn't anything possible? If I can travel across the galaxy to find the girl I thought I'd lost forever, can't we find a way to live together at last?

The *Freefall*'s in the final stages of preparation for takeoff, the gravitational drive engaged for its journey to Tau Ceti e.

Sofie breaks away from a conversation with her team and takes my hand, pulling me away from the crowd. She reaches up and delicately, almost shyly, gives me a kiss.

"You ready?" I ask her.

"For anything," she says, and smiles.

I grip her hand as the ship rumbles and then rises. The planet that held us prisoner falls away, and we're soaring into the space between worlds. But it's a short flight, and we won't need deepsleep. We can sit by a window, and tell each other stories of the places we've been, and watch the everlasting stars as they guide us home.

Acknowledgments

Eternal thanks to:

My superstar agent, Liza Fleissig of Liza Royce Agency.

My cosmic editor, Karen Wojtyla, and her stellar assistant, Annie Nybo.

My galactic genius copy editor, Brian Luster.

My celestial publicist, Katy Hershberger.

My out-of-this-world cover designer, Greg Stadnyk.

My astronomical friends within the YA writing community, especially Kat Ross, who read an early draft of the manuscript and provided invaluable feedback; Jen Rees, who offered editorial assistance on the revised draft; and S. Alex Martin, who helped me with the trickier science.

My dazzling children, who've rocketed from picture books to YA before my very eyes.

My heavenly readers, for whom I first embarked on this voyage.

And Christine, for showing me the stars.

Author's Note

The Science of *Freefall*

M any of the places, events, and technologies in *Freefall* are based on known (or at least probabilistic) science. These include:

Tau Ceti e. An "exoplanet" (a planet that orbits a star outside the solar system), this is the fifth world circling the star Tau Ceti, approximately twelve light-years from Earth. We don't know much about this planet, but some consider it within the "habitable zone" (the range of orbits around a star within which a planet might possess Earth-like properties, particularly the presence of liquid water), which is why many science-fiction books have been written with the Tau Ceti system as a setting. Shortly after I completed writing *Freefall*, scientists announced the discovery of a possibly habitable planet orbiting Proxima Centauri, the star closest to our own sun (only 4.24 light-years away), but for the purposes of the story, we can assume that Cam's society determined this planet not to be suitable for human habitation.

The Executor *and the* Freefall. Spaceships that travel at sub-light speeds, and thus would take thousands of years to reach the nearest stars, are typically termed "generation ships" (because multiple human generations would be born and die during the course of their journey). But with the deepsleep or suspended-animation technology described in this book, the passengers on my two starships are able to stay alive throughout the thousand-year voyage. Technically, to travel twelve light-years in a millennium, these ships would have to be moving at speeds far in excess of current automated (much less occupied) spacecraft. But that brings me to:

The gravitational drive. In other words, a drive that "locks onto" and amplifies the gravitational field of its target star. Strictly speaking, that's impossible: Artificial gravity can be created only through linear or rotational inertia, and the "slingshot" method utilized by automated spacecraft such as *New Horizons*, which acquired a "gravity assist" from Jupiter to increase its velocity on the way to Pluto, wouldn't be adequate to power a ship across the galaxy. Though the drive envisioned in these pages isn't a warp drive, which requires immense mass to warp or bend space, I've made my starships massive to assist the illusion of their actually manipulating a star's gravitational pull.

Biofeedback. There's nothing fictional about the ability of some people to exert conscious control over involuntary functions such as heartbeat and breathing. The pod-and-deepsleep technology in *Freefall* is, however, an admittedly fictionalized exaggeration of the biofeedback process.

Nanotechnologies. Engineering microscopic machines to perform medical and other tasks is one of the frontiers of present-day science. In *Freefall,* nanotechnologies have many applications, from performance enhancement to biomechanical drone warfare.

There are many other aspects of *Freefall* that I've made no attempt to explain scientifically—mysteries that, as Cam suggests, perhaps *can't* be explained that way. And as I see it, that's the job of science fiction: to use the known and plausible as a means of exploring the unknown and perhaps unknowable.